Scarred

To: Desiree
Thank you for
your support!
Hope you enjoy!

~ Marie
xo

Scarred

The Anderson Brothers Series
Book 1

MARIE LONG

Scarred
(The Anderson Brothers Series, Book 1)

This book is a work of fiction. Any references to historical events, real people, or real places are used fictitiously. Other names, characters, places, and events are products of the author's imagination, and any resemblance to actual events or places or persons, living or dead, is entirely coincidental.

Cover design by Najla Qamber Designs

Printed in the United States of America

10 9 8 7 6 5 4 3 2 1

ISBN: 978-0-9863019-0-2 (paperback)
ISBN: 978-0-9863019-1-9 (eBook)

To all of my male friends and colleagues who let me pick your brains in helping me make this my best book ever. You rock!

ACKNOWLEDGMENTS

Thank you, first and foremost, to my Lord and Savior, Jesus Christ, for giving me the creative talent to write. Without Him, none of this would have been possible.

Thank you to my friends and family, especially my parents, for always being so supportive of me in everything I do. I appreciate you and love you very much.

To the awesome staff at Red Adept, thank you for working miracles on my manuscript and helping me to better myself as a writer.

To the Dragon's Sandbox—you know who you all are. Thanks for all of your honest and helpful critiques to help me get this manuscript the best it could be.

A very special thanks to Marie Hall. You are one of the reasons why I wanted to write a New Adult story. Thank you again for all that you've done.

Thank you to the reviewers who took the time out of their busy schedules to read and review this book. Reviews are essential to writers, and I am grateful for every single one.

Lastly, to you, the reader. Thank you for allowing me to share my story with you.

Scarred

CHAPTER 1

I CAN'T CONCENTRATE. EVEN THE WHIRRING OF AIR wrenches and the buzzing of shop gossip is drowned out by that voice in my head again.

His voice: *"Boy, sit the fuck down now!"*

I cringe.

"Don't move or say a fucking word, understand?"

I bite my lip. He sounds so close.

Something hits me on the forehead, snapping me back to reality. I hiss and blink a few times and stare up at the underside of a car—the chassis of a sedan, to be exact. Damn, I zoned out again. Tumbled into memories I've been trying to bury for years.

Fuck him. Fuck the world.

The wheels of the hardwood dolly squeak as I roll out from under the car and stand. I toss my wrench in the open toolbox and wipe my dirty hands on a towel. Dabbing away the sweat from my forehead, I frown. That sweat certainly wasn't from my hard work. I glance at the car next to mine and watch Samuel doing some wiring under the hood.

He stops for a moment, rummages through our toolbox, and pulls out a set of pliers. Instead of returning to work, he furrows his eyebrows at me. "Everything all right, man?"

I nod. "Yeah, fine. Just so damn tired today." It's mostly true, and I emphasize the point with a deep yawn.

Samuel smirks. "Heh. Yeah. Glad tomorrow's Friday. Got a date with this honey I've been dying to go out with. Name's Mona. Always wears these short-shorts over that big—no, *huge*—round ass of hers. God bless A*meri*ca!"

I roll my eyes. Tomorrow, Mona is his booty call. After that, who knows who he'll be in the mood for? I don't understand why the chicks he dates even give him the time of day.

I haven't had a date in months, much less a girlfriend. But then again, I'd stopped trying after the last girl. I was apparently cramping her style because I wanted to get to know her a bit more rather than fuck her the very same night I met her. Why the hell is that so wrong? I wanna be with a girl who knows how much she's worth instead of how much of the goods she has to show so I'll jump in bed with her.

Samuel waves a hand in front of my face. "Yo, Dom!"

I blink back to reality again.

"What the hell, man? You look like shit."

Frowning, I shove Samuel's hand away and head toward the main office. "I told you I'm fine. It's time for me to clock out. Can you finish getting this catalytic converter installed?"

"Yeah, sure." Samuel shrugs. "Oh, by the way . . . "

I stop short of the office's glass door and look back.

"Better talk to Frank before you go. He was asking about you earlier."

I look through the glass door and see Frank, our boss, leaning back in his swivel chair with his feet propped up on his paper-filled desk. He's yapping away on the phone while he plays with the tangled cord.

I look back at Samuel. "Asking about me for what?"

Samuel shrugs again then sticks his head back under the hood and resumes wiring. "I dunno. You were taking a piss when he came looking for you. Told me to tell you to go see him before you clock out."

I blink. "And you're just telling me now?"

"Sorry, man. I forgot."

Shit. A meeting with the boss is never a good sign. Then again, everything else in my life always seems to go to shit, so why not my only means of income? Sighing, I enter the office. It's big enough to accommodate a grungy, magazine-ridden couch and a desk. The room feels nice and cool after working on cars all day.

Waiting for the boss to hang up, I check my cell for missed calls. No one—not even my roommate, Chris—left any messages.

Probably too busy fucking. I dream of the day when I can finally get a place of my own. But this job, especially with my college expenses, doesn't pay enough to make Seattle rent on my own.

Frank hangs up the phone. Without taking his feet off the desk, he folds his dirty hands over his large belly, which pokes out slightly between the buttons of his oil-smeared blue shirt. He rocks back in his chair, making it squeak, and looks at me. "Dominick. I'll make this quick."

I suck in my breath and start anticipating where this little talk is headed—and how much money I have saved, which garages might be hiring . . .

"There're going to be some changes around here," Frank says in his deep voice. "Money's getting tight, and I've been receiving a few customer complaints lately."

I blink. *Complaints?* Not from *my* work, I hope. I know cars like the back of my hand. Been working on them since I was seven. "What—what kind of complaints?"

"Just a few things—little things that I take very seriously. Like, one customer complained that his radio was tuned to some rock station when he got his car back after an oil change. He's a religious man and was offended by the—and I quote—"devil music" coming from his own radio. There's no fucking reason to be touching the radio if you're doing an oil change."

"I didn't mess with the radio, man," I say, shaking my head. I don't even listen to rock.

Frank stiffens and glares. "Did I say you did? Is there something you're not telling me?"

"No. Sorry for interrupting."

His face relaxes. "Had another complaint two days ago that a customer's warning lights were still on after she had her engine serviced. She thought there was still something wrong with the car, and after she brought the car back to have it re-inspected, Paul discovered that the warning lights just weren't manually turned off. Careless shit like that is something I can't stand. Time is money. If you're going to work for me, then put a little pride in your fucking work, right?"

I nod again, more stiffly this time. What's he hinting at? There are only five employees at Frank's Garage, but as far as I know, we all get along, work hard, and don't cause problems.

Frank pulls his feet off the table, straightens in his chair, and looks at me carefully. He places both hands on the desk. "Time is money, and all these kinds of complaints are bad for business—bad for *my* reputation. I'm letting Sam go today, so that means work's gonna get crazy for a while with just the four of you. But I know you guys can do it."

Samuel? I know he's always talking about how much he loves ass and tits, but I never thought he'd be the one to cause problems for the shop. Without Samuel, we're going to be short-staffed, and that's totally going to up the workload. Boy, Thursday's really turned to shit.

I leave the office in silence and walk around back, where my red sport bike is parked. After slipping on my helmet, jacket, and gloves, I kick the bike awake and zip toward the south side of Montlake as fast as I can, taking alternate routes in order to bypass the evening rush-hour traffic. When I arrive at the two-bedroom duplex at Springview Commons, I park my bike behind a tall wooden fence around the side. I pull off my helmet and pat my jeans pockets for my key. Going in through the door into the kitchen, I listen for sounds of my roommate, but hear no one. Either Chris is really gone for a change or he's asleep. Curiosity gets the best of me, so I creep through the hallway to his bedroom door, which is cracked open slightly, revealing some of the large posters of pin-up girls and his favorite pro football players plastered on the walls. I get a whiff of sex and booze tainting the room's stale air. Not needing to see any more to know what he's been up to, I climb the stairs to my room and shut the door. I strip out of my work clothes and plop down in bed in my boxers. Heaving a deep sigh, I close my eyes and try to relax after a long day.

The visions return.

I see *him* again.

"You want it? You gotta beg."

"But Pop—"

"What did I fucking say?"

I shudder and open my eyes. *"What did I fucking say?"* I repeat in a quivering whisper.

CHAPTER 2

FRIDAY MORNING, MY PHONE ALARM GOES OFF, BLASTING
the song, "1st of tha Month". I wake up at my desk with my
face smushed onto the open pages of my engineering textbook. Groaning, I grope for the phone and disable the alarm.
Morning light filters through the closed blinds on my window. I also hear rain. *Damn. Hope the weather lets up before I
leave.* I drag my ass out of my room and to the half-bath to
take a piss, but I find the door locked. *What the fuck?* I
pound on the door.

"Just a minute!" a woman yells.

I seethe. *This is ridiculous.* I can't even use my own damn
bathroom when I want to! Another reason why I desperately
need to get my own place.

Two flushes later she exits, decked out in one of Chris's
oversized football jerseys. It reaches down to the middle of
her thighs, the kind of thighs I like—well defined, like she

works out. She's surprisingly cute with a naturally full body that some skinny, flat-chested chicks would pay thousands for. She scans me up and down with her deep brown eyes lingering below my waist for a couple seconds too long. She smirks. "Oh, hi. You must be Dominick."

I nod. "Yup." Her nipples harden beneath the shirt. Her tits are perky, and part of me wants to have some fun with her, but I know better. Despite the tightness in my boxers, I tear my gaze away from her and look beyond her to the bathroom. "You done in there?"

"Uh, sure." She sounds surprised as she steps aside. "You doing anything tonight?"

I try not to laugh, because her question sounds so pathetic, so desperate. And I hate a desperate woman. My own mother was desperate, and she got hurt. Bad.

This girl would probably love it if I got rough with her. Even more if I hurt her like the "bad boy" she probably thinks I am. But I'm better than that. I'm not some horny punk like the guys she's probably had before me. I'm not playing that game. Not even batting an eye, I pass her by. "Dunno." I shut the door in her face.

Sure as hell ain't going down that *road again.*

By the time I head out, the rain's let up. It's Friday, my light class-load day. Physics lab, electromagnetics, and then off to work. I'm a routine guy. Doesn't take much to make me happy. Maybe that's why I was never desperate for a girl, unlike most of my friends.

After my last class, I head out of the engineering building and to the parking lot, where my bike is parked. I don my gear and rev the engine, garnering a few admiring glances from both male and female students walking by. Others scowl at me or hold their ears, but I don't care. My pipes are pretty loud and can be heard almost a quarter of a mile away. I head downtown.

By one thirty I arrive at Frank's, and by the somber looks on my coworkers' faces, I know Samuel's already gone. There's only four of us now—me, Paul, Larry, and Nate—and there's a ton of shit to do on the cars we have.

Damn, we need help.

Some of the guys in my motorcycle club are looking for jobs. Matt, the club's VP, got laid off from stocking shelves.

A towel plops over my head. I tug the towel off, my nose wrinkling from the odor of oil and old gasoline.

Larry stands in front of me with a smug look on his face. Besides Frank, Larry's the oldest out of all of us in both age and experience, so he usually has no problem with ordering us college kids around. He's cool, though. Pretty laid-back in most cases. Always keeps us busy with small projects and helps us when we need it. "Hey, you ready or what?" he asks.

"Yeah, sure, man," I say, approaching the whiteboard where our daily assignments are posted. Today I have to change brake pads on an old pickup truck, repair struts on a car, and do three scheduled oil changes. Only easy projects today, and that's likely Larry's doing. His present to me heading into the weekend. God, I love that man. Frank, on the other hand, doesn't give two shits and fills our names in anywhere.

I retrieve a spare toolbox and a dolly hanging on the wall of one of the occupied bays and go outside to where the wheelless truck sits on some blocks. The sky is overcast and a light drizzle is just enough to keep the ground damp. I fish through the toolbox for a wrench and a flashlight, lay back on the dolly, and roll myself under the front of the truck. My mind wanders while I'm under here, unscrewing bolts, and I feel at peace. There's no one to bother me. Just me and my thoughts. Most of the time, that's more of a curse than a blessing. If I let my mind go idle for too long, those *other* thoughts start to take hold.

Thoughts I would rather forget.

I try planning my weekend. No new movies coming out, and I damn sure don't want to stay home with Chris. He'll most likely have all of Seattle's women in our apartment. Maybe I'll ride up to the Cascades, or the Cougar Mountain trail. I need to clear my head somehow. Or maybe I can go see my uncle. But then I remember that he's still taking care of Mama.

A bitter taste forms in my mouth.

She cried when I called her sometime last year. Cried over *him*. That son of a bitch. And I still don't know why. He did nothing for our family. So many times I'd wished my Uncle Adam was my father instead. I'd stopped talking to Mama since then, and ignored her calls.

I'm tired of her damn crying.

A bolt hits me in the forehead. I curse and rub the painful spot, then start unscrewing the next bolt.

"So careless. So careless."

I grit my teeth. I hate that voice.

"Know what I do with careless little boys like you?"

I suddenly release my grip on the wrench, which somehow still stays in place on the bolt.

"Come here, Dominick. Let me show you."

"No," I mutter softly.

My phone vibrates, startling me, and I barely miss whacking my head on the chassis. I roll out from under the truck, and check the name on my phone before answering, "What's up, Chris?"

"'Sup, dude. Sorry to call you while you're at work, but, uh . . . you think you can get a box of condoms on your way home?"

"*What?*"

"Yeah, I only got two left. *Definitely* not going to last me the rest of the day."

"Didn't your girlfriends come prepared?"

"Nope. They thought they were gonna get a free ride, saying they're on the pill and all that, but I didn't buy it. I've heard the horror stories. That's baby mama drama just waiting to happen."

"Why don't you go out your own damn self and get some? Who the fuck do you think I am, your mother?"

"Dude, I would if I could, but I can't be leaving these chicks unattended while I run out to the store. Besides, my license is still revoked."

I grit my teeth. "That's your own fault for not paying that parking ticket."

"No, that fucking cop was being an asshole. Look, man, I swear, I'll pay you back. This is so embarrassing, but—"

"When the hell did I become your personal errand boy?" Closing my eyes, I let out a sigh. "If you need some so bad, then use mine. There's a box under my bed."

Silence. "Um . . . I already used those."

My eyes go wide. "*What*? That was a 12-count box!"

"I've been using them since last week since I knew you weren't."

That motherfucker! "You've been sneaking into my room without my permission?"

"Dude, I only went to get condoms. I swear. I kept forgetting all week to go to the store after work, and now I have these two anxious chicks here, and . . . damn! I need to introduce you to Melanie. She's got *amazing* legs!"

The left side of my mouth twitches. "I don't want to know who the fuck they are. Keep them out of my room. And you stay the hell out, too."

"Noted. So, you gonna run by the store for me, or what?"

I exhale and abruptly hang up. Of course I'm going to get more condoms—for me. I swear, this time I'm not going to break down like a little pansy and give him any. Sometimes I hate being the nice guy.

My phone vibrates again. This time I get a text.

THX MAN URE DA BEST

He's already on to me, damn it.

Attempting to fight down a smile, I reply:

fuck u

I stick my phone in my side pocket and slide back under the truck. Not even five minutes pass before the phone vibrates again. Grumbling, I snatch it out.

Another text from Chris.

O btw, got tickets 2 ur bro's gig 2nite. wanna go?

Cringing, I shove the phone back into my pocket and return to my work. I never particularly care to go anywhere with Chris, because it usually means I'll be spending my time watching him pick up every girl around. Maybe I'll go to the club, if only to see Kevin.

Finished with all my work, I pick up the toolbox and dolly and return them to the shop.

Larry, who is fixing a radiator, stops and wipes his hands on a towel. "All done?"

"Yup." I hang the dolly back on the wall.

"All right. Five minutes till quittin' time. You have a good weekend."

The way he says that sounds like he wants me to leave early, have fun. I take that cue without hesitation and head out.

On the way back home, I stop at a convenience store. It's rush-hour traffic, and the place is near the interstate, so it's pretty busy inside with tons of people packed into the tiny store. I stand on line with a box of condoms tucked under one arm and stare idly at the nine people ahead of me. Of course, an old man at the head of the line decides to pay with plastic and takes forever to punch in his information on the card reader. I sigh heavily and watch customers enter and mill about the store.

I just want to go home.

After what seems like forever, I'm finally the second person in line. The bell over the door jingles, followed by the sounds of hurried footsteps. A girl comes running up to the counter in a panic. Several customers in line give her dirty looks. The girl appears slightly younger than me—nineteen, maybe twenty.

"Excuse me, is there a working pay phone anywhere? It's an emergency and my cell's dead!" she says frantically.

While punching buttons on the register with one hand, the clerk points to the entrance with the other and says, "Outside around the corner."

"Thanks." She spins on her heel and rushes out.

The troubled look on her face makes me curious. *Is she alone?*

When it's finally my turn, I quickly pay and leave, hoping the girl hasn't left yet. Why am I even worried about her, anyway? I don't know her. With my luck, she probably has some jealous boyfriend waiting in the car for her. He could be waiting to beat the living shit out of a stupid punk like me for nosing around in her business.

I discover the girl around the side of the building at the pay phone, which looks like it's been out of commission for years. She wipes sweat from her forehead, adjusts the dark blue headband she's wearing over her cornrowed hair, then fishes through her purse and jeans pockets, probably looking for change. After stuffing the box of condoms in my backpack on my bike, I walk over to her. She looks up at me briefly before resuming her search.

I pull a quarter from my pocket and hand it to her. "Here."

She looks back at me with raised eyebrows, then at the quarter, but doesn't take it.

"Or you can use my cell, if you like," I say. I glance over my shoulder, anticipating her jealous brute of a boyfriend— because a beautiful girl like her couldn't *possibly* be single— grabbing me from behind and slamming me against his car, but all I find are people going in and out of the convenience store, not paying either of us any mind. I turn back to the girl.

She looks at me hesitantly. "I . . . "

"I'm just trying to help here. That's all. You said it was an emergency, right?"

"Yes." She takes the quarter meekly. "Thank you." She turns away from me and picks up the receiver.

Of course, I want to ask her what the emergency is, but that's none of my business. Maybe if I wait long enough, I'll get an opportunity. This girl looks different from the ones Chris brings home every night. Hell, she looks different from some of the college girls I've seen in the past couple of semesters. She actually covers her assets rather than advertise them.

Again, I look over my shoulder for some rough-looking guy heading in my direction, but cars go by, and random people continue entering and leaving the convenience store. I hear the clicking sound of the coin being inserted into the phone, and I whip my head back around.

"Hi, I need a tow truck right away . . . "

My concern for this girl gets a little deeper.

"Yes, I have roadside service under my dad's name," she says. "I'm uh . . . " She pauses and looks around briefly, then returns to her conversation. "I'm at the ShopMart on Fifteenth, but my car is further away . . . Denise—Denise Ramsey . . . All right, thank you." She hangs up the phone and spins around, casting me a thankful look.

I try not to smile. Denise Ramsey, I assume, is her name. And she apparently has car problems.

"Thank you so much," Denise says. "I'm very sorry. I wish I had some change to pay you back."

"Naw, don't worry about it," I say, waving my hand dismissively. "So what happened to your car?"

Denise shrugs. "I don't know. I was driving along and suddenly everything just cuts off without warning. I coasted to a stop and the car wouldn't start any more."

My mechanic mode kicks in. "Sounds like a bad battery. Or the alternator."

Denise's eyes dull. "Oh. How expensive is something like that to fix, you think?"

"It depends on the seriousness of the problem."

She sighs. "I guess I'll be without a car for a while. I don't get paid for another week."

I chew my bottom lip. I know I could fix whatever was wrong with it—though, depending on her car, an alternator might be a bit of a pain. Denise seems like a sensible girl I might like to get to know. "Denise, was it? My name is Dominick. I'm a mechanic at Frank's Garage, over on Mercer Street."

"You're a mechanic?" Denise blinks, then gives a short laugh. "That's convenient. But there's no way I'll be able to afford any car repairs right now."

Frank certainly won't approve, but Larry never minds whenever I bring my bike over there to service after-hours. So long as I don't use the shop's parts, Larry is usually cool with it. I figure I will probably have to explain about Denise's car, though. "I think I might be able to make it all work out if you bring it by the shop. I just need to talk to a coworker about it."

Her eyes light up, but that excitement quickly fades. "No, I should probably get it towed back to my house until I can afford the repairs."

Smart girl. Never trust strangers. "All right. I completely understand. You don't know me, and I don't know you. That's smart. But please know that I'm just trying to help. You are always welcome to stop by the shop and see for yourself whenever you like."

"Thank you." She nods.

"Mind if I wait on the tow truck with you? I'd rather not see you waiting out here all by yourself like this."

She arches an eyebrow at me. "I happen to be a grown woman. I don't need adult supervision."

Ouch.

"But I don't mind the company, and you *did* loan me a quarter." She smiles reassuringly, perhaps realizing she sounded harsh.

I exhale. I barely know this girl, but she's got me curious. I step aside to give her some space, and then lean against the wall of the building, stuffing my hands in my pockets. "I hope you don't find it creepy or something for me to want to ensure that an attractive woman like you is safe." I mentally kick myself. *Did I really just say that?*

Thankfully, she doesn't appear put-off by the comment. Her expression, however, turns coyer. "I don't really find it *creepy*. Though, I can only wonder what is going on in that mind of yours that you would take time out of your busy schedule to wait on a tow truck with me."

My smile slowly returns. "Have you never heard of chivalry?"

She laughs. "Yeah, I heard it's dead."

"Eh, well, there are still a few of us guys out there trying to keep it alive." My phone vibrates in my pocket, and I pull it out. Chris's number blinks on the screen. I ignore the call and send him a text message saying that I won't be coming home anytime soon. If he's that desperate for a quick fuck, he'll find a way. I stuff the phone back into my pocket.

Denise looks away and out toward the road, perhaps searching for the tow truck.

"So where were you headed, if you don't mind my ask-ing?" I ask.

She looks back at me. "Home. I have a big test to study for on Monday."

"You're in college?" Relief spreads over me. She's most likely legal.

She nods. "I'm a junior at UDub. What about you?"

"Sophomore. I go there, too." Maybe this means I'll be seeing her around. Get to know her.

"What are you studying?" she asks.

"Electrical Engineering. You?"

"Wow, that sounds intense. I'm Liberal Arts."

"That's cool. So do you work?"

"Yeah, but only part-time. I write fashion and lifestyle ar-ticles for an online community."

"You're a blogger?" I raise my eyebrows, and she nods.

"If you'd call it that. But it's fun work. And helps pay rent."

I'm about to ask her more about work, when a set of headlights shines on us. I didn't realize how dark it had got-ten already. A quick check of my phone reveals the time—7:19 p.m.—and a text notification—most likely from Chris. I ignore the text and re-pocket the phone. Denise walks over to meet the tow man, who gets out of a big black wrecker with spinning orange and yellow lights on top. He scribbles something on a clipboard before handing it to her.

"Sign here, here, and initial here," Tow Man says, point-ing.

While she's filling out the paperwork, he gives Denise one of those wolfish looks. I push myself off the wall and move closer to her, in an almost protective manner. Tow Man shoots me a dirty look, but says nothing. Finished writing, Denise hands the clipboard back to him.

"Thank you, Miss Ramsey," he says, taking the clipboard and returning to the truck. "Hop in and you can direct me to your car." He opens the passenger-side door for her and waits.

She glances back at me then turns and climbs into the truck.

I'm certainly not about to leave her alone with that guy. I return to my bike as I watch the truck leave the parking lot and head down the street. I follow the truck from a short distance away, keeping the orange-yellow lights in sight. Soon, it turns down a road that is less traveled this time of evening. The truck slows and veers off to the grassy shoulder and in front of a white sedan. I park my bike behind the car and watch as Tow Man gets out and begins hitching up the front of the car to the wrecker. He shoots me another dirty look but says nothing. Denise hops out of the truck as well. She notices me and waves. I smile and wave back.

"Where would you like your car towed, Miss Ramsey?" Tow Man asks.

Denise brushes her fingertips over her lips as she contemplates the now-hitched car. Then, she looks over to me and stares for a long time, as if she is considering something. Dropping her fingers, she says, "Frank's Garage, please."

CHAPTER 3

I LEAD THE WAY TO FRANK'S GARAGE, AND WHEN I ARRIVE, I notice most of the lights are on and someone's moving around inside behind the shut glass bay door. Larry's working overtime again. I swear, he's the hardest-working man I've ever met. Why isn't he the boss instead of Frank?

The tow truck stops in front of the shop. Larry pulls up the bay door just enough to duck under. I park my bike while Denise and the tow man get out of the truck.

Tow Man hands Larry a clipboard, and Larry signs off on it.

As Tow Man unhitches Denise's car, Larry grabs my arm, and I wince. Damn, he's got a strong grip. He pulls me over toward the door to the office.

Larry looks at me, bleary-eyed. "Dominick? What the hell's all this?"

"Can't seem to get enough of this place, y'know?" I say, rubbing the back of my head.

Larry simply stares. "Look, I've gotta finish replacing a timing belt, so—"

"Larry, don't be mad or anything, but this girl was having car problems, and I told her she could bring it by here for me to look at. I think it's the alternator. I can probably fix it myself. I just need the shop light."

Larry frowns. "If Frank comes by here and sees you . . . "

"I'm just doing a favor, that's all. Trying to be a good guy here."

"Don't bullshit me, boy."

I sigh and look toward Denise, who is watching Tow Man secure the chains back on the wrecker.

"Goodnight, Miss Ramsey," Tow Man says with a smile and flirty tone as he opens the driver-side door.

I clench my jaw. *Phony bastard.*

Denise smiles back at him, but unlike his fake-ass one, hers looks genuine. "Goodnight, sir, and thank you."

Tow Man hops in and speeds off down the street.

A sudden smack to the back of my head lurches me forward. "I'm talking to you, Dominick! Don't you fucking ignore me!"

I turn back to Larry and stare at him. His overworked, bloodshot eyes are glaring. *Oh shit.* The last thing I want to do is make him angry. He used to fight Golden Gloves in his younger days. Rubbing the back of my head, I mutter, "S-sorry, man. Got distracted there for a minute."

"No shit." Larry folds his arms over his chest. The muscles in his forearms and biceps bulge menacingly.

I don't know where to look. "Yeah, so, uh . . . can I use a small light to work on Denise's car? I promise to stay out of your way, and I won't use any shop parts."

"Damn right you won't use any shop parts," Larry says through clenched teeth. There's a long pause. Then, sighing heavily, Larry uncrosses his arms and thumbs over to bay two. "You can use the one hanging on the wall over there. The one with the orange cord." He walks back under bay one's raised door and lowers it, but doesn't shut it completely. His head disappears under the hood of an SUV.

Smiling, I hustle over to Denise. "Sorry about that. I just had to straighten some things out. It's all good now."

Denise tilts her head curiously. "Are you sure it's okay for you to be doing this?"

I nod curtly. "Yeah. And if I get in trouble, well, then I get in trouble. But Larry's cool about keeping quiet about me working after hours. It's not like I get paid overtime or anything."

"Ah . . . payment. About that . . . "

"Naw, we'll talk about that when I finish. Now, I'm gonna need you to steer while I push your car close to the bay there. Can you do that?"

Denise smirks. "I know how to steer a car, if you can handle the weight."

Beautiful, smart, *and* sassy.

I go behind the car while she gets in. Grunting, I push it up to bay two's closed glass door.

Denise pops the hood while I lift the bay door a little, grab the metal work light, and feed its long orange cord through the bottom of the partly open door. I almost do a double-take when I notice the transmission. *Holy shit, she drives stick? That's hot.* First girl I've met who knows how to drive one.

The battery looks good, so I move on to the alternator.

"How bad is it?" Denise asks. Her voice is close.

I glance up and realize she's standing beside me, leaning in a little. Her braids drape over her shoulders, down to her chest, where her scoop-neck shirt reveals a slight peek of the thin lace of her bra. I exhale slowly and feel my pants tighten. *All right, Dom. Keep it under control.* I clear my throat. "Uh, let's see here . . . " Hauling my attention back to the alternator, I move the light around as best I can. I already see problems, but hopefully it's not as bad as I thought. "Looks like you have a little corrosion around the connectors, and a loose wire around your alternator. Nothing major, but that could be why you couldn't start the car."

"Think you'll be able to fix it tonight? I'm really going to need the car tomorrow to go to a study group. Or maybe I should just take the bus instead—"

"No," I say quickly. "I'll make *absolutely sure* your car is ready for tomorrow."

"All right. So, how much is all this going to run me?"

Scratching the back of my head, I glance over at bay one, where Larry is still tinkering under the hood, oblivious to us. Business is business, but technically, I'm not on the clock, so this doesn't really count as business, does it? I mutter, "Don't worry about it."

She blinks. "Quit playing. I can't let you do all this for free. I mean, you work here and all that, right?"

"Yeah, but this is my own personal time. Favor for a friend, you know? But if you're gonna insist on paying me, then . . . how about dinner?" I bite my tongue as soon as the words are out of my mouth. What the hell was I thinking, asking her that?

Denise snorts a laugh. "Dinner? As in a date?"

I deflate a little. I'm such a fucking idiot. "Uh, no . . . not really. Sorry, I was way out of line there."

She doesn't reply. Just awkward silence.

Shit! I blew it! I'm hopeless.

"How long is this repair going to take?" she finally asks, as if she hadn't heard me.

I swallow a lump in my throat and turn away, sticking my head back under the hood. I can't even look at her any more. "Uh . . . about two hours, maybe?"

"All right. I guess I'll go study in the meantime." She rounds the back of the car.

I glance in her direction, careful not to make eye contact. She opens the trunk, and pulls out a large, tan messenger bag. "You can use the office, if you like," I say, pointing to the office entrance. "There's a couch in there."

She slams the trunk shut. "Thanks."

She leaves, and I start on the repairs. My hands work practically on their own while my mind wanders.

What the hell just happened? Why couldn't I have met someone like Denise before? She's not only physically attractive, her intelligence and self-respect make her that much more beautiful. And it's clear she knows her worth.

I exhale, stop working, and wipe at my palms. My thoughts have made them sweaty.

The connections and wires are all repaired, and I realize two and a half hours have flown by. I get in the car and start it up. The motor hums, and I smile.

"Yes!" I hiss, doing a little fist-pump.

I glance through the glass of bay one. Larry's still hunched over the SUV, working away. I swear, that man is a machine.

I shut the car off then head to the office. Denise is sprawled on the couch among a mass of papers. A thick textbook sits open beside her. She looks up from a spiral-bound notebook in her lap, her eyes full of anticipation like an excited puppy. "You're finished?"

Nodding, I dangle the keys. "Yup. Should be good to go now."

She beams and springs up from the couch. "Oh, thank you so much!" She scoops up her books and papers and hastily stuffs them into her bag.

I hold the door open, and she brushes past in a hurry, snatching the keys from my hand. For a split second, I catch her scent. *Pear.*

She tosses the bag in the passenger seat, climbs into the driver's side and starts the car. "It works!"

I grin. "'Course it does. I fixed it."

She gives a little hollow-sounding laugh.

Things suddenly feel awkward. What happens now? She leaves and I never see her again? I don't want her money, and she *did* thank me for fixing her car, so what else would I expect?

Maybe the club. Or a movie. Or—

"So, dinner?" she says.

My heart stops for a second. My mouth goes dry. I try to speak, but my voice cracks.

Denise smiles at my apparent idiocy.

"Dinner," I finally manage to mumble.

"Tomorrow?"

I swallow again. *Oh shit! This is real!* "Y-yeah, tomorrow's good."

"How does Jade Fusion sound? We can meet there, or I can come get you, if you want."

I take a deep breath. This is ridiculous. I know how to do this. "No. I'll pick you up around seven. That okay?"

She pauses, then nods slowly. "Okay. I'll be waiting." She turns and fishes through her purse, then pulls out a small pocket notebook. She scribbles on a page then tears it out. "Call me tomorrow when you're about to leave," she says, handing the paper to me.

I take the paper, which carries a hint of her alluring pear scent. Her name and phone number are written on it. Her handwriting is gorgeous. "Thanks, Denise. I will," I say, smiling.

She backs out of the lot and drives off.

I sigh, watching until her taillights are gone.

I got her number! I got her fucking number!

My heart does flip-flops. I fold the paper in a neat square and place it in my wallet. *Damn right, I'm gonna call you.*

I re-coil the light cord, gather the tools from the toolbox, and return them to their proper places in the shop.

"She's quite a catch," Larry says from behind me.

I wheel around. Larry's still under the hood. "Huh?"

"The girl. What? You think just 'cause I'm under here that I don't know what's going on?"

"I was just doing her a favor."

"Pretty big favor." Larry pulls his head out from under the hood. "Repairing alternators ain't easy. You charge her?"

I frown. "No."

His face goes rigid. "'No'? Look, Dominick. This is a business. Don't do that again."

"I couldn't charge her, man. I knew she didn't have that kind of money on her. Besides, I didn't use any shop parts to fix it."

"You used these lights, didn't you? And those tools?" Larry frowns. "Look. I won't say anything to Frank, but next time, you need to either treat her as a customer, or do that shit at your own house, got it?"

I nod once. "Yeah, man. Sure."

Larry sighs and rubs his forehead. "Sorry, kid. I'm just tired from having been here all day trying to get caught up with these repairs. It sucks being short-staffed."

"It really does," I mutter. "I wish Frank would hire more help already."

"Hopefully soon. But for now, we'll manage like we always do. This ain't the first time this shit's happened."

Larry is always optimistic. Part of the reason I always look forward to coming to work. In his eyes, there's always hope no matter how bad it gets.

It was the attitude of a father—a *real* father, like I always wanted, but could never have.

CHAPTER 4

It's almost eleven thirty by the time I get back home. I'm surprised when I go inside not to hear any women's voices. Maybe Chris went to the gig. But when I enter the living room, I find Chris on the couch in a T-shirt and boxers, playing one of his football videogames on the big-screen TV.

"You're still here?"

Chris says nothing and doesn't take his eyes off the TV.

"So where are all these girls you went on about?"

He finally pauses the game and glares at me, his feathered brown hair whipping across his flushed face. "Gone! They got tired of waiting."

I frown. "Well, I got more condoms. Here." I toss a few packets from the box at him and they land on his lap. Sometimes it's fun messing with him like that.

He growls, brushes them away, and resumes his game. "You're such an ass, you know that?"

"Hey, I'm just paying you back for the shit you pulled earlier. Going into my room without permission and using up all my condoms like that. What the fuck is wrong with you?"

"I have needs, you know."

I roll my eyes. "So do I."

"Whatever, man. I know and you know those weren't getting used. Last time you had a girl was, what, two months ago? And that lasted all of, what, half a day?"

"Felicia?" I curl my lip. "Good fucking riddance. She was begging to go down on me within five minutes of meeting me."

Chris shakes his head. "Dude, I still can't believe you rejected her over that. She had a perfect ass, perfect tits . . . she was gorgeous!"

"Gorgeous, but not my type. Anyway . . . " I pin him with a glare. "We going to my brother's gig or what?"

Chris pauses the game again and looks back with a raised eyebrow. "What? You still wanna go? It's almost midnight, and I gotta get ready. By the time we get down there it'll almost be closing time."

I shrug and head for the stairs. "Well, if nothing else, I can see my brother again. Look, if you don't wanna go, that's cool."

"Ehh . . . "

I give him time to think about it while I hop in the shower, shave, and go through my closet for some decent club wear—a gray button-down shirt, black pants, and some matching shoes. Returning to the living room, I find Chris still on the couch in his T-shirt and boxers. There's a ticket on the arm of the couch with a sticky note with my name written on it. Frowning, I swipe it and head to the kitchen. Guess he made his decision.

"Later, man," Chris calls as I grab my motorcycle jacket off the back of one of the kitchen chairs.

Downtown Seattle, at Club 88, cars are parked everywhere, including in the designated overflow lot. I glimpse the hood of Kevin's black hatchback sports car, which is parked behind the building. It's great to see that Big Bro has a full crowd tonight. I park in a space far too small for a car, but perfect for my bike. I take off my gear, set it atop the bike seat, and smooth out my clothes. I don't know why I got this dressed up when I only intend to see my brother. I haven't seen him in a couple of months.

Approaching the entrance, I hear Kevin's house music thumping. I show my ticket and driver's license to the bouncer standing outside, and he lets me in. Strobe lights and fog welcome me as I enter. The place is packed. People are dancing amid the swirling, sparkling lights of mirror balls. Off to one side is a bar with hot chicks in skimpy outfits serving drinks. I look beyond the dance floor to the stage, where Kevin is manning his deejay station. He has a pair of thick headphones around his neck, and he's busily working the upbeat house tunes, spinning vinyls like the pro he is.

He's one of the few deejays around these days who still works in vinyl.

As I watch my brother do his thing, dancers bump and jostle me. Some apologize, while others are completely oblivious. I'm not mad; it's a club, after all, and I'm not in the mood to start a fight.

I head to the bar and order a rum 'n Coke. Drink in hand, I weave through the crowd and find a vacant seat on a white couch against the wall. The couch faces the stage, giving me a pretty good view of Kevin. I take a long sip of my drink and bob my head to the music.

From the corner of my eye, I see a group of girls start to meander toward me. I don't acknowledge them. One of them, however, gets bold and walks by me, bumping my leg with hers, probably deliberately. She's dressed in a short, skintight, cherry-red dress with a neckline that shows off every bit of her big tits. I'm sure if Chris were here, he'd be all over her.

Though Red is still near, I casually swirl my drink as I watch the stage. She finally plops down next to me on the couch. She smells sweet, like roses. But while she looks and smells good, I'm not interested.

Red crosses her legs, and the bottom of the dress hikes up her thigh about five more inches. "What are you drinking?" she asks.

I take another sip, pretending to be oblivious to her bait. "Rum 'n Coke."

She leans over like she's about to whisper in my ear, but I can tell it's really to show off her goods.

And I can't help but look. *Are those even real?*

"You should do a boilermaker," she says.

"Naw, I gotta drive tonight."

Nearby, Red's group of girlfriends giggle and talk to each other, all the while taking turns looking in my direction.

"Can I help you?" I say to her, annoyed.

"Well, I was going to ask *you* that." She winks.

I am so ready to blow her off, but then I think about Chris. I hate to say it, but I think this girl would be perfect for him. She would surely get him out of his funk. I down the rest of my drink. "Give me your number, and I'll let you know."

Red gives me one of those satisfied kinds of looks. I'm sure she's probably bagged plenty of guys this way. She scribbles her number down on an unused napkin, then her name beneath it—Adrienne. She has nice handwriting. Might actually be a smart girl under that painted-on dress. Chris could certainly use one of those types for a change.

Smiling, I fold up the napkin and stuff it in my pocket. "Thanks."

Red—Adrienne—is still gawking. "You're going to call, right?"

"Yeah, sure."

The music fades to silence, and the crowd cheers. I check the time on my phone—almost two a.m. Adrienne hops up from the couch and rushes to her friends. I get up as well and head to the stage, snaking my way through the sea of people in hopes of losing Adrienne for good.

The club's emcee comes out on stage. "Last call for alcohol, folks! Next Wednesday we'll be having DJ Trype on the ones and twos for an old school trip-hop night. As always, ladies, dress to impress!"

Much of the dance floor crowd thins as people head to the bar to get their last drinks. I hop up on stage and make my way to Kevin, who's packing away his vinyls and equipment.

"Hey, what's up, man?" I pat him on the shoulder.

He flinches and starts, looks up at me, and then beams. "Yo, Dom!" He sets down his records, and we do our secret handshake followed by a shoulder bump. "I *thought* that was you I saw out there in the crowd."

Other than my uncle Adam, Kevin's the only family I'm really close to. He's the only one who truly understands the shit I went through.

Then, as now, he's the only one I ever trusted.

We break off the hug. "What's going on, man?" Kevin asks.

"Nothing much. Working like a motherfucker." Without even asking, I begin helping him pack up his equipment. I'm the only one he ever allowed to touch his stuff. All along, he trusted me as much as I did him. He's always there for me to talk to.

"Yeah, I hear that." Kevin sets his sleeved vinyls in metal crates. "Sorry I haven't called lately. I've been busy with a bunch of shit for the past month."

I unplug a wire from the main mixer and begin wrapping it in a neat coil. "What happened?"

"My girlfriend fucking backstabbed me. Because of her, I'm about to get evicted from my apartment."

"*What?*"

"I got called to do a gig to fill in for one of the DJs that got sick, and I let my then-girlfriend, Justine, stay at my apartment. Rent was due, but the landlord had gone out to lunch by the time I had to leave, so I gave the money to Justine to give to him when he got back. She left with my money and never came back. Now the damn landlord has charged me *double* for being late. It's utter bullshit. I owe the landlord almost two thousand dollars now! If I can't pay up in four days, I'm gonna get evicted."

Frowning, I set the coiled cord in a milk crate with the others. I hate seeing Kevin so miserable. "Damn. That's messed up, bro. Anything I can do to help?"

Kevin shakes his head. "Naw, I'm straight. I think after tonight's gig, I'll finally have enough to pay the bastard. This whole ordeal has been such a fucking pain. Here's a tip, li'l bro. Don't get famous, else the crazy gold-digging bitches'll come crawling outta the cracks like roaches. They think I'm banking just 'cause I'm supposedly a "famous deejay" or some shit. Well newsflash! I make just enough to pay the bills and not much else.

"I'm not nearly as 'famous' as some of the guys down in Cali or over on the East Coast. Hell, there's even international sensations out there. I'm a nobody compared to them. What the fuck did I ever do to deserve this?"

"Don't worry about it, man," I say. "You know I got your back."

Kevin gives me a small smile. "Yeah, yeah, I know. So, who was that girl you were talking to?"

I snort. "What girl? I came here to see you."

"Kinda hard to miss T and A dressed in red." He laughs.

I punch him in the shoulder. "She wasn't my date. But I *do* have a date tomorrow—or should I say, later tonight. Her name's Denise. And man, is she amazing! Smart, smells like pears, dresses so sexy . . . "

Kevin whistles. "That's great, man! How long have you two been dating?"

"I just met her. But I'm a little scared of what might happen if she were to ever find out about—"

"Hey." Kevin puts a hand on my shoulder. "Don't let that shit get in the way of your own happiness. That's exactly what *he* would have wanted. Remember that. Don't let that sick motherfucker get into your head."

Biting down on my bottom lip, I exhale through my nose. Kevin's right, of course. But sometimes, some nights, I can't control that demon in my head. "I just . . . You know how sensitive some girls can be. What if she gets grossed out by that shit?"

"Dammit, Dom. What did I just say? You're a damn good man, and the honeys would kill to have someone like you. You're nothing like Pops, and never will be. Get that shit straight right now."

I stuff the headphones and microphones into a duffel bag and zip it closed.

"Remember what Uncle Adam said to you at that dinner for your high school graduation? 'You have to keep moving through the dark tunnels of life no matter what. Because at the end of that tunnel, you'll eventually find light.'"

I smile. "Yeah, I know, man. I try every day."

Finished packing, I help Kevin carry the stuff out to his car. Kevin arranges the equipment in the cramped backseat and trunk so that everything fits perfectly. Satisfied, he hops in the driver's side and starts up the car. He cranks down the window and asks, "You gonna be around next week?"

"Should be. Got an electromagnetics test next Friday, so I'll be studying for that."

Kevin nods. "Well, we'll have to catch up on things before then."

I look at him a little more seriously. "Have you decided whether or not you're gonna finish school next semester?"

"No idea." He shrugs. "I'm just trying to worry about my current shit first. Need to get that straight before I worry about school."

I sigh but don't press the issue. It bothers me that he's only seven credits away from graduating but isn't following through. "All right. But don't let me graduate before you."

Kevin ignores me. "I'll call you later, li'l bro. Take it easy." He plugs his music player into his sound system and cranks up the volume. Familiar house music blasts through the speakers, making his entire car vibrate.

"You too," I say, though he probably can't hear me. I watch him drive off, his tires screeching around a corner. Even when he's out of sight, I can hear the deep, thumping bass.

CHAPTER 5

I WAKE UP REFRESHED, AFTER HAVING A DREAM ABOUT Denise. I grab a set of clothes from the closet and head downstairs to the shower. I don't hear the TV on in the living room and wonder if Chris is still sulking in his room. He must be miserable, not having been able to sleep with a girl for a change—and on a Friday night, even. Serves him right for messing with me.

Leaving the bathroom, clean and dressed, I discover Chris lazing around on the couch in his T-shirt and boxers, munching on cereal while he watches Saturday morning cartoons.

"Hey, man, you just gonna sit there all day?" I ask, heading to the kitchen.

Chris munches loudly, but doesn't reply.

I pour myself a bowl of cereal and join him on the couch. "You should've come with me to the club last night. Ran into some hot chicks that would've loved to take you home."

He glares at the TV, still chewing.

I wave the napkin Adrienne gave me in front of him. "I even got one of their numbers."

Fuming, Chris slams his plate down on the coffee table, milk sloshing out of the top. "What the fuck, Dom? Gonna rub that shit in my face now?"

"Nope. Not my type. Got nice tits, though." I let go of the napkin and watch it flutter onto his lap.

Chris picks it up and stares at it. "'Adrienne' . . . You managed to get her *number*?"

"Yup. Got it while thinking how to help your sorry ass yet again." I smile a little at the shock on his face.

Chris gets a hold of himself. "Dude, you did this for me? I . . . thanks. Sorry for being such a dick about things."

"Mildly speaking." I finish my cereal.

"You said she's got nice tits? What're her measurements?" Chris's eyes widen with intrigue.

"Uh . . . I dunno. Forty inches, maybe?" I throw some random number out there. I'm definitely *not* a boob connoisseur.

He looks thoughtful for a moment, then narrows his eyes. "Chest or band?"

"What?"

"Chest, then." He does some counting on his fingers. "The way you make it sound, she's pretty big, so I'm thinking maybe around a thirty-five band." His eyes suddenly go wide. Dude! You realize that's probably a double-D cup?"

I blink. Several times. *Did he just calculate her bra size in his head?* It amazes me that Chris practically has this down to a science.

"Are they real?"

I shrug. "Never said they were real. I honestly have no idea. Guess you'll have to find that part out yourself, now won't you?"

"Damn right, I will!" He springs up from the couch and marches to his room, napkin in hand.

The old Chris is back. Never thought I'd actually be glad about it.

Noon rolls around and I can't take it anymore. It's seven hours till my date with Denise, but I really want to call her to hear her voice again. I dig the folded paper out of my wallet and hastily dial her number. She answers on the third ring.

My heart pounds. Her voice is beautiful on the other end. "H-Hi, Denise. It's Dominick."

"I thought I told you to call me when you're about to leave?"

I bite my bottom lip. I can't tell if she's just joshing me or really annoyed that I called too early. "Sorry, uh, if you're busy, I can go . . . "

I'm met with silence on the other end. *Did she hang up on me?*

"No," she finally says, and I exhale a quiet sigh of relief. "I got back from the study group not long ago. But I have to go do laundry in a bit."

"Okay. Well, I'll let you go do that. You still up for the date tonight?"

"'Date?' I thought we specifically agreed on 'dinner,' not a 'date.'" I can practically hear the smile in her voice.

"Isn't it the same thing?"

"Not quite, but I'll let it slide for now. So we're still on for Jade Fusion?"

"Yep. I'll see you around seven."

"I'll be waiting. Later, Dominick."

I open my mouth, trying to think of something more to say, trying to think of a way to keep hearing her voice for a little while longer, when I'm met with the buzzing sound of the ended call.

My heart swells with excitement. How ridiculous is this? I feel like I'm back in high school on my first date. I haven't gone out on a date—a *real* date—in months, maybe even a year. The few girls I ended up with since starting college turned out different than I expected, and they all moved on to the next guy.

But Denise seems genuine. Like the girl I always wanted in my life but could never get.

With seven hours to spare, I can't keep still. I call the restaurant and make reservations, and then rummage through the clothes in my closet for the white button-down shirt that has my motorcycle club's emblem embroidered on the left side. The graphic is small and abstract, like a tattoo design. I also find a pair of casual black pants. With the clothes draped over my arm, I head to the kitchen, grabbing the iron and ironing board from the hall closet along the way. While I'm unfolding the ironing board, Chris's door creaks open from down the hall.

Chris stops at the kitchen doorway, his phone in one hand, and a bright smile on his face. I've not seen a smile that wide on him in a very long time. He'd been in his room all morning on the phone, so I assume his chat with Adrienne went well. But as soon as he notices me ironing, his glow turns to curiosity. "Holy shit, we have an iron?"

I roll my eyes. "You mean *I* have an iron."

"Right. So what's up with this?"

"I told you, I have a date tonight. We're going to Jade."

"The Asian place?" He whistles. "All the girls seem to like eating there."

"It's got atmosphere."

"Heh. Well, you must really love this new girl or something."

I smile. *Sure feels like it.* I turn the heat setting to Delicate to iron the shirt. "What's up with you and Adrienne?" I look back up at him in time to see him beaming again.

"Well, at first, she was like, 'who's this creepy guy calling me?' so I let her know what was up. Put the charms on her, y'know."

I guffaw.

"She wondered where 'the guy from the club' was, and I told her you were my roommate, but a bit of a flake, and to not expect you to call her."

I reset the iron and glare at him. "You what?"

"Hey, I had to think of something, dude." He shrugs. "Anyway, we swapped pics, and she sounded totally interested. Even said I was hot! Can you believe it?"

Picking up the iron again, I resume pressing my shirt. "No, I honestly can't believe it."

He gives me the finger, but I ignore it.

"We're going to the movies tonight, then to one of her girlfriends' house parties." Chris's face lights up. "Dude! You should bring your new girl, too. We can make it a double date."

I gawk at him. "You can't be serious."

Chris laughs. "I'm telling you. We can show off our hot new chicks at that party."

"Naw. I'm taking things slow. I'm not gonna fuck up this date. And how the hell do you know if Adrienne is hot? You haven't even seen her."

"I told you, we swapped pics. Holy shit, she looks amazing!"

I shut the iron off, set it aside, and carefully fold my shirt and pants. "How do you know the picture is even real? She could've manipulated it or something."

"Nope. This pic is as real as it gets. Look!" He shows me his phone.

The picture is his current wallpaper. It's definitely Adrienne. She's wearing the same red dress from the club. She strikes a teasing selfie pose, angling the camera in such a way that it looks like the top of her dress is barely covering her tits. The peaks of her nipples create small beads beneath the fabric. I wonder if she took that picture last night? Probably intended to send it to me whenever I called. I'm glad it's Chris who got the pic and not me. "Yup. That's definitely her, all right."

Chris nods. "No kidding! Oh, and her boobs are a single D, not double. She looks between thirty-five and thirty-eight inches. But they are most definitely all real."

I arch an eyebrow. "You can tell all that from a picture?"

"Of course I can! I've seen and felt enough of them to know the difference."

I shake my head. "Right. Well, hopefully, for your sake, she's a keeper." I pause and cast him a look. "You *are* going to try and keep her, right?"

He stiffens. "I dunno. That depends on her. Why are you so insistent on me keeping a girl? It's getting old."

"Because, frankly, I'm sick of your shit every time you dump a girl the day after sleeping with her."

"I don't dump them. They dump me." He grimaces, perhaps realizing how utterly pathetic that sounds.

"Yeah," I say, "they dump you because they find out you were sleeping with five other girls just hours before them."

"Dude, get off my back about it, all right? I've yet to find 'the one,' and I'm not ready to settle. Not everyone's all prim and proper like you, Dom."

I grunt. "I'm far from being a saint, but I also don't want to be known as a guy who fucks anything that moves, either."

Chris narrows his eyes at me. "What the hell are you trying to say?"

"I'm saying to just give Adrienne a chance, will you? Please?"

"Well, she's my new wallpaper now, so that's a start, ain't it?" He looks at his phone, and the annoyed look on his face lifts.

I've known Chris since high school, and he never sets a picture of a girl as his wallpaper unless he's really interested in her. Perhaps there is hope for him, but I'm not holding my breath. "Fair enough."

"I told her to come by here. She'll be over in an hour or so."

My jaw drops. "What? Why the hell did you do that?"

He gives a light shrug and heads for the living room. "She insisted on coming over. Who am I to reject a girl with such beautiful boobs who thinks I'm hot?"

"You've lost it, man." I shake my head.

"What can I say?" Chris says from down the hall. "That girl makes me *crazy*! Now help me clean up the living room, will you?"

Chris? Cleaning? Maybe he really has *gone crazy.*

The five hours remaining feel like an eternity. I sprawl on the couch with the TV on, but I'm too distracted to watch it. I can't stop thinking about Denise. I want to call her again, but I restrain myself. The last thing I want to do is creep her out with my constant calling. Besides, she's probably busy doing laundry. I wonder what she's gonna wear to dinner.

A sudden knock at the door makes my heart race. I spring up from the couch, rush to the door, and peer through the peephole.

It's Adrienne.

She knocks again, and Chris suddenly yells from behind me, "Got it!"

I jump and spin around. *Where did he come from?*

Chris, wearing one of his favorite pro football jerseys, pushes me aside. "I told you, I got it."

I take the opportunity to disappear. "Keep her away from me," I mutter then head for the stairs. I hide in the stairway and listen. When I hear the door open, I peek around the corner.

Adrienne enters wearing a short denim skirt and a white spaghetti-strap camisole, which strains to accommodate her large tits. She furrows her thin, penciled eyebrows at Chris as she slowly walks around in black, open-toe stilettos, assessing him like a doctor diagnosing a patient.

I could swear I see Chris wipe some drool from the side of his mouth.

Adrienne finally stops in front of him. "Chris?"

He gawks at her, as if she has him under some magical spell. "Yeah . . . That's me," he says breathily.

She grins. "You look even hotter in person."

You've got to be shitting me.

"Yeah?" Chris winks. "Well, you know. I aim to please."

"So where's that flakey roommate of yours? I kinda wanna put my foot up his ass for not calling me like he said he would." She says this so innocently, it's a little frightening.

"Ah, you just missed him. He's a bit unreliable and scared as shit of girls. Especially the beautiful ones."

I clench my jaw. *Fuck you.*

Adrienne flicks a lock of her ebony, red-streaked hair from her face. Her stylish bob looks like she just left the salon before coming here. "Shame, 'cause he was cute. Probably has a nice ass, too. Too bad it's going to have an imprint of my foot on it when I see him again." She crosses her arms and cocks a hip.

Chris's eyes are clearly drawn downward, most likely to her tits. "Uh . . . y-yeah, Dom's such a dick, isn't he?" He looks up for a moment, and then his gaze drifts downward again. "Can I, uh . . . get you something to drink? Water? A beer? Milk?"

I roll my eyes. *Oh for fuck's sake.* He's going to blow his chances before the date even starts.

Surprisingly, Adrienne laughs. "No, thanks. I am a little hungry, though." She leans up against the back of the couch, her arms still crossed. "How does Chinese sound?"

Chris manages to lift his eyes again. "Sounds great. So this is officially a date, then?"

"It's lunch." Adrienne uncrosses her arms. "You're not just some guy looking for a one-night stand, are you?"

"Yes—I mean—no! *Hell no!* Fuck it, let's go eat." He takes Adrienne by the arm and leads her out the door.

I remain in my hiding place and listen to the muffled sounds of car doors slamming and an engine starting. The sounds fade into silence, and I come out from hiding.

I can't believe that actually worked.

CHAPTER 6

Six thirty can't come fast enough. I fiddle around with the GPS maps on my phone to find the quickest route to Denise's house. She lives only ten minutes away, and not far from downtown, where the restaurant is. I give myself one last check in the mirror and remember to grab a spare helmet out of the closet on my way out. As I start up the engine, I suddenly have a thought: what if she's afraid of motorcycles? I guess if she refuses to ride with me, we could just take her car. I'm willing to do whatever it takes to spend time with her, but I hope she won't be scared to ride.

The traffic in town isn't bad for an early Saturday night. I reach Denise's house about fifteen minutes early. Her neighborhood is quiet and quaint, with picket fences in front of almost every house. I park my bike along the curb, set my jacket and helmet on the seat, and head up the walkway leading to her small, white house. I ring the bell and stuff my hands in my pockets. Beyond the screen door, an inner door opens.

It's not Denise.

The woman steadily chews her gum while she stares at me with cold, calculating, dark brown eyes. She looks older, maybe early-to-mid forties. She tilts her dreadlocked head and looks down her nose at me. "Yes? Who're you?" she asks in a thick, Caribbean accent.

I clear my throat, trying not to let her stare faze me. "Hi, I'm Dominick. I'm supposed to pick up Denise. Is she here?"

Dreads blows a small, pink bubble. "Denise, eh?" She raises an eyebrow, then cranes her neck and looks beyond me. "So where's your ride?"

I thumb over my shoulder. "There."

She blinks. "You shittin' me, right?"

I shake my head, but before I can answer aloud, footsteps approach and Denise appears behind Dreads. She pushes past her and opens the screen door. Denise wears a blue dress over black leggings. Her hair is cornrowed in the front, with the back twisted out into a cascading ponytail of thick, curly hair. Her smooth, caramel face doesn't look made up, but her full lips glisten with some kind of sparkly, peach-colored lip gloss. The only jewelry she wears is a pair of small silver hoop earrings and a silver necklace with a charm in the shape of a *fleur de lis*. My heart skips several beats as I take her in. When she smiles at me, I practically melt.

God, she's beautiful.

"Hi, Dominick," Denise says to me as she steps outside. She's wearing black flats, perfect should we go on an after-dinner walk.

Dreads places a hand on Denise's shoulder, stopping her. "Hey. You're not actually going out with this carless dead-beat, are you?"

I lift an eyebrow. *Deadbeat?*

Denise looks back at her. "I just met him, Lauren. He fixed my car, and we agreed on dinner."

Dreads—Lauren—pops her gum. "He fixes cars and doesn't have one of his own? What's wrong with that picture, hmm?"

I frown. I have a driver's license, but I didn't want a car when I came to college.

"What are you talking about?" Denise asks, looking back and forth between me and Lauren.

Lauren points outside. "Look at what he intends to drive you around in . . . or should I say *on.*"

Denise follows Lauren's direction and gasps. "A *motorcycle?*" She looks back at me and pales. "You've got to be out of your mind, Dominick!"

I grimace. This was *not* how I wanted our night to start out. "There's nothing to worry about, Denise. I'll make sure you're perfectly safe. You can even use my jacket so you don't get cold."

"'Ey, now," Lauren interjects. "She's not gettin' on that thing! It's a death trap. What kind of man fixes cars and doesn't have one of his own, anyway, hmm?"

Is this woman her roommate or her mother? I don't feel like arguing with Lauren. "We can take your car if you want, Denise," I say in a calm voice, ignoring the other woman. "I don't own a car. I've had other passengers before, though, and I've kept all of them safe."

Denise doesn't respond.

Damn it. I'm fucking this up.

"'Other passengers,' hmm?" Lauren says. "Other girl-friends?"

It takes everything I have to keep my cool. She could very well be Denise's mother.

Denise turns away from me. Her shoulders slump, and she seems disheartened, a little fearful. *She doesn't trust me.* I'm not sure what to say or do.

"Lauren, let me talk to Dominick in private, please." Denise says.

Lauren scoffs. "You've gotta be shittin' me, D."

Denise shakes her head. "Please."

Lauren gives me the stinkeye. Sucking her teeth, she reluctantly spins on her heel and disappears inside, shutting the inner door behind her.

I exhale quietly, relieved to be alone with Denise. Being this close to her makes my heart beat faster. Her fresh scent, a mix of pears and cocoa butter, tickles my nose. Everything about her arouses me.

"Sorry about that," Denise says. "Lauren can be like a mother hen sometimes. She's a friend of the family, and going back to school for her PhD, so we ended up as roommates. She's always looked out for me since I was a kid."

I make a sour face. "But you're a grown woman. You don't need that kind of . . . supervision."

She smiles. "She means well. Really, she does. She's just had some issues in the past. I shouldn't say." She pauses and bites her bottom lip. "Just go easy on her, all right?"

I shrug. It sounded serious, but it's none of my business, and I'm not gonna pry. "Fine."

"So, about that motorcycle . . . "

I sigh deeply. "I just thought that—"

"We were going to Jade Fusion. Does it look like I'm dressed to ride a damn motorcycle?"

I cringe. *Not really, but you do look stunning.* "Look, if you really don't wanna ride, we can take your car."

She looks thoughtful. "Were you really expecting me to get on that thing?"

The fact that she doesn't acknowledge my previous comment tells me that she might possibly be reconsidering. God, I sure hope so. "I didn't know what to expect, but I had hoped you might have been feeling a little adventurous tonight."

"It looks dangerous."

"Life is dangerous sometimes."

"What if I fall off?"

I chuckle to myself. Her fear and denial are more than obvious now. "I won't let you fall off. Trust me."

Her thin eyebrows rise. "I barely even know you."

"True, but how else will we get to know each other if we don't take chances?"

With pursed lips, she looks hesitantly at my parked bike. "I don't know. Maybe we *should* just take my car."

"Up to you," I say with a shrug. "But . . . " Slowly, I reach for her hand. I can't help it—her hand is so close to mine, I can feel her warmth. Gently, I glide my fingers over hers, and feel her soft, smooth skin. "I promise you everything will be okay." I look down at her hand and don't feel inclined to let go. Not yet. Not at all. I want to kiss her hand so badly, but she seems surprised enough by my actions.

Her eyes drift to mine, then down to our hands. Thankfully, she doesn't pull away. "Okay. Just this once. I'm holding you to your promise. I better not fall off." She smiles slightly. "Let me grab my purse."

I exhale. It's progress in a big way. She's trusting me. I let go of her hand and watch her disappear back inside the house. I hear voices rise from within, and then Denise comes back outside, looking slightly annoyed.

"All right, let's go," she says.

I keep my thoughts about their argument to myself and lead Denise down the walkway to my bike.

She runs her hand along the red tank and over the seat. There's hesitation in her eyes.

Smiling reassuringly, I unlock the extra helmet from the side of the bike and hand it to her. "Here. You need to wear this."

She gingerly takes the helmet and stares at it. It's a black-and-white full-face helmet with gold-colored abstract designs on it. There are signs of obvious wear on the helmet, but it's otherwise fully functional. She slips it on over her head—and over that fantastic hairdo that she'd probably just gotten done—and I help her. The helmet is a little big but seems to fit her well enough. After securing the strap under her chin, I look her over. "How's that?"

She pulls up the face shield and grumbles, "I can't believe I'm doing this. This is totally going to mess up my hair."

I laugh. "It'll be fine. Your hair is beautiful regardless."

She rolls her eyes and shakes her head.

I shrug out of my jacket and hand it to her. "Here. So you won't get too cold."

"Thanks," she says, taking it. "But what about you?"

"I'll be fine." *I'm already hot just thinking about you sitting behind me.*

She slings her small square purse across her body and puts on the jacket.

I slip on my helmet and mount my bike. "Come on." I motion to the raised back seat for passengers. "Sit in that spot behind me."

"How do I get on?"

I point to the foot pegs on either side of the lower frame, near the back tire. "Put one foot there, swing your other leg over, and sit."

"Geez, glad I wore pants," she mutters, and I chuckle.

She hesitates a moment before managing to heft herself up. That whiff of pears and cocoa plays with my senses again. "Am I sitting right?" she asks, her voice muffled from the helmet.

I look behind me and nod. "Good. Now, keep your feet there, wrap your arms around my waist and . . . " I fall silent as I feel her slender arms around me. Her hands squeeze my abs, and I feel the softness of the rest of her body pressing against my back. I swallow a lump in my throat. My groin tightens.

"Am I holding too tight?" she asks.

I swallow again. "N . . . No, not at all. Hold as tight as you need to, and keep your arms around me."

"Don't worry, I don't intend to let go."

I beam so wide my cheeks hurt. I am not about to complain about her holding too tight. Her touch is electrifying.

I start up the engine and slowly ease away from the curb. Denise clutches my abs and stomach tighter, nearly making me gasp for breath. But the feeling does more than startle me; it gets me harder. Riding on a motorcycle with a hard-on is absolute torture. Why does she have to be so amazing? I don't think I'll be able to concentrate on dinner at this rate.

I take all the side streets and make it to Jade Fusion a little after seven. There's an unreserved parking space right outside the restaurant that's just big enough for a bike to fit. I maneuver my way into the space, throw down the kickstand, and shut off the engine. While I take off my helmet, I wait for her to get off the bike.

"And this is why I love to ride," I say, gesturing to the parking space I managed to squeeze into.

She stumbles a little as she dismounts, but I reach out for her hand to help steady her. She fiddles with the snaps and loops of her helmet, and pulls it off. The helmet has done little to mess up her hair. All of her braids are still intact, and her naturally curly ponytail is still full of life, just like her.

She peers at herself in one of the bike's mirrors and brushes the front edges of her hair with her fingers.

I chuckle. "Your hair's fine. You look great." I get off the bike, hang my helmet over the other mirror, and set hers on the seat. Taking her hand, I lead her to the restaurant's entrance. A waiter standing outside the doors and dressed in a chic black suit casts Denise and me a questioning look as we approach.

"Good evening. Do you have reservations?" he asks.

I nod and give him my name. He walks behind a podium and checks a clipboard sitting atop it. Then he nods and scribbles a line across the page with a yellow highlighter. "Ah, Mister Anderson." He smiles. "Thank you. Please enjoy your experience at Jade Fusion."

The smell of marinated beef and steamed vegetables engulfs us as we enter, making my stomach growl. The restaurant is dimly lit, with jade-green lights creating an upscale, modern Asian-fusion atmosphere. I've only been here a handful of times, since it's not exactly a place mechanics go to on their lunch break.

A waitress escorts us to a table, next to one of the restaurant's many windows overlooking the busy city streets. The table is set with two wine glasses and silverware rolled in black cloth napkins. Two black leather-bound menus are set where the plates would be.

I pull out a chair for Denise.

"And here I thought chivalry was dead," she says, smiling at me.

Returning the smile, I seat myself. "I'm glad I was able to change your mind. So what did you think of the motorcycle ride?"

"All right, I'll admit it. It wasn't so bad. At least I didn't fall off."

I wonder if she'll want to ride again. "See? I told you. It's fun. And relaxing."

"It is."

"Think of all the other fun and adventurous things you might be missing out on."

She raises her eyebrows. "Oh? Like what?"

"Like . . . " I rub my chin. " . . . maybe going to a movie with me after dinner."

She chuckles. "How about we just get through dinner first?"

"Fair enough." I smile sheepishly.

I scan the single-page menu. Though the restaurant is somewhat upscale, the prices are fairly reasonable. "You like this place?" I ask Denise, and she looks up from her menu.

"Yeah, it brings back memories," she says, glancing around the place dreamily.

"Old dates?" I wonder how many guys before me have taken her here. I mean, what guy wouldn't want to take a beautiful girl like her out to dinner?

She gives me a dumbfounded look, then covers her mouth and chuckles. "You think I came here on dates?"

It's my turn to look dumbfounded. "Well, why else would you come to a place like this?"

"This wasn't always a restaurant, you know. It used to be Anastasia Beaumonte's Dance Studio. I used to come here to do ballet."

My jaw drops. "You do ballet?"

"*Did*," Denise says. "Only in elementary and middle school before Miss Beaumonte died and the place shut down."

"Sorry to hear that. I bet you were really good at it."

"I was okay, I guess." She tries to fight down a smile, and I know she's being modest. "Anyway, I never really got back into it since I didn't have the time. And I really loved Miss Beaumonte. I didn't think I would ever find another teacher like her."

"Well, some things you never forget."

The waitress returns with a tray of water glasses and a bottle of wine. "Would you two like to try our special Riesling tonight?" she asks, setting down the glasses of water.

"Sure," I say just as Denise adds, "Please."

"I will need to see your IDs, please."

I flip my driver's license from my wallet, and Denise does the same. As the waitress scans them, I peer at Denise's ID, hoping to get a glimpse of her birthdate, but I can't see shit.

"Thank you," the waitress says and fills our wine glasses a quarter of the way with white wine. I release a breath I hadn't realized I was holding. She's twenty-one, at least. Thank God I won't be drinking alone tonight.

Denise and I place our dinner orders, and the waitress disappears again.

"I saw you looking," Denise says, smirking.

I blink. "Huh?"

"Trying to know how old I am. Or were you just trying to sneak a peek at my horrible picture?"

I never even thought to look at her picture. But I suspect it was anything *but* horrible—unlike mine. This girl doesn't look like she takes horrible pictures. "Well, uh, you know, it's impolite to ask a woman her age, so . . . "

"Yeah, if they're insecure about it. Honestly, age is just a number."

I smile. This girl is really one-of-a-kind. "All right, then. How old are you?"

"Twenty-one and proud. You?"

"Twenty-two." I pick up my wine glass. "A toast?"

Denise lifts an eyebrow. "To what?"

"To . . . ballet. Yeah."

She chuckles and picks up her glass. "You're crazy. Fine. To ballet."

We clink glasses and take a sip. The wine is a little dry for my taste, but Denise seems to enjoy it.

"So what about you, Mister Mysterious?" Denise asks, with a lick of her lips that really gets my motor revving.

I set my glass down. *She wants to know more about me— perhaps my past—but there's nothing there I would want to talk about.* "Well, I'm an engineering major at UDub."

"Yeah, you told me that already." She leans her elbows on the table and rests her chin on her fists, staring at me intently.

Oh damn, that look. She obviously wants to know something personal about me. I pick up my water glass. "Did I already tell you that? Okay. Hmm . . . " I take a small sip to hide my discomfort.

"Are you from Seattle?"

"Not originally, no. I was born in the Bronx and moved to Renton when I was three."

Her eyes glitter. "The Bronx? As in New York? Wow. I'd love to visit New York someday."

"I'm sure one day you will." I grin. "Lots of ballet shows on Broadway."

"So, let's see. You ride motorcycles, fix cars, study engineering . . . you must've totally been a jock or something when you were growing up."

I chuckle. "Well, I did play football my junior and senior years."

"Really? Wow, never would've guessed football. Maybe basketball or soccer."

"My brother played basketball. He was really good. He was on the varsity team all four years of high school. Ended up with a full ride to UDub, where he became a legend for three years. He could've gone pro." *But he had to go and throw it all away by dropping out.*

"Why didn't he?"

"He lost interest." I take another sip of water to hide my frown. I'm not sure if it's true or not, but that's what he always told me whenever I asked. But part of me has always thought otherwise. I see the guilt and regret in his eyes every so often. He sacrificed his dream. *Because of me. Because of the shit at home with Mama. Because he knew how miserable*

I'd been in that house alone with her and Uncle Adam. And those memories.

Those fucking memories . . .

"So why did you choose engineering, of all majors? Did your parents put you up to it?"

I set down my water glass. It's leaving a bitter taste in my mouth. "So what kind of movies do you like?" I ask, hoping she's willing to take the hint.

She pauses and looks at me strangely, but to my relief, she lets the life story thing rest. "I like action," she says, then picks up her water glass. "The more car chases and explosions, the better."

"I like action movies, too."

The waitress returns with our food—Mongolian beef over rice with steamed vegetables for me and teriyaki chicken with a salad for Denise. The food is excellent, and we eat in silence, occasionally looking up and shooting little glances at one another. Denise still looks damn good, but sometimes I think I see a little frown between her eyebrows, like something's bothering her. I hope it's not the food. I *really* hope it's not me.

We both finish, and I check my phone to see what movies are playing. "Let's see . . . there's a movie that came out last week that's supposed to be pretty good. Lots of action in it. It's starting around 9:55. Wanna check it—" I look up and notice Denise has her arms crossed, and she's jiggling her foot under the table. I can see the tablecloth bouncing. "What's wrong?" I ask, shutting off my phone.

Denise looks down and starts fidgeting with the table-cloth. "Just nerves."

I scratch the stubble of my beard, trying to make sense of it all. "Are you . . . not enjoying yourself?"

"First dates always make me nervous. You know, having dinner with a complete stranger."

"Are we really complete strangers? I mean, we can get to know each other little by little."

She runs her finger around the brim of her water glass. "Yeah? You don't seem to like talking about yourself very much."

Yeah, because I don't want to gross you out with my past. "What else can I say? I'm just a normal guy."

She chuckles, and I relax a little. "A 'normal guy'? No, Dominick. Normal guys don't do what you do."

I purse my lips, wondering what her past boyfriends did to her to make her so defensive. "Well, I guess I'm not a normal guy, then. I'm trying to do this right, you know. No obligations, no one-night stands. Just a quiet dinner and a movie afterward. That's all."

"That's just it. No obligations? Let's be real, Dominick."

Of course she doesn't trust me—maybe she doesn't trust guys at all. I guess in a way that's smart, but now I'm even more curious about what her past boyfriends must have done to her to cause this icy shield. I don't want to lose my cool in front of her, but she is starting to push the wrong buttons. "Yeah, no obligations. I've treated every girl I've met like this—or at least I've *tried* to," I say, trying to keep my voice calm. "And you know what? They didn't want it. I was too boring for them. Old-fashioned. They were *expecting* some sort of obligation." The anger begins rising in my chest. *I don't understand why some of you chicks prefer guys who treat you like shit.*

Her eyes widen, and she gapes at me. "So what are you saying? That I don't appreciate this?"

I take a deep breath. I had gone off on her, and I didn't mean to. "I wasn't talking about you in particular. I won't lie, I've had other girlfriends in the past. But none of them lasted longer than a few days. It was either because they wanted a one-night stand or because they felt like I was cramping their style."

She stares at her half-empty water glass, which is covered in condensation. She idly runs her finger down the side of the glass, catching the water droplets.

Fuck going to the movies tonight. I'm too pissed.

The waitress returns with the bill, and I stick three twenties in the black leather holder and hand it back to her, telling her to keep the change.

"Can't a girl be curious?" Denise asks once the waitress leaves again.

I frown. *Cautious, you mean.* It's not fair for me to generalize like this. Denise is very smart. I should appreciate that she wants to know more about me instead of just spreading her legs to a stranger. "Hey, I'm sorry. I just . . . want you to trust me. I wanna be the best guy I can be for you. The fact that you trusted me enough to ride on the back of my bike meant a lot. And sitting here having dinner with a beautiful and intelligent girl like you means everything."

Her head tilts to the side and she smiles, her cheeks turning a slight shade of red against her smooth, caramel skin.

"I know we've only just met," I say, "and you feel like you barely know me, but I like taking things slow, no pressure."

"I guess. It's just weird. Most guys I've dated wanted to get into my pants the very first night."

I frown. In truth, I do want to get into her pants, and I feel horrible for thinking that, but I can't help my urges. Denise may have given up ballet in middle school, but she still has that luscious dancer's body.

"Thanks for dinner, by the way," she says, and I realize I hadn't responded to her previous comment.

"You're welcome." I nod.

"We should get lunch sometime or maybe an early breakfast before classes."

An opportunity to spend more time with her? Hell yeah. But I'd never seen her on campus before. "What's your schedule like?"

"I have a nine-thirty sociology class and a two-hour world literature class starting at 11:10 on Mondays and Tuesdays, then the rest of the week are all afternoon and evening classes."

I make a mental note of her schedule. "All of my classes are in the morning, starting at eight, and the last one ends at 1:10. I go to work after that."

"That's convenient."

I shrug. "Eh, it works. I don't have much of a social life on the weekdays because of it, though. Hey, in June my motorcycle club is having a community cookout to raise money for a member's little girl who has cancer. Would you be interested in coming out?"

"I'd love to. I'm sorry to hear about the poor little girl."

"We're hoping it'll be a big turnout so we can help the family out."

"It's two months away, but I will try and make plans to be there."

A quick check of my phone shows 9:52. I slide out of my chair and extend my hand to her. "I might as well take you home. Let's do a movie next time."

She takes my hand as she stands. Hers feels soft, smooth, and warm. "Next time sounds good."

We leave the restaurant and get back on the bike. She doesn't seem afraid this time as we ride through town and back to her house. She gets off, shrugs out of the jacket, and stands at the curb.

"Thanks for dinner. And the motorcycle ride. It was nice."

I put the jacket on and become engulfed in her warmth and cocoa-pear scent. I smile from underneath my helmet, but realize she probably can't see it, so I give her a thumbs-up instead. "Anytime. Maybe I'll see you Monday?" I wonder if my voice sounds muffled to her.

She nods, my only indication that she can still understand me. "Yeah, sure." She gives a little wave of her hand, though I can see from the look on her face that she's troubled about something. "Hey, Dominick, I—" She looks away. "Never mind. Bye."

Before I can say anything more, she turns and heads for the front door. I frown. *Bye, Denise.*

I wait until she's safely inside before I leave. Her troubled look remains etched in my mind. I know that look. She wants to trust me but doesn't think she can.

He haunts my dreams again.

"Turn around."

I shudder and feel my eyes burn with fresh tears, but I hold them back. I'm not gonna let them fall. Not in front of him.

"Only little pansies cry," he says. *"If you're going to be a little pansy, then I'll treat you like one."*

He spanks me on the ass. Hard. I yelp, but I hold the tears back. He pushes me face first to the floor and kneels down behind me. I just want it to end.

The sound of the front door slamming downstairs jerks me out of my sleep. Staring blindly at the darkness, I lie still in bed and listen to the sounds of two sets of footsteps. I check the clock on my phone. 4:45. Damn, way too early. I recognize Chris and Adrienne's low voices, which are suddenly cut off by the sounds of Chris's bedroom door closing. With a sigh, I get out of bed and retrieve my music player and noise-cancelling headphones from the desk. The walls are thin, and once they get going, I'll hear every moan and groan from their fucking. Slipping the headphones on, I lie back in bed. I start up the player to a random hip-hop song and close my eyes, letting the music take over while I try to relax. I mull over my dreams—nightmares—and my date with Denise.

That look of doubt on her face. Like tonight didn't even matter.

Who knows if I'll see her on Monday? Maybe by then she will have forgotten all about me. Just my luck, she will have moved on to someone else. Like they all do.

CHAPTER 7

I WAKE UP LATE, DESPITE MY TROUBLE SLEEPING LAST NIGHT. I couldn't stop thinking about Denise all night, and she remains on my mind even now.

I totally fucked up last night.

I check my phone, curious if she's called, but there's nothing. Not even a text. I know I shouldn't be worrying about it. I mean, it's too early to tell whether or not she's interested in me. But even as I think the words, my heart aches at the thought that I might never see her again.

Why should I even care?

Because there's something about Denise—something genuine—that draws me to her.

I swipe the screen on my phone and check my email. Buried within the notices and announcements sent by the university, I spot a newsletter from one of the local nightclubs with the subject, "Don't Miss DJ Kevitron!" and quickly open it. Kevin is scheduled to be the featured deejay there tonight from ten till two. After last night, I feel like confiding in my brother. He'll help me get out of my funk.

The house is quiet, even when I leave the bathroom, showered and dressed, but based on Chris's shut door, he's still home. He and Adrienne must've went on pretty late last night.

I'm too pissed to worry about it. My stomach growls, and, deciding to leave my depressing shit at home, I head over to Loriano's, my favorite pizza joint in Seattle, and one of the few local eateries open on Sundays. The place is not as crowded today as it is during the week, but it's still busy. I buy a giant slice of their famous "big-as-your-head" pizza and a beer, and then head to an unoccupied booth near the back of the restaurant. I stare at my cell phone screen—again—and think about Denise—her perfect smile, ebony eyes, cornrowed hair, and pear scent.

Her number stares back at me from the call log. I shove the phone back into my pocket.

If she wants to talk to me, then she'll *call.*

My gut sinks. What if I freaked her out? So many scenarios run through my mind that I can't concentrate on lunch. I force a bite of the hot pizza and relax as I savor the truly authentic, New-York-style taste. My eyes drift up to the ceiling where a TV hangs showing the sports channel. Professional basketball scores scroll across the screen along with highlights of last night's games.

My phone vibrates in my pocket, and I reach for it. I whip out the phone and pray it's Denise, but I hesitate to look at the lit-up screen. I inhale, finally take a peek, and exhale. *Damn.* Just a text from Chris.

Adrienne's a keeper! :)

I'm glad to see that Chris found some stability for a change. It's about damn time. And yet, here I am, wallowing in self-pity, deep in a love funk that would rival one of Chris's past episodes. As I polish off my beer, someone slides in my booth and sits across from me. It's Alonzo, my M/C club's road captain. His girlfriend, Lindsey, works here as a waitress.

"The hell you doing here, Genius?" Lonz says with a bright smile.

I cringe. *Genius.* I'll never get used to that nickname my club brothers gave me once I became a full-fledged member. The guys always get on my case about how crazy I was to major in engineering. But still. "Genius" is the last thing I consider myself.

He folds his arms and rests them on the table. The short sleeves of his white T-shirt hike up his thick forearms. The Chinese dragon tattoo on his left forearm gave him his nickname, Dragon.

I pocket my phone. "Nothing much. Just having a late lunch. What's up with you?"

He arches a salt-and-pepper eyebrow. "Alone on a Sunday afternoon? What the hell's going on with you?"

Lonz is about the same age as Larry, and like Larry, it's always difficult to hide things from him. Damn old guys. I lower my gaze to my half-eaten pizza. "Nothing, man. Just thinking and killing time 'til tonight. Gonna see my brother."

"You two ain't tired of each other yet?" He laughs.

I try to laugh as well, but it's hard. "Who the hell do I talk to about personal shit?"

"Well, you *do* have other family besides your brother." He pats the embroidered patch of the club's grim reaper emblem on the left side of his leather vest.

I shake my head. "I'd rather discuss it with blood."

"Suit yourself, but if you intend to live out the rest of your life in this social funk, well, it's not healthy, I tell you." He motions Lindsey over, and she brings us a pitcher of beer and two frosted mugs. The two of them kiss, and she goes on her way.

"I'll be all right, Lonz," I say.

Lonz tops off both mugs and slides one my way. "So Darryl says he saw you last night downtown carrying a girl on your bike." He takes a long swig.

I frown. "Eh, I was just taking a chick home. Her date had a little too much to drink." I reach for my beer.

Lonz eyes me from over the brim of his glass. "Bullshit. Who is she?"

"I don't wanna talk about it," I say, my shoulders slouching.

"Trouble already?"

"I told you, man, I don't wanna talk about it."

Lonz sets down his half-empty mug, leans his head in close, and lowers his voice. "If it really *is* true and you finally found someone, then that's great. It's about damn time."

I'm not sure if he had meant that as a joke or compli-ment, so I stay silent.

"You're bringing her to the cookout in June, right?" Lonz asks.

I shrug. "I dunno."

"You should. She'll have a good time." He picks up his beer and chugs the remaining contents.

"I don't think so." I tighten my grip around the handle. "Anyway, it's only been one date."

"So take her out on more dates." Lonz looks at me a little more seriously, though a hint of a smile is still eminent. "You're a good man, Dominick. She's lucky to have someone like you."

His words are comforting, but he has no idea what hap-pened last night. "I don't think she's interested, Lonz." I look at him sadly. "She doesn't trust me."

Lonz stares at me a moment, then shrugs. "Then let her get to know you better so she can."

"It's not that easy. I wanna take things slow, but I'm not sure she wants that."

"Stop overthinking things, boy. You know, I thought that about Lindsey, too, when I first met her, but we talked little by little. And now, I wouldn't trade her for nothin'."

"That's all well and good for you, man, but that's not the norm in this fast-paced college life." I tip back my beer and finish every last drop.

"No, you haven't met the right one yet. That's college life. Enjoy what's out there as much as you can, while you can, so you can settle down later."

"I don't want to settle down until I find a girl I know won't end up breaking my heart."

"You're living that make-believe shit. You twentysome-things are all about taste testing. Seeing what's out there. That's what it's all about, right?"

I rub the back of my head. "I guess." *So maybe it's just me who's not normal.* I think about Chris and the many different women he's brought home almost every night. Why did that shit always piss me off?

Instability, like Pops, that son of a bitch. He broke Mama's heart. Bad. Drove her insane to the point where she didn't even care about us—about *me*. And frankly, I stopped caring, too.

My phone vibrates again, snapping me out of my thoughts. I pull it out and check the screen. Disappointment fills me when I see it's another text from Chris.

Goin 2 another house party tonight with Adri.

u and denise wanna come?

Grimacing, I stick the phone back in my pocket without replying. I look across the table at Lonz, who lifts an eyebrow. I shake my head and say, "It wasn't her."

He slides out of the booth. "Whatever, man. I expect to see you and your girlfriend at the cookout. No excuses."

"She's not my girlfriend. And honestly, I don't know what's going to happen in two months."

"Well, you better show. Come up with a reason to bring her. Trust me, it will do you both a bit of good."

Before I have a chance to respond, he turns and leaves, stopping only briefly to pay for the beers and to kiss Lindsey goodbye.

I remain in my booth alone, staring at my now-cold, unfinished pizza and wonder if perhaps I still do have a chance with Denise after all.

CHAPTER 8

I HEAD DOWNTOWN TO CLUB RIYZE. IT'S AFTER TEN, AND the line out the entrance nearly wraps around the block. I'm glad to see my brother has a lot of fans. Standing on line, I can feel the familiar thumping beats of Kevin's house music. "DJ Kevitron" posters are plastered all over the walls outside the club. Across the street, a bus stops and lets off a group of people who are dressed for the club. Spread on the side of the bus is an advertisement for a new action movie that looks pretty good.

Denise loves action movies. I'd love to take her to see it.

The line shuffles along quickly, and I soon reach the front. After showing the bouncer my ID, I head in and push my way through the sea of well-dressed bodies toward the large raised platform forming the stage where Kevin's set up at his deejay mixer. The smell of alcohol mixed with sweat, cheap perfume, and cologne hangs in the air. There's barely room to walk, much less dance, in the tight confines of the dance floor. After several minutes of squeezing my way through the crowd, I finally make it to the foot of the stage and gaze up at Kevin. He's wearing an oversized red hoodie with the words "Urban Fantasmic" written in graffiti-style letters across the front. A black baseball cap is flipped backwards on his head. With one hand, he holds one end of a pair of thick headphones to one ear, and with the other, he messes with the mixers. His head bobs in time to the bass beat, which vibrates the floor. The pumped-up crowd cheers and hollers at the stage, some of them raising their hands—sloshing drinks and all—in the air while they move in place to the music. I keep my eyes on Kevin, hoping he will notice me, but with all these people around, that's unlikely.

I make my way to the bar for a drink. After several minutes of inching my way through the jam-packed area and waving down one of the scrambling bartenders, I'm finally sipping on a rum 'n Coke. I look for a spot where I can stand against the wall, but it's impossible, so I head upstairs to the Blue Room. The room is literally tinted with blue lighting and has a huge glass window overlooking the dance floor and stage. There are three couches in the room, all of them occupied by couples. I cringe at the sight of one of the couples making out. Makes me remember my fucked-up date with Denise.

Fortunately, there's standing room. I wander over to the window and peer out at the people below. The music's not as loud up here, but the thumping bass still vibrates the room. As I nurse my drink, a group of girls nearby starts giggling.

Then I hear a familiar voice and fix my gaze on the opposite corner of the room.

"I know! Can you believe he just surprised me like that all the way from Chicago?"

Denise!

Butterflies swarm my stomach when I hear her beautiful voice. She doesn't notice me as she talks among her girlfriends, who all have drinks in their hands. Denise is dressed in a short—but not too short—backless, silver, sparkling dress that shows off her long legs. She truly has a beautiful body, and I want her. But then I replay last night's ordeal and realize I can't.

Maybe she's just here for girls' night out. I can at least go say "hi," right?

I gulp the rest of my drink and wander over to her. Her pear scent immediately triggers my senses. The girls stop talking as I draw near, and look to me, their eyebrows raising. Denise's mouth opens slightly, and her eyes widen a little.

"Hi, Denise." I smile, locking my gaze on her.

"Dominick!" she says, then looks around nervously.

"You look nice tonight."

She smiles. "Thank you."

Her girlfriends continue to watch me carefully, and I nod politely at them. But I keep my attention focused on Denise. "Hey, I saw there's a new action flick playing next week. Would you like to go see it with—"

A figure suddenly looms behind Denise and places both hands on her bare shoulders. She flinches and turns around. "Oh! You scared me."

A guy steps into a pale blue light that filters down from the ceiling. He looks about my age and height, physically fit, with a goatee on one of those pretty boy faces that girls fawn over. He's dressed sharp in a navy blue button-down shirt, crisp pants, and shoes that look brand new. He leans over and kisses Denise on the cheek, then casts a charming smile at her girlfriends.

"You fine ladies need a refill on those drinks?" he asks, and then his eyes cut to mine and his expression hardens. "Oh, sorry, man, didn't see you there."

I clench my jaw. The sweet taste of my drink lingering on my tongue turns bitter.

Denise steps aside while hooking her arm with Pretty-boy's. "Dominick, this is William. William, Dominick."

"Hey," William says, lifting his chin a little.

"'Sup." I return the gesture. My gaze flits to Denise, who's now huddled up against him, seeming to enjoy that closeness a little too much.

The butterflies get stronger. I hope to God this isn't what I think it is.

William glances to Denise. "What are you drinking, baby? I'll get you a refill."

Denise grins and downs the rest of the amber-colored concoction. "You mean you've forgotten my favorite drink?"

Running a hand through his short, twist-out 'fro, William returns the grin. "Hmm. Long Island Iced Tea, right? Ain't been *that* long."

I stiffen. *That long? Since what?*

William leaves, and I feel inclined to do so as well. This feels too awkward. "So, uh . . . I guess I'll see you around campus sometime?"

Denise nods, her beautiful smile never faltering. "Sure."

"Okay, well, I'm gonna go downstairs for a while."

Her smile fades.

I turn away from the group and head downstairs.

It has to be true that they're together, because the truth is supposed to hurt, right?

So my suspicions about last night were right. None of it mattered to her. It was all a lie. How could I have been so fucking stupid?

I'll vent my frustrations out on Kevin. He's the only one who will listen. The only one I can trust.

I remain downstairs until closing time. The crowd starts filing out of the club, Denise and William nowhere in sight—probably long gone by now.

Thank God.

I hop on stage to meet Kevin, who's busy breaking down his deejay equipment and setting it back in the carrying cases.

"Great show tonight, bro," I say, slapping him on the back.

Kevin pauses from wrapping up a cord. "Hey, Dom. Thanks."

I slip a few used records back in their sleeves and place them in the crates with the rest. "I got an email saying you were going to be here tonight. Of course I wouldn't miss this shit for nothing, especially when it's at one of my favorite clubs in Seattle."

"Aw, thanks, man. Yeah, it was pretty packed tonight. I'm sure I'll be back here again real soon."

"You know I'll be here."

Kevin beams. "Hey, you bring your girl?" He turns and looks out at the thinning crowd.

I stop packing away the records and feel a lump forming in my throat. "Naw, I think she's seeing someone. I fucked up bad, man."

Kevin quirks an eyebrow. "What happened?"

"I don't know. Last night started out okay. We went out for dinner. It was nice. But then she started asking me questions. Trying to pry into my personal life. I get it. She's trying to learn more about me. But I don't want to talk about my fucked up past over a nice dinner."

Kevin frowns. "No. You don't need to tell her that shit. She doesn't need to know. That's personal shit."

I sigh and rub my hands over my face. "I don't know what to do, man. I'm really attracted to her, but she obviously wants nothing to do with me. I should just move on, but . . . "

"It's hard to let go, especially when a chick does crazy shit to you—crazy *good* shit, that is. You didn't fuck her, did you?"

I grimace. "Seriously, man? It's only been one date."

"So that's a 'no.' That's good, then. You have nothing to lose. Just move on."

I resume packing the records to keep my hands busy. "Maybe nothing according to Denise, but I feel something whenever I see her. No other girl's ever done this to me, man. I can't explain it."

Kevin shakes his head and begins unhooking cables from the mixers and turntables. "Love's not a one-sided thing. You're a great guy, Dom. But she isn't the one for you. If she's not interested, then move on."

He always makes it sound so simple—and maybe it is. Maybe I'm just thinking too much on it.

"But then again," he says. "Since it *was* only the first date, maybe you just need to give it another shot."

"I was going to. I was about to ask her out to the movies, when her *date* showed up." I scowl.

"Oh. Maybe she moved on."

I sigh. *Maybe . . .*

"Hey, just 'cause she's not interested doesn't mean there's something wrong with you," Kevin says.

"Oh yeah? Then why the fuck can't I ever keep a damn girl?"

"It ain't your fault, man. There's someone else out there for you." Kevin carefully places a turntable in one of the crates.

But I don't want someone else. I want her. I twist my lips sideways in thought.

"I know that look," Kevin says. "It's the 'I don't give a shit what my brother's saying, I'm gonna do whatever the hell I want' look."

That's partly correct—I *don't* give a shit—but I *do* want to listen to my brother. He's never let me down before. "All right," I finally say. "I'll leave her alone."

Kevin just nods and resumes packing away the rest of the equipment.

When we're all done packing, I help him load his car, which is parked behind the club. After we finish, Kevin slams the hatch shut. "Thanks for helping, man," he says, then gets in the car.

I nod. "Anytime. And thanks for the advice."

"Eh, you know what you gotta do." He starts up the engine and puts it in gear. "Later, li'l bro. Take it easy."

"Later."

I watch him speed down the street until his car rounds a corner and the taillights disappear.

There are still a few club-goers milling around the building and in the parking lot. I don't see Denise or her friends.

She's long gone, and never coming back.

I return to my bike and begin slipping on my gear. A group of girls nearby spot me and wave, smiling. I catch their gazes and wave back. At least I can be polite. Afterward, I mount my bike and reach for my helmet.

"Dominick?"

I pause just as I'm about to slip the helmet on, and look toward Denise's voice. The butterflies return.

She comes running, waving, from a small cluster of people in the lot, grinning wide.

My stomach does flip-flops as she stands before me. I catch a whiff of her intoxicating pear scent. How the fuck am I supposed to move on from her?

"Oh, hi," I finally say in a piss-poor attempt to sound casual.

"I totally didn't expect to see you here tonight." She doesn't look the least bit guilty.

"Likewise, but it was good to see you again." I glance over to the cluster of people nearby and recognize some of them as the girlfriends who were with her earlier. When they meet my gaze again, they all break into a giggling fit.

"My God, he's looking at us! Stop being so obvious, Alexis," one of them says.

I return my gaze to Denise, who is looking at me apologetically.

"Sorry about that," she says. "My friends are crazy sometimes. They invited me for drinks tonight, so I decided to come. But it seems that their real agenda was to see DJ Kevitron. They all have a thing for him."

I laugh. "DJ Kevitron's my brother."

Denise blinks, then covers her mouth in shock. "Are you serious? Well don't tell my friends that."

"I wouldn't think of it. What about you? You have a thing for him, too?"

She shrugs. "Not really. I mean, he's all right. But I'm sure he's got enough girls chasing him."

"True that." I exhale, relieved to know that she doesn't care much for my brother. It would be all sorts of weird otherwise.

She twists her lips like she's trying to fight down that beautiful smile of hers. "Hey, um, can I ask you a weird question?"

I blink. Totally unexpected, but I'm all ears. "Sure. What's up?"

She bites her bottom lip, then gives me a somewhat sly, shifty-eyed look. "What's the engine displacement of your bike?"

I blink. Several times. *Really* unexpected, but fucking hot as hell. Did she just ask me something about my bike? Something *mechanical* about my bike?

"Uh . . . " I stammer.

She tilts her head to the side. "Don't you know?"

I open my mouth to answer, then stop myself. *Wait.* What if William put her up to this? Maybe he's thinking about getting a bike, too, to impress her. "Yeah, I know. I'm just . . . well . . . a bit surprised that you'd be interested in that kind of thing."

By the look in her eye, I know William has nothing to do with this. "I was looking up your motorcycle online. Ever since you took me on that ride, I've been curious about them. You were right about how I'm missing out on some awesome fun things."

"You're thinking about getting a bike?" I ask, with raised eyebrows. I'd fucking explode with happiness—and slight worry since she must be new to riding—if she is.

She grimaces. "I don't know. Probably not anytime soon. It was fun riding on the back of yours, though."

I chuckle. "I'm always up for riding if you are. As for the engine displacement, it's 600cc."

"Oh." She nods thoughtfully. "I saw your motorcycle on a review site. It was named one of the top ten sport bikes last year due to its 'incredible handling and rider feedback.'"

God, I think I'm about to have an orgasm. "Yeah, it handles well because the chassis is lightweight and the engine is balanced."

"I'm thinking about writing about motorcycles for my next lifestyle article. Maybe even incorporate some fashion trends with it. I saw some pretty sweet jackets for women riders."

A thin layer of sweat forms on my chest and up to my neck. My heart's pounding. Call me a fool, but there's no fucking way I'm ever moving on from this girl now. "That'd be cool. I'd love to read the article when you finish."

"I'd love to get your input, though I don't know how savvy you are with women's fashion."

I laugh. "Well, uh, I'll do my best to help you."

She looks over her shoulder, then back to me. "Hey, I need to go, now. Let's talk more about it later. Enjoy the rest of your night." She turns and begins heading back to her group of giggling friends.

She's leaving, the tease. Shit! "Ah, Denise?"

She stops and looks back at me. "You wanna do breakfast tomorrow before class?" I ask hopefully, my voice cracking as I try mentally to ease the pain of my hardness.

She scrunches her face slightly. "I don't know yet. We'll see. My ride's here now, so I gotta go. Bye, Dominick."

Dumbfounded, I watch her leave, the pain in my pants quickly disappearing on its own. *Did I really just get shot down?*

When she returns to her friends, a black sedan decked out with shiny rims and a custom paint job pulls up to the curb near the group. Denise waves goodbye to her friends, hops in the passenger side, and rolls down the window, still chatting away with the other girls. I glimpse the driver—William. He leans over to her and kisses her on the cheek. She smiles and seems to enjoy it a little too much.

The tires squeal, and the car speeds off.

Fuck my life.

CHAPTER 9

I SEE DENISE RUNNING—RUNNING FROM FACELESS MEN WHO want to hurt her. *Kill* her. She wears that same sparkly silver dress from the club. But she's barefoot now, rather than in those matching heels. I stand on one side of a glass wall, watching her run toward me. The men are gaining on her. She hits the wall and presses her hands against it. I stand before her, putting my hands against hers. But I can't feel her. I call to her, but she can't hear me. The way she frantically looks around, I don't even think she can see me, either. I pound on the glass wall, yelling her name, but she still can't hear me. The group of men catches up with her, and, like a trapped, defenseless animal, she spins around, her back flat against the wall. I continue pounding on the glass, harder and harder, but it still won't break, and she still doesn't seem to hear me. As her assailants draw closer, they become recognizable.

All of them bear my father's face.

And that's when I wake up in a cold sweat.

Happy fucking Monday to me.

I don't think I've ever had a dream like that before, and I've no idea what it means. But I have to talk to Denise *today*. Hell, I have to talk to her *now*! I don't give a shit if she's seeing Prettyboy William. My usual morning of getting ready for class is marred by the dark thoughts of that dream.

Physics class is dismissed five minutes early, and I head straight for Padelford Hall, where Denise's world literature class will be ending soon. I plop down on one of the benches outside and wait for her. That stupid dream still haunts me, and the ugly memory of it zaps my appetite, so I decide to skip lunch today.

While I wait, I text Larry, letting him know that I'll be a few minutes late for work, and he texts me back with the okay.

When I look up from my phone, I spot Denise among a cluster of other students walking out the front doors. My eyes trace the blue sweater she wears down to her short floral-patterned dress, which reveals her long, slender dancer's legs. Her messenger bag is slung across her, and she cradles a spiral-bound notebook in her arms.

So beautiful.

I realize I'm ogling her, and I hop off the bench before she can get away. "Denise?"

She stops and looks in my direction, her forehead furrowing. Then her face softens. "Oh, hi, Dominick. Don't you have to go to work?"

I glance around briefly, eyeing passing students who seem oblivious to us. I step closer to her. "I do, but I wanted to see you."

She averts her gaze to the ground. I could swear she's blushing. "Dominick, I . . . "

She looks even sexier when she's flustered. I want to hold her and let her know it's okay. "Can we talk? Just for a moment? There's something that's been on my mind and I—"

"Sorry, Dominick. I have to go. I'm meeting someone." She turns to leave.

I tense up. *William, I bet.* But the longer I have to wait to talk to her, the more that crazy shit's probably going to keep haunting me. "Five minutes. I promise. That's all, I swear."

Glancing over her shoulder, she purses her lips, her nostrils flaring slightly. "Fine. Five minutes, and that's all."

Five minutes is all I need to let her know how I feel. I gesture to the bench. She sits, but scoots to the edge and looks at me expectantly.

I sit beside her, but not too close. "Okay." I say in a low voice as I fish for the right words. "First of all, I want to apologize about the other night at dinner. I didn't mean to make you upset or uncomfortable. I just . . . totally overreacted when you started asking me personal questions. I was out of line, and I'm sorry."

Her eyebrows rise. "I just wanted to get to know you. Isn't that what people do on first dates?"

Hearing her say "date" makes me feel even shittier that I fucked it up. "I guess. I'm a complicated guy, and I didn't want to run you off. But it seems all I managed to do was make things worse. I'm sorry, Denise. I really am."

She stares at me as if I'm crazy. Maybe I am.

I take a deep breath. "I know it's only been a few days, but I . . . I like you, Denise. And I want you to be happy. You're really beautiful, nice, smart, and hell, you like motorcycles." I manage to get a hint of a smile out of her with that last bit. "Anyway, I don't want some stupid guy to take advantage of you."

She scoffs. "You sound like my father."

Ouch. "Well, can you blame him?"

"No, but sometimes he acts like I'm going to spread my legs to the world. It's annoying."

"I think your dad just wants the best for you, that's all."

Her face softens slightly. "Look, Dominick. I'll be all right. Does this have something to do with last night?"

"What?" I blink. "No."

"You're a terrible liar."

I sigh. "Okay. Maybe a *little*. Should I be asking who that guy William was?"

Her expression remains unchanged. "He's a . . . a friend from high school. I haven't seen him in five years. We were going out back then, but then he moved to Chicago, and . . . "

The left side of my mouth twitches. *Friend.* I'm pretty sure she means "boyfriend." But I don't care who the hell he is. This isn't high school anymore. "Right, so about last night.

I'm sorry. I should've called to see if you wanted to come to the club with me."

Denise shakes her head. "Don't worry about it. It was girls' night out."

Girls' night out, huh. Does she think I forgot about Prettyboy that quickly? "Still, I mean. I would like to get to know you more. You wanna ride with me down to Cougar Mountain on Wednesday?"

Her perfect, beautiful smile returns. It makes me glow inside. I can never get enough of it. "I'd love to, but . . . " Her expression shifts abruptly, and she looks at me the same way she did when I took her home from dinner Saturday night. *Guilt. Regret.*

"'But'?" I ask.

Denise bites her bottom lip and stares straight at me. I can tell she's wrestling with something in her mind. Something big. There's a hint of fear in her eyes. Doubt. "What do you do when you're faced with the past again?"

I swallow. *The past.* Does she mean William? That's an odd question to ask, but a question that I'm no stranger to. I wish I could forget about the past. The hurt. I think carefully about my response. Her question sounds almost like a cry for help. I've asked that question of Kevin so many times before. And he's always answered the same thing: *You gotta fight to win, because the past will always try to drag you down.*

"What do I do?" I say. "I keep reminding myself that the past doesn't matter. The past'll always try to drag me down. But I have to fight through it. Fight to win." I look at her, concerned. The question is on the tip of my tongue. "Is everything okay with you?"

She nods without hesitation. "Yeah. I'm just . . . stressed about how I did on my world literature test today."

Bullshit.

But despite how "stressed" she's really feeling, her face manages to brighten again. My heart beats faster, pounding away in my chest. I just want to hold her. Comfort her.

Kiss her.

I look down to her hands in her lap. "I'm sure you did fine on your test," I say softly. Then I slowly place my hand atop one of hers.

She doesn't appear fazed by my gesture. *Progress.*

She looks down at our hands and places her other hand on top of mine. I hold my breath. Her hands are smooth and warm.

"I'll be okay, Dominick. I appreciate everything you've done, fixing my car, and taking me to dinner and stuff. You're a cool guy. Way different from other guys I've met."

I beam. "Thanks. I try. Hey, I like you, Denise. A lot. I said that already, didn't I?" I chuckle softly. "I hope that maybe, you know, we can make something work."

"Maybe." she says with a bit of uncertainty.

I give her hand a brief, gentle squeeze. William pops into my head. Fuck him and his shitty-ass car and everything else he's probably got to impress her with. I stare at her face, cast into shadow by the shade trees. She stares back intently at me. I gaze longingly at her full, glossy, peach-tinted lips. What I wouldn't give to kiss them. To taste her.

Slowly, I pull back my hand. *No, not now.*

"I need to go," she says in almost a whisper, her face flustered. *I wonder what's going through her mind right now?*

"Yeah," I say breathily. I watch her retrieve her world literature book and re-sling her bag crosswise over her chest. "Since you're busy Wednesday, do you wanna do something on Thursday?" I ask.

She rises from the bench and turns to leave. "I . . . I don't know yet."

"Right," I mutter. "Sorry, I just realized it's been longer than five minutes."

She looks over her shoulder and, to my surprise and relief, smiles. Maybe she's not too upset with me. "It's okay. I'll see you later."

I watch her walk away. She may not do ballet anymore, but she still has a gentle, flowing dancer's gait. It's not until she disappears into a crowd of students that I finally exhale. *Bye, Denise.*

My back pocket vibrates, and I'm shaken back into reality. *Oh yeah. Work.* I swipe the phone out and check for messages.

Shit. It's Larry.

FEW MINUTS LATE MY ASS!!! WHER TEH HELL RU BOY!!!!!!

Cringing, I text a quick *omw* as I bolt toward the lot where my bike is parked.

CHAPTER 10

I ARRIVE AT FRANK'S LATER THAN I MEANT TO, BUT I DON'T see Larry. Probably went to take a piss. As I walk toward the whiteboard hanging on the wall in bay one, the office's side door suddenly swings open and Frank comes storming out.

"You're late. What the hell, Dominick? Oversleep? Wanna end up like Sam, too? Don't think for a minute I won't hesitate to get your ass replaced!"

I nod, frowning. "It won't happen again, man. I swear." Frank's a bastard most of the time, but this time his anger is justified. I'm sure Larry is plenty pissed at me, too. Frank returns to the office and slams the door behind him. Checking the whiteboard, I see I'm assigned a clutch replacement job. Pretty complicated, at that. It must be Frank's doing.

The sports car is up on the lift in bay two, and Nate is already working on it. Sighing, I approach him.

"Yo, Nate. I got this," I say, as he removes a bolt from one of the drive shafts.

Nate casts me an annoyed but relieved look. "It's about time. Where the hell were you?"

"Out," I say, and leave it at that. "But I'm here now, right? So you can take a break."

Nate rolls his eyes. "Right. Fuck up in front of the new guy, will you?" He shoves the air wrench at me.

I blink. *New guy?* But before I can ask about it, Nate walks away.

Has Frank found someone already? I look toward the office. Larry might be in there, too.

"I'm tellin' you, man, I tapped some of that at the party last night." Paul says from the first bay.

I glance over to the SUV on the lift, where Paul's busy setting the wheels.

"Marissa? How was she?" Nate asks, joining him, and shouting over the whine of the wrench.

Paul whistles. "Sweet mother of God, she's amazing. She gets all kinky when she's drunk."

The two of them laugh, and I tune out the rest of their conversation. Usual shop buzz.

The office's side door creaks open, but I don't bother turning away from my work. I'm in deep shit as it is for being late. I might as well not add to it by idling around.

" . . . yeah, I'm pretty good at poker, but an ace at darts—at least, that's what my girl says."

I freeze. *That voice.*

"No shit?" Paul guffaws. "Man, don't you know I'm the *king* of darts?"

I peer over to bay one. Nate, Paul, and another guy stand on the other side of the lifted car, only visible from their torsos down.

"We'll have to see about that," the familiar-sounding guy says, then laughs.

No . . . It can't be.

The office door opens again, and a set of workpant-covered legs approach the group.

"All right, you guys," Larry says, then pauses. "Dominick! Get over here!"

I jump, and my heart starts pounding. I set down the wrench and hustle over to the group. Rounding the back of the SUV, I halt. All eyes are drawn to me, including the new guy's, who looks more amused than anything.

William.

Fuck me.

"If you all haven't formally met yet, this is William Porter," Larry says with a wave of his hand. "Today's his first day on the job, so make him feel welcome."

I watch Nate and Paul shake his hand, but I remain where I am. *No, he can't be working here. Why the fuck is he working here?*

"The quiet one over there is Dominick," Larry says, gesturing to me.

William strokes his goatee. "Oh yeah, it *is* Dominick. What's up?"

Larry lifts an eyebrow. "You two know each other?"

"You could say that," I say, holding back a sneer.

William laughs. "Yeah, ran into him at the club last night."

Larry crosses his arms and nods slowly, giving me one of those calculating looks as if he knows something's up.

William steps forward and extends his hand. "Well, good to meet you again, bro."

I exhale through my nose. *The feeling's mutual, asshole.* For now, I swallow my pride and paint on a smile that would convince even Larry. "Yeah, you, too," I say, shaking his hand. My hand is getting crushed in his. Damn, he's got a strong grip, but nowhere near as strong as Larry's. Squeezing back, I match his strength as best I can, but all he does is smirk as he finally lets go.

"All right. Now that the intros are done, get back to work." Larry thumbs at my car. "William, since you and Dominick seem to know each other, I'm putting you two together, so Dominick can fill you in on how we do things around here."

William nods. "Sure thing."

Watching Larry disappear back into the office, I grit my teeth. Was Larry being sarcastic? I guess this is my punishment for being late.

Looking sideways at William, I frown. Why does God hate me right now? Of all the mechanics' shops in Seattle, William had to choose this one. Sighing, I put on my poker face as I walk back to the car.

"Damn, can't believe I'd run into you again," William says, following me. "I mean what are the odds?"

Against me, apparently.

"Small world, isn't it?" he says.

I scowl. "*Cramped* is more like it." I grab for my air wrench but end up picking up a drill instead. Growling, I toss the tool aside and pick up the correct one. Damn it, I can't even concentrate.

William looks at me and laughs. Fucking stupid laugh.

"What's so damn funny?" I snap, whipping my head back around to look at him.

He stops laughing and holds his hands up in surrender. "Nothin', man. Nothin'."

"Good," I say, removing the final bolt holding the drive shaft. I toss a drain pan underneath the car. "Pop that bolt and get that shit drained."

He looks at me, amused, then steps under the car and begins fiddling with the bolt. "Gotta say, man. I never thought in a million years you were a mechanic."

My left eye twitches. What was that supposed to mean? "Yeah, you don't look so mechanically savvy yourself either, Pret—William."

William catches the bolt in his palm and holds the drain pan up just as amber-colored fluid pours steadily out of the car. He slowly sets the pan back on the ground while the fluid continues draining. "I worked in a shop in Chicago back in high school," he says, apparently not noticing my slip.

"Yeah? So how'd you end up here?"

William steps out from under the car. "Well, I'm a Seattleite, but I had to move with my parents to Chicago when I was a junior in high school. I went to Chicago State for about a year, then transferred to UDub this semester."

The fact that we go to the same school makes me cringe. "Oh, cool," I say with little enthusiasm. "I go there, too. Sophomore."

"Heh. So am I. Truth is, my high school sweetheart's still here."

I roll my tongue around in my cheek.

"She's still as amazing as I remembered her. Hasn't changed one bit. That look on her face when I surprised her last night at the club was priceless."

"So were you two still talking after you left Seattle?" I ask.

"At first, but then it got harder. I mean, long distance relationships suck, you know?"

No, I don't really know, but I've heard the horror stories. I check to see if the fluid has completely drained. "So it's been a while since you've seen her? I would think she's forgotten about you by now."

He chuckles. "Fuck no, she didn't forget about me. She kissed the shit out of me, actually. That girl's got amazing lips."

I narrow my eyes. I'd like to *punch* the shit out of him. I've got an amazing left hook.

"So, how do *you* know her?"

His question irks me. It's none of his fucking business how I know her. "I see her around campus sometime."

William furrows his brow, and then nods thoughtfully. "Oh, I see. So who's your girl?"

That was none of his business, either. I've half the mind to tell him it's Denise, but that'd probably make her forever pissed at me if he ever relayed *that* to her. This asshole seems like the type that probably would.

"You gotta be kidding me," he says again. "No girl?"

Shit. I guess I was silent for too long.

"You're a mechanic," he says. "You know chicks are into guys who are good with their hands, right? So what's the problem?"

I roll my eyes. "There's no problem. I'm just a busy man."

He guffaws, obviously seeing right through my bullshit.

Denise was right—I'm a *terrible* liar.

CHAPTER 11

I CLOCK OUT AS SOON AS SIX O'CLOCK HITS. I CAN'T GET OUT of there fast enough. Revving the engine on my bike, I speed out of the parking lot. This day has gotten shittier and shittier. I'm ready to strangle William. String him up by his fucking dick for bragging about Denise in my face. Of course, she's amazing. But seriously, what does she see in that guy, anyway?

At least there's one thing she and I have in common. She likes motorcycles, something he hadn't talked about. But it seems obvious that she likes him, not me. The thought of her having put her beautiful lips on his fucking face makes me sick to my stomach.

I park my bike and storm through the kitchen door. The house is quiet again, and just as I'm wondering where Chris might be, my phone vibrates. I slip it out of my pocket and check the screen.

A text from Chris. He seems to send them at the most inconvenient times.

Yo, spending the nite @ Adri's.

Scowling, I hurl the phone against the wall. The impact sends the back cover flying off and the square battery popping out. There's a small black scuff on the drywall. I don't care if I practically destroyed my phone. I've had it for over three years, so it's probably about time I upgraded, anyway.

"Fuck my *life!*" I yell, stomping up the stairs. I should be happy for Chris. It's what I wanted, right? This is the second day in a row that he's stayed with the same girl. A new record. I've not seen a girl make Chris this happy in a long time.

So why the hell can't *I* be happy?

I slam my bedroom door and lean against it. Closing my eyes, I sigh. I'm angry, jealous, and sad all at the same time—mainly sad. And yeah, very jealous. Uncle Adam's words ring through my ears. That tunnel is dark—so dark, I'm getting lost. I don't know if I'm going forward or backward.

I have to move on. She doesn't want a guy like me. Take it like a man and move on.

I flop on the bed and lay back, staring up at the still paddles of the ceiling fan. Maybe I should just give up the chivalry shit. It's only brought pain. Be a bad boy like all these bitches like and take what I fucking want—her.

No!

My left eye twitches.

God, no. Did I just think that? I hate thinking like that. *He* would love that. Love that I'd become just like him by thinking that shit. No. I'm not going to give that son of a bitch the pleasure.

You'll never win. You hear me? Burn in Hell you piece of shit. Tears sting my eyes. I just want to be a normal guy, meet a great girl, and spend the rest of my life with her.

I just want to be happy, but fuck those thoughts.

Fuck my life.

I hop out of bed, return downstairs, and retrieve the discarded phone. I pop the battery back in, and once I snap the cover shut, the phone turns on, no problem. The thing's been dropped, smashed, and even run over by a car, and the only damage was a tiny little crack on the upper corner of the screen. And the thing still works. I call Kevin. It's still a few hours yet before he'd go to a club if he's working tonight.

"'Lo?"

I sigh, relieved to hear his voice. "Hey, bro. You working tonight?"

"Yeah, gonna head out to Blue Xscape around nine. Something up?"

I slowly walk up the stairs. "I need to talk, to vent."

He stays silent, though I can faintly hear his breathing, so I continue. "I've been thinking bad shit again. Thinking about hurting people. Thinking about Pops—"

"Don't you start with that shit, Dom," he says. "You're better than that."

"I'm such a screwup."

"It's about a girl, isn't it?"

I don't reply.

"That girl you told me about . . . Danielle, right?"

"Denise," I say as I rest my hand on the doorknob to my room. "And yeah."

"So what's the problem?"

I sigh. "I met her piece-of-shit boyfriend. *William*."

"Seriously, Dom? You're gonna just let him take her from you?"

"She can like whoever she wants, Kev. I just wish it wasn't *that* guy."

"She likes him, huh?"

"Yeah." I think back to that night I took her home. She looked unsure of herself, about to say something, but she didn't. Could it have been about him? "I don't know what to do, man," I say, heading into my room. I plop down on the bed with a solid bounce. "Worst of all, I have to work with William, and today, all he talked about was her."

"If she don't want you, then you need to find yourself a new girl. Come to the club tonight, li'l bro."

My throat tightens. I was afraid he'd say that.

"Dom?"

"Yeah, I'm here. I—"

"Hey. You wanna forget about her? Then get your ass to Club Xscape tonight."

"But, Kev—"

"No 'buts' unless they're attached to cute girls."

With a long sigh, I nod. "Fine. I'll be there around ten."

"Don't bullshit me, either, or I swear, I'll never let you live this down."

"All right, damn it. I told you I'd come!" I snap through clenched teeth. Kevin can be persistent sometimes, but I can't help but love him for it.

We both hang up, and I toss the phone next to me on the bed. I'm too exhausted to think clearly any more, so I shut my eyes and take a nap. Even in my dreams, all I keep seeing is Denise's smiling face, and I can't get the smell of pears out of my mind.

Club Xscape is nearly as crowded as Club 88 was last night. On stage, Kevin is set up, doing his thing. It's always great to watch my brother do what he loves.

I head to the bar and get my usual. Leaning with my back against the high countertop, I scan the crowd of mostly college students and recognize a few from my engineering classes. I'm supposed to be forgetting about Denise, but I can't help but hope that she's here.

Familiar girlish giggling breaks me out of my thoughts. Taking a long swig of my drink, I look over to a group of four girls nearby. I recognize them—Denise's friends. I gasp. *Could she be here?* I look around the crowd but don't see her.

A thin petite girl breaks from her group of friends and approaches me. Her short, purple hair falls in small wisps across her ghostly white face. She wears an oversized, off-the-shoulder top revealing tattoos on her arms and chest, hip-hugger jeans, and brown boots with fur. She's got a metal ring in her bottom lip, as well as scores of other piercings in both ears. After looking me up and down, she smirks. "Hey, you're the guy from the other night. The cute one on that awesome red bike."

I finish my drink. "Cute one, huh?" I say, smirking back.

Purple Hair giggles and takes my hand. "It was unanimous. My friends wanna meet you."

My heart pounds as she tugs on my arm. I reluctantly follow her to the rest of the group of girls, who all have their eyes on me.

Purple Hair releases my hand, and I shove both of them in the front pockets of my hoodie. "Hello, ladies."

One of the girls, a curvy Latina with long curly hair, chews on her fingernails, fighting back a smile as she stares.

Another girl, dressed in a purple halter top and jeans, gazes at me, her mouth slightly open. She's a bit on the chubby side but wears the weight very well. She looks toward the stage, then back to me. "You look a little like DJ Kevitron."

"Oh whatever, Trinity," Latina says. "You think every hot guy looks like DJ Kevitron."

I never thought we looked anything alike. "Well, actually, he's my brother." *Oh shit. I wasn't supposed to tell them that, was I?*

All of the girls' eyes go wide. "Oh my God! It's Kevitron's brother!" they squeal.

I wince. Is this the kind of thing Kevin gets every night? "So, any of you guys seen Denise tonight?"

All excitement slowly leaves their eyes. Then, one of them, a tall, full-figured girl wearing a black dress says,

"She'll be here soon. She and I were supposed to come together, but William called and ended up taking her instead." She scrunches up her face a little. "How do you know Denise, anyway?"

I sigh. I can't seem to get away from that bastard. I should leave while I can. "Oh, I, uh, fixed her car."

Purple Hair elbows Trinity, giving me a discreet wink. "Hear that, Trinity? He's not only Kevitron's brother, but he's also a mechanic."

Trinity licks her sparkly, glossy lips, and looks anxiously at me.

William *did* say something about chicks liking guys who are good with their hands.

"I am so jealous of Denise right now," Latina says. "She's getting all the hot mechanic guys after her."

"And one of them happens to be Kevitron's *brother!*" Trinity exclaims.

I think I'm grinning like a fool. Their flattery is beyond overwhelming. Denise has some cute girlfriends. But none of them are quite like her. "I'm Dominick, by the way. Sorry for not introducing myself before."

Black Dress plays with one of her braids. "I'm Cherie."

"And I'm Alexis," Purple Hair says, eyeing me like a piece of meat.

"I'm Bianca," Latina says and gives me one of those kissy-faces.

Trinity still can't stop staring and smiling. Her smile reminds me of Denise's.

Bianca shoves her forward playfully. "Stop staring, *chica*, and go get him."

Trinity squeals, and I grab her as she stumbles in her pumps. Her soft, curvy body presses into mine as I steady her on her feet. I smile awkwardly at her. She looks back at me, mortified, then turns to her friends, who are snickering. "Oh my God, Bianca! I almost fell!"

"Right into his arms," Bianca says, grinning devilishly, and the other girls laugh.

I scratch the back of my head. This is such an awkward moment.

Alexis pokes me in the bicep. "Hey, Dominick. Can you get us some drinks?"

I frown a little. I don't want to give these girls the wrong idea, but the fact that they're Denise's friends means they'll most likely be talking to her about me at some point. And I'd rather not be labelled the biggest asshole they've ever met. I guess I have some time to spare before I split. "Okay," I say, nodding. "What do you guys want?"

"Tequila Sunrise for me," Cherie says.

"Me too," Bianca says.

"I'll do a Malibu," Alexis says.

"Long Island iced tea," Trinity says.

I smile at Trinity, remembering that it's also what Denise likes.

Damn it!

I head to the bar, wave down a bartender, and order the drinks. As I wait, I turn and people-watch again. Denise's friends are still huddled in their little group, occasionally stealing glances in my direction. I wave at them. They seem like a good bunch of girls, but the more I stay around them, the more I think about Denise.

I suddenly smell pears. *She's here!* My eyes dart left and right, searching eagerly. Then I spot the couple walking toward the group of girls. They must've walked right past me while I was daydreaming.

The drinks all prepared, I skillfully carry the four glasses back to the waiting group. I slow my steps as I near Denise, eyeing her from behind. She's wearing an oversized blue plaid top over black leggings, which shows off every bit of those great legs, all the way up to the bottom of her beautifully round ass. I reluctantly look from her to William, who has his arm draped around her shoulders.

Frowning, I brush past them and deliver the drinks to the other girls. "Here you go, ladies," I say, trying to focus on them. But Denise's pear smell is too distracting.

The girls all fawn over me as they take their drinks.

"Thanks, Dominick. You're a really good guy." Cherie says.

"No problem," I say.

Denise gasps behind me. "Dominick? What are you doing here?"

Just hearing her call my name makes me smile. I turn to her. "I should be asking *you* that," I say with a bit of a laugh.

William rubs her shoulders, and I frown. "Taking my advice, I see, Dom." He smirks.

I shoot him a glare. I just want one moment with him to break those fingers that are touching her shoulders. "What advice? I came here to see my brother."

William raises his eyebrows. "Your brother?"

Trinity beams. "Can you believe it? Dominick is DJ Kevitron's brother!"

"No shit? Well, your brother is pretty damn good on those ones and twos," William says.

I stare coldly. "He's all right." My gaze drifts back to Denise. Her face is slightly taut with concern, as if something is on her mind. Damn, I wish I could talk to her.

William kisses her on the cheek. "Want something to drink, baby?"

Denise smiles slightly. "Sure. The usual."

"Okay. Be back in a sec."

I watch him make his way to the bar, and I turn back to Denise, who's fixed on the rest of her friends. My mind is crawling with so many questions. I don't even know where to begin.

"So how's it going with you and William?" Alexis asks.

I keep quiet and listen.

Denise looks nervously at her girlfriends. There doesn't seem to be a spark of happiness in her eyes. "We're all right." She hesitates, glances to me, then looks to her friends again. "Can we not talk about that here?"

I arch an eyebrow slightly. Is something going on with them? There's so much I want to ask her, but it's probably none of my business.

"Sorry. I was just curious, you know?" Alexis says. "After he surprised you the other night. It's been what? Five years?"

Denise shakes her head firmly. "Please."

I lick my lips. Something's definitely going on. And I'm standing so close to her, I'm about to go crazy that I can't touch her. I look over my shoulder and notice William returning with drinks. Sighing, I turn back to the girls. "I think I'm gonna head out."

Trinity gasps. "What? Already?" She grabs my arm, pulls me into her. "We didn't even dance."

I stumble forward and look back at Denise guiltily. William arrives with her Long Island iced tea.

I gently pull my arm away from Trinity. "No, sorry. I can't. I've, uh, got a big electromagnetics test to study for next week." I add with a smile, "But I'm sure Kevin—er, Kevitron—would love to meet you all."

Trinity's eyes light up. She glances toward the stage, then back to me. "Can I see your phone for a minute, Dominick?"

I blink at the question. "Uh, sure." I dig the phone out of my back pocket and fumble it in my sweaty hands.

She plucks it from me, swipes the screen, types something, and then hands it back. "Call me, okay?"

My eyes wide, I take the phone and stare at the screen. Her name and number is saved in my contacts.

Bianca and Cherie tease and make catcalls at her.

"Aw, c'mon, guys." Looking embarrassed, Trinity turns away from me and nurses her drink.

I shouldn't have gotten her number like that, especially with Denise standing right there as it happened. Stuffing the phone back into my pocket, I look sideways at Denise, who doesn't seem at all offended. In fact, I don't think she even cares.

I'll be a dick if don't call Trinity.

I can at least give Trinity a chance, right? Denise keeps good company. They all seem like good girls who like to have fun.

"Hey." William slaps me on the back of the shoulder, interrupting my thoughts. "See you at work tomorrow."

I freeze. *He touched me. That bastard touched me.* It takes everything I have not to grab that hand and break it in several places. Shrugging him off, I spin around and give him one of my poker-face looks. "Yup."

Denise blinks. "What? You two work together?" She looks to William for confirmation.

William grins at her. "Yeah, just started at Frank's Garage today, baby."

Her mouth opens like she's about to say something more, but then closes, and she nods thoughtfully.

I wish she'd smile again. Something is on her mind. Something not good. But I can't let anyone know this shit's getting to me. I finally break away from the group and, after casting a quick wave to Kevin, head home, deciding to make it a point to call him sometime tomorrow. My mind continuously wanders to Denise and that look I saw on her face.

I know that look all too well.

It's the look of regret.

CHAPTER 12

TUESDAY'S DIGITAL SYSTEMS CLASS LETS OUT PROMPTLY AT 9:10, and I have thirty-five minutes to spare before circuits lab starts. I hustle to the sociology building where Denise will be going to her nine-thirty class. I can't get my mind off how troubled she looked last night.

Perched on a handrail of the wheelchair ramp next to the stairs leading into the building, I watch students go by, paying no attention to their conversations. Then Denise approaches. Her beautiful dancer legs are covered with flared jeans, but she walks just as gracefully. She wears a yellow sweater over a white, scoop-neck shirt, and the light winks off the silver *fleur de lis* necklace lying at her throat.

I catch myself before falling backward off the handrail. Thankfully, no one notices my near-spill. "Denise!" I call as she begins walking up the steps. "Over here."

She stops and looks in my direction. A hesitant smile tugs at her lips. She fidgets with the strap of her messenger bag and approaches me.

"Hey," she says. The corner of an issue of *Street Throttle Racer* magazine peeks out from under her bag's front flap.

"Did you see some of the decked-out sport bikes featured in this month's *Street Throttle Racer*?" I ask, pointing.

Blushing, she hastily tucks the magazine deeper into her bag. "Not yet. I just picked it up."

"You'll be amazed." My face gets hot. *Okay, focus, Dom. You know why you're here.* Taking a deep breath to calm my nerves, I slide off the handrail and stand before her. "So, I thought we could talk for a bit."

Her smile slowly falls.

"You looked a little distant last night," I say, watching her face. "Is everything okay?"

She nods. "Everything's fine, Dominick." She avoids my eyes and fidgets with the strap of her bag again.

Bullshit. Why do I have this sudden feeling of déjà vu? "All right. Well, I was wondering if you were still up for doing something with me tomorrow."

"I'm sorry, I can't. William is . . . " She pauses, like she's backtracking on something she was about to say.

"Yes?"

She bites her bottom lip. "I . . . I'm busy tomorrow, sorry."

I frown. "Okay, maybe next time, then."

She turns. "I have to get to class now. See ya, Dominick."

I sigh as I watch her leave. I know she's intentionally avoiding me, but her hesitation has me more concerned. At this rate, I'm not going to get much out of her, but I know someone who might.

I retrieve my phone and scroll through my contacts to Trinity's name. I stare at the name with sadness and regret, but a little bit of hope.

No. I can't use her to get to Denise.

I head across campus toward the engineering building, keeping my eyes focused on the phone screen. *If I'm gonna do this, it's gotta be all or nothing.*

Denise is never going to talk to me. This is a lost cause. With that, I manage to convince myself enough to guide my thumb to the "dial" button.

Trinity answers on the second ring.

"Hey, Trinity. It's Dominick."

"Dominick! You called!" She sounds so grateful and happy. She's probably been burned by guys in the past who never called her.

"Yeah," I say, a little half-heartedly. "You wanna come over and watch movies with me tonight?"

Work goes by quickly for a change. I'm even able to ignore William's shit. Having something to look forward to, like tonight's M/C club meeting, takes the sting out of William's little jabs. Charles, who's hosting this time, lives on the far western side of Montlake, near the Bay. Getting there from work around this time is usually fast and easy. It's also a beautiful ride.

The driveway is already filled with parked sport bikes and cruisers when I get there, so I squeeze into a small space along the curb. The front door opens as I head up the long, shady cobblestone walkway, and Charles appears in the doorway, wearing a black T-shirt with the club's logo and name—Phantom Saints—printed over his heart.

"'Ey, Genius!" Charles greets me with a crooked grin.

"'Sup, Ghost," I say, as we do our special handshake and he steps aside.

Inside, I'm greeted by the smell of beer, sweat, and cigarettes. The drab white walls of the living room are covered with flags, pennants, tapestries, posters, and plaques, mostly awards won from past motorcycle shows and community events. Most of this stuff belongs to all of us, but Charles is the only one with a house big enough to hold it all.

The overhead fan's light illuminates the large room in a hazy, yellow glow. The rest of my club brothers lounge around on chairs and couches, and some are sprawled out on the floor, drinking, smoking, and shooting the shit. Charles's girlfriend, Xiang, had gone out with her friends like she always does whenever Charles hosts, so we have the house to ourselves. All eyes turn to me as I find my usual seat on one of the couch's armrests.

"'Sup, Genius?" Randy, the club's sergeant-at-arms, says with a small salute.

I salute back. "Tracer."

Alonzo tosses me a beer. As I pop open the can and take a swig, I scan the rest of my brothers. All of us are college students except for our president, Troy, a.k.a. "Lone Wolf," Alonzo, Charles, and Randy. These guys are like a second family to me. There's nothing we wouldn't do for each other.

I spot a picture of Charles and Xiang sitting on the kitchen counter. She's a beautiful thirty-five-year-old Chinese woman who looks like she's twenty. Next to the picture sits a cute little heart-printed tote bag and a stray bottle of pear body spray. A female has certainly made her mark here.

I stare at the bottle. *Pears . . .*

My mind isn't all there even after Troy calls the meeting to order. While he goes down the list of news, upcoming rides, and events, my thoughts are on Denise.

Why the hell did I invite over the best friend of a girl I like? "Genius!"

I blink back to reality. The meeting is over, and everyone's just hanging out, talking. Is it almost eight already? I look over to Shane.

"You're coming to the Xi Rho Nu party next Friday, right?" he asks.

"Party?" I blink. "Oh, damn. I forgot."

"How the hell can you forget about *that*? It's Andrew's twenty-first birthday! You know how we do things."

I'd only met Andrew once through Shane. He's a pretty cool guy—outspoken and loves to have a good time, much like Shane.

Matt, who's reclined next to me on the couch, his feet propped up on the coffee table, tilts his head back and exhales a long stream of white cigarette smoke. He scratches the blonde stubble on his chin. "I thought you said you have to have a date for that party?"

"You do," Shane says, nodding, then he cuts his eyes to me. "Wait, don't tell me you're *still* single, Genius!"

I feel all eyes bearing down on me. "Naw, man. I'm just . . . it's complicated right now."

Jason, sitting on the floor across from me, lets loose with a loud belch. "I call bullshit." He crushes the empty beer can in his fist.

Troy laughs. "Gettin' a bit rusty, Genius?"

I scowl. "Naw! I'm just taking it easy right now." I glance back at Shane. "I'll let you know, all right?"

Shane crosses his arms, giving me a skeptical look.

"Of course he's going. He'd be a pussy otherwise," Lonz says.

Randy, Shane, and Darryl break out in laughter.

I fail in fighting back a smile, so I flip them all off. "Yeah, fuck all you guys."

Randy shakes his head as he lights up a cigarette. "I don't know how the hell you're going to survive your last two years of college, not enjoying some of those beautiful twentysomething honeys."

I grimace. "They wouldn't give you the time of day, old man."

Everyone laughs, including Randy.

"Yeah? I don't see you doing any better. How long has it been? A year? Five years? High school?"

The guys whoop, and I fall silent, unable to think up a good comeback.

"So," Shane says, "I'll be manning the door at the party. You better come, or I'll embarrass your punk ass all over campus." He smirks.

Giving Shane the stinkeye, I chug the rest of my beer and wipe my mouth with the back of my hand.

Marco's phone suddenly goes off, and he pops up from one of the couches. "Shit! Gotta go, guys."

Charles whistles. "Booty call!"

We all laugh, and Marco's face reddens. He flips us all off as he makes his way to the front door. Thank God the attention's no longer on me.

The sound of Marco's sport bike rumbles outside and then fades away.

Gregg takes a pack of cigarettes from inside his vest and slaps it in his palm a few times. "Time for me to split, too." He pulls one out with his teeth and heads to the door.

"Right behind you," I say, sliding off the armrest. "See you punks later."

Outside, I spot Gregg mounted on his bike, having his smoke. He tips his head in my direction.

As I reach for my jacket, Lonz comes out the door and approaches me. Rolling my eyes, I heave a heavy sigh. *I'm not in the mood for a damn lecture.*

Lonz eyes me sternly and folds his arms across his chest.

"C'mon, man, I gotta—"

"You weren't all there at the meeting," Lonz says. "We talked about this at Loriano's didn't we? I thought you were gonna have that shit under control?"

God, I hope Trinity's not waiting on me. "I do have it under control, Lonz. I found someone else, and I got a date with her tonight."

He arches an eyebrow. "You don't sound too happy about it."

I grit my teeth. Damn these old guys and their innate ability to spot bullshit. "I just met her, all right? I don't know how it's gonna go down. Why are you so concerned about it anyway?"

"It's *you* I'm concerned about. You think I don't notice the way you drag your ass around? Keeping your head in the clouds and not paying attention to tonight's meeting?"

"I was paying attention."

"Then when and where's our next poker run?"

Shit. Did they mention a poker run?

"Exactly, Genius," Lonz says when I take too long to respond. "You got till next month's meeting to get it together, or else I'll see that you're demoted back to "Prospect." And believe me, I will. That's a promise."

Glaring, I slam the helmet over my head. "Noted." Without another word, I crank the engine and zoom off.

CHAPTER 13

To my relief, Trinity's not waiting outside when I return home. Hopping off the bike, I rush through the back door into the kitchen. As I toss off my gear, I hear the TV in the living room and Chris cursing. Entering the living room, I spot Trinity curled up on one end of the couch. She watches Chris, who sits on the other end, playing his football videogame. She doesn't look the least bit entertained.

"Chris? Trinity?"

Trinity turns and gasps. "Dominick!" She hops up and rushes into my arms as if I'd just rescued her from death by boredom.

I huff as she slams into me, her soft, curvy body pressing against mine.

"'Sup, dude," Chris says, not looking up from his game.

Trinity wraps her arms around me and squeezes tight. She rests her head on my shoulder. *Way too clingy for my taste.*

Tensing, and smashed into her, I can't help but look down at how her jeans pull tight across her rounded ass, and she rises up on her toes to grind against me a little bit. I gently pull away enough to breathe, and as I do, her purple, snug-fitting shirt smoothes out as her large tits bounce back into place. She falls back to her heels, her feet covered in blue socks with cartoon cats.

"It's about time," she mutters. "I don't think I could take another minute of listening to him swear at that damn game."

"Aw, come on, you son of a bitch! He ran out of bounds!" Chris yells at the TV, slamming his fingers on the controller buttons.

I unwrap Trinity's arms from around me, march over to Chris, and swipe the controller from his hands.

"Dude! What the fuck?" Chris says.

"Sorry, man. I need the TV. Movie night." I power off the game console.

Grumbling, Chris gets up and leaves. "Fine. I'm gonna call Adri. Keep it down in here, you two."

I flip him off while his back is turned.

Trinity snorts and covers her mouth. "You two are hilarious."

"He's cool once you get to know him. He's been my best buddy since high school. Anyway." I look apologetically at her. "I didn't mean for movie night to start out like this."

"What are you talking about? I'm just glad you're here."

I sigh. "How long were you waiting?"

"Not long. The bus dropped me off about fifteen minutes ago."

I retrieve the thick binder of movies from under the TV. "So what kind of movies do you like?"

"Mm . . . thrillers and comedy mainly."

I idly sift through pages of white-faced discs with hand-written labels. Looks like Chris acquired some more movies. My mind drifts elsewhere. I feel like such an ass for almost standing her up. My fingers pull out a random disc. "Ever see *The Shining?*"

Her eyes light up. "That's a classic! Let's watch it."

I pop the movie into the player. "Get comfortable. I'll make some popcorn. Want something to drink?"

She curls up on the couch. "Some water's fine."

Returning to the kitchen, I search the cabinets for the box of microwave popcorn. The sound of the TV fades to a dull buzz. Tonight feels weird, as if it's not supposed to be happening—at least, not with Trinity.

Denise is supposed to be the one on that couch.

I tear open the popcorn pack and throw it in the microwave. I know things probably won't work with Trinity, but how the hell do I tell her? She and Denise are friends, for God's sake. Sighing, I grab a beer from the fridge and fill up a glass of ice water.

The popcorn done, I carry it and the drinks back to the living room. I hand Trinity her water and then plop down on the couch.

"Thanks," she says.

I put the popcorn bag between us. I don't want to give her any ideas. But she takes the bag, sets it on the floor, and scoots close to me.

I try to enjoy the movie, my beer in hand, but her constant shifting has me nervous. *What is she thinking right now?*

She lays her head on my shoulder and watches the TV for a moment. "I can't believe this is happening. Me watching movies with DJ Kevitron's brother."

I can't help but laugh. "Is that all I am to you?"

"Of course not." She idly traces her finger along the top of my thigh. "I, uh, kinda have a confession. So, I think it's cool you're his brother and all, but I was wondering, if, um . . . you can hook me up with him?"

I gawk at her. Wow, she's obsessed with him, all right. "What?"

She smiles apologetically. "Don't get me wrong, Dominick. You're a pretty cool guy, but I know you're into Denise. Let's be real here."

I blink. "Wait. How do you—"

"Oh, come on. It was pretty obvious when my friends and I saw you at the club, and when you talked to Denise that night outside. Judging by the way your eyes were ready to pop out of your head and the line of drool about to fall out of your mouth, we figured you have a thing for her."

I huff. "I was *not* drooling."

"You *totally* were." She prods me in the tricep with her finger.

"All right. Fine. So I *might* have a bit of a thing for her. Does Denise know?"

She shrugs. "Maybe? I mean, we didn't tell her anything. Not with her thing with William."

William. I lower the TV volume and turn to face Trinity. "What's going on with Denise and William, anyway?" I ask, trying not to dry-swallow.

She shakes her head. "I really shouldn't say anything about her personal life, but I don't care for William. He kinda creeps me out, y'know? But he loves Denise, and Denise loves him, too, I think, so that's all that matters."

"You 'think'? What about him creeps you out?"

"He's a frat guy. One of the obnoxious types. The ones that think girls are supposed to be nothing but arm candy."

"What frat is he in?"

"Xi Rho Nu, I think. At least, that's what I overheard him telling Denise before. Not sure if it's true or not. Maybe he's trying to impress her or something."

I scowl. *What is that asshole up to?* "I have a friend in Xi, but he's not like that."

"Denise is my best friend. I just want her to be happy." She fidgets with the couch cushion. "It hurt her when he had to move to Chicago."

I lower my voice. "You have no idea how much I want to fuck up that guy."

Her lips twist into a smirk. "You're jealous."

I scoff at that. "Well, how the hell does someone like William get someone like Denise?"

"He was a smooth talker in high school. And a soccer jock. Denise always had a thing for jocks." She covers her mouth. "Oops. I wasn't supposed to say that."

Well, shit.

"Don't tell her, okay?"

"Don't worry, I won't." So Denise likes jocks, does she? "Y'know, I was a jock in high school, too. So was Kevin."

"Really?" She bites her thumbnail.

I nod. "I played football. Kevin played basketball."

"That's cool. I like you, Dominick. You seem like you'd make Denise happy. And you're a jock. That's always a plus."

"So I guess the question is, how do I get her to want me?"

She shrugs. "I don't know. I should stay out of it. She might think I'm conspiring behind her back or something. I guess technically I am." Her smile returns when she looks at me.

I place my hand atop hers. "You're an amazing girl."

She rolls her eyes. "Mhmm."

"Seriously, you are. And thanks for telling me all this, by the way. I swear, I won't say anything to anyone about it."

"Thank you." She blinks, as though suddenly coming to a realization about something. "Wait. Did you say Kevin played basketball?" Her eyes widen.

I furrow my brow. "Uh, yeah. Like two minutes ago."

"*Your* brother? DJ Kevitron?"

"Yeah."

"Oh my God. Does he still play?"

"Sometimes he plays pickup games at the parks. Why?"

"I want to watch him play. You know how sexy that is? Wait, of course you don't. God that sounded so weird. Okay, um . . . never mind. So yeah, can you talk to him for me?"

I just stare at her, speechless. This girl is not only into his music but his athletic skills, too. And she's a big girl. He *loves* big girls. Holy shit, maybe she *would* be perfect for him. "I'll see what I can do."

She beams, then kisses me on the cheek. It's a light, gentle peck that I can tell was intended to be a friendly gesture. "Thank you." Looking back at the TV, she reaches down and grabs a handful of popcorn. "Ooh! Turn up the volume. One of my favorite parts is coming up."

I crank it up, but right now, not even an axe-wielding psychopath can distract me from my thoughts.

CHAPTER 14

WEDNESDAY AFTER WORK, I CATCH UP WITH KEVIN AT HIS apartment in Eastlake. He finally got his mess straightened out, and everything's all good. He's not working tonight, and it's pouring outside, so we hang out and shoot the shit. His wall-mounted TV is tuned into a basketball playoff game.

I'm sprawled on the couch, a bottle of beer sitting on the floor, as I fiddle around with the circuit board of one of his broken mixers. The mixer had finally breathed its last due to overuse, and I'm trying to repair it. It's not the first time Kevin's asked me to repair some of his deejay equipment. Besides, what better way to get some hands-on study time in for my circuits class? I occasionally look up from my project to the TV, but I'm not really paying attention to the game. My phone vibrates. It's a text from Chris asking if I want to meet him over at Chauncey's for a few drinks. I ignore it for now while I decide. "Whatcha doing tonight, bro?"

Kevin kicks his feet up in the recliner. His shirt's off, revealing the string of tribal tattoos covering the left side of his arm, all the way up to his shoulder, across the side of his neck, and down to his pec. "I dunno. May go down to the park for a while after the weather lets up. Get in on some pickup games."

I pause to take a long swig of beer, remembering him playing 'ball for the Huskies. "Have you thought about finishing school this fall? I mean, c'mon. It's just one semester and that's it. You're done."

He glares. "Shut the hell up about that already. I'll finish when I finish, so get off my fucking back about it."

I arch an eyebrow at him. He's not usually this pissy at me. "You okay?"

He says nothing and scowls at the TV.

"Kev? Come on, man."

His fingers dig into the fabric of the armrests and his knuckles whiten.

Now he's starting to scare me. "Kev . . ."

He looks daggers at me, bangs the footrest down, and stands. He storms out of the living room, and the door to his bedroom slams so loudly the framed basketball posters on the living room walls shake.

I set the detached circuit board aside. *The hell?* I jump from the couch and rush toward his bedroom. "Kev? Kevin!" I knock lightly. "Kevin." It's been a long time since I've seen him act like this. And that was when *that shit* happened.

He doesn't respond, so I slowly open the door a crack. In the midst of the deejay equipment and album-filled bookshelves lining all four walls, Kevin sits on the edge of his unmade bed with his face buried in his hands.

I enter his room. "Kev," I say softly. "Talk to me, man."

His phone slides from next to him on the bed to the floor. When Kevin doesn't stir from his spot, I walk over and pick it up. The screen wakes up, revealing the list of recently missed calls. I spot a name that makes me seethe.

Michael.

I haven't talked to my oldest brother in years, and I damn sure don't miss him.

"He called again this morning from New York," Kevin says. "I didn't answer."

"Good." I toss the phone back on the bed. "Maybe he'll take the hint."

"He's got the balls to keep calling, I'll give him that."

"Can't you block his number?"

"I did. Three times. But he kept calling me from a different number each time, so I gave up. He's been calling from that number more often now, so I just saved it and make sure not to answer whenever it comes up."

"What do you think he wants?"

"I don't know, I don't care. And neither should you. I'll never forgive him for running like a scared bitch when we needed him."

"Yeah." I stare at the wood-grain patterns on the floor.

"Hey, sorry for freaking you out before. I'm just . . . Every time I see his name, I wanna punch something. I've been angry all day about it."

I put my hand on his shoulder. "Let's go to Chauncey's."

Kevin lies back in bed. "Ehh . . . "

"C'mon, man. I think you and I can both use a couple drinks right about now. Hell, I'll drive, if you want."

"No. *I'll* drive." Kevin lies there with his hand over his eyes. "Gimme a minute."

I nod and return to the living room. While waiting for my brother, I finish the rest of my beer, do as much as I can with the circuit board for the time being, and catch the final few minutes of the game.

My mind's so numb right now, I don't even wanna think.

Chauncey's is pretty busy by the time we arrive. With the place being only blocks away from campus, it's one of the most popular bars, and our favorite hangout spot. Kevin finds a space across the street to park, and we get out, hustling across the street as rain pelts us.

"You know, you look ridiculous wearing those at night." I point at his sunglasses.

Kevin adjusts his ball cap and stuffs his hands in the pockets of his brown hoodie. "I don't give a fuck. I'm not in the mood to deal with fans right now."

Dim lights and the smell of stale beer welcome us as we enter. The groups of college students that frequent here are standing or sitting around in their usual spots. Kevin and I find two empty stools at the bar, near where a bunch of frat guys are playing darts.

"You're Miss Dee Dee tonight, li'l bro," Kevin says with a smirk, and then points out the vodka to Olivia, the bartender.

I roll my eyes. It's an inside joke Kevin and I have whenever we go out and drink. The one who's named "Miss Dee Dee" first is responsible for driving, so they're not allowed to get hammered.

"Whatever you say, Miss Daisy," I say, and order my usual.

Olivia fills three shots and slides them in front of Kevin. He downs the first one in a single gulp, and then winces and hisses through his teeth.

I spin around in my stool so my back's against the counter and watch the crowd at the dartboard. I recognize a few guys from Xi Rho Nu. The girls watch each guy who takes aim like predators assessing their prey. I look sidelong at Kevin, who quaffs his second shot. "Hey, Kev. You still single?"

Kevin looks up. "What the hell kinda question's that?"

"An important one, 'cause . . . well, I met this girl at the club the other night, right? Name's Trinity. Pretty sexy. Thing is, she's one of Denise's friends. She knows you and I are brothers."

"Mmhmm." Kevin downs his third shot and then signals Olivia to fill up three more.

"She's cool," I say. "But I don't think we'd make a pair, y'know?"

"What? You can't like her?"

"Not anything more than friends. I mean she already knows I have a thing for Denise. But the moment I mention your name her panties practically drop."

Kevin smirks. "I tend to have that effect on the honeys." Three more shots slide his way. He picks one up and tips his head back, emptying shot number four.

"She's a good girl who's looking for love, bro. You should talk to her."

"Naw. I'm done with relationships for a while. Not after the shit I went through with the last one."

I shake my head. "Seriously, I don't think she's anything like that. She's Denise's best friend, and from what I've seen, Denise doesn't hang out with skanks like Justine."

"Justine was worse than a skank." Shot number five disappears quicker than I can blink.

"Trinity loves the fact that you play basketball," I say.

"You told her that?"

"Yeah. And she thinks it's hot."

"Does she, now?" He traces his thumb across his smiling lips.

"Yup, and she said she wants to watch you play sometime."

"Play what?"

"*Basketball!*"

He nods absently. Has the vodka already started to kick in?

"Oh, and she's a bit chubby, too."

He looks sidelong at me. "So?"

"'So'? I thought you were into chubby girls?"

"Who told you that?" Kevin quickly reaches for a shot glass and puts it to his lips.

"You did . . . and that's empty."

He blinks and looks into the glass. "Oh, shit. So it is." He picks up the sixth shot instead.

"Right, so"—I pull out my phone—"you should give her a chance, bro. She idolizes you. Just think how happy it would make her for DJ Kevitron, the all-star basketball player, to be her boyfriend."

Kevin rolls his eyes. "No. She's probably just another groupie. She only *cares* about DJ Kevitron, the all-star basketball player. Not plain ol' Kevin."

"I don't think she's like that. Gimme your phone."

"No."

Sighing, I copy Trinity's name and number from my phone onto a square napkin sitting on the counter. While Kevin gulps his seventh shot, I stuff the napkin in the front pocket of his hoodie.

Kevin coughs. "What the hell, man?"

"Trust me, bro. Call her. Please."

He sighs heavily but says nothing and gestures to Olivia to fill up two more shots.

I tried.

The darts crowd suddenly erupts in cheers, and I turn my head to the commotion.

"Gimme those darts! Let me show you how this shit's done."

William.

The asshole stands up from behind the crowd where he was sitting and swipes a handful of darts from a nearby frat guy wearing a dark green shirt with Greek letters on the front. William makes a stupid face at someone I can't see, then looks seriously at the dartboard. He pauses, then throws a dart. It narrowly misses the bull's-eye, but it's the closest I've seen out of all who tried. He throws another, and that one makes its mark.

"Bull's-eye, baby!" William does a fist-pump and the other players cheer and congratulate him. A frat guy wearing a Xi Rho Nu shirt hands him a full mug of beer.

"Damn, you never said anything about being a beast at darts," the Xi guy says.

William smirks. "No one asked." He returns to his seat.

The crowd disperses revealing William's date.

Denise!

My heart sinks. She and William sit at a tiny table. She holds a glass of amber liquid. Probably her usual Long Island iced tea.

William looks in my direction and squints. I spin back around on my stool and nurse my drink. "Fuck. Fuck. *Fuck!*" I say through clenched teeth.

Kevin plays with one of his empty shot glasses. He hasn't touched his two new shots and doesn't appear too buzzed yet. But I know that won't last much longer. "What?"

Lowering my head, I whisper, "William's here. *With Denise.*" I discreetly thumb over my shoulder in their direction.

He looks over his shoulder and tips his sunglasses down slightly. "So that's her, huh? The girl that swept my baby brother off his feet?" He chuckles, turns back and sets his sunglasses back into place. "Meh, she doesn't look right with Fratboy."

I growl. *No shit.*

"It *is* you!" someone says from behind me.

My anger quickly ebbs when I recognize the familiar female voice: Adrienne. There's a sudden tightness in my throat, and I turn to her. *Shit.* I forgot Chris said he was going to be here. And I hadn't thought about Adrienne being with him, too.

Her hands on her hips, Adrienne glares at me with murderous eyes.

Kevin casts one brief look her way, then turns back and nurses his seventh shot.

I clear my throat. Trying to play things cool. "Hey, Adri."

She slaps me, and my head whips to one side. I'm staring at Kevin, and the side of my cheek stings. Bad. *Did she really just slap me?*

"Don't you 'hey Adri' me!" she growls.

I place my hand to my cheek. I've never been slapped by a girl before. But I probably deserved it, given that I'd passed her number off instead of calling her like I said I would. Denise just totally did it for me. I wasn't interested in other girls. My gaze drifts over to Denise, and she and William are looking in my direction. In fact, the small commotion Adrienne managed to cause has most of the people in the bar watching us.

"That's for thinking you can pass me around to your friends like a fucking whore!" Leaning her face closer to mine, Adrienne prods me in the chest. Her breath reeks of alcohol.

I wrinkle my nose. "Ugh, you're drunk. And I was *helping* a friend. Not passing you around."

"You piece of shit!"

I wince.

She leans back and teeters a bit.

Kevin looks over his shoulder again, this time a bit more amused. "Damn, you fuckin' her, too?"

"Hell, no!" Another quick glance in Denise's direction, and she's still watching me, this time with narrowed eyes. God. Why does Denise have to see this? I can already guess what's going on in her head—thinking she was just another flavor of the week for me or something.

"You're lucky Chris is good in bed, else I'd be kicking your sorry ass right about now," Adrienne says.

I open my mouth to protest, but Kevin suddenly bursts out laughing. I glare at him. I'm glad *he's* enjoying himself, at least. I've half a mind to blow his cover for being such an ass.

"Speaking of Chris, what the hell's taking him so long? Is he jerking off in the bathroom or something?" Adrienne mutters, wandering off to an empty table.

With the commotion dying down, people in the bar lose interest and turn away.

Someone slaps me on the shoulder, and I snap my head up. *William.*

"Hey, Dom. Here's a tip: Girls don't like table scraps."

I clench my fists. The bastard's got balls, I'll give him that. My fists shake as I hold back the urge to knock his head off.

No, not in front of Denise. I calm and give a quick flick of my nose with my thumb. "Yo, Willy, here's a tip: Mind your fucking business." The last thing I want to do is get kicked out of here because of this asshole, but damn it, I'm not about to stand here and let him talk to me like a bitch.

William shrugs and laughs. "Well, damn, just trying to help, geez. And you wonder why you're still single." A few of his frat buddies nearby laugh.

Grinding my teeth, I elbow Kevin. I'm ready to leave before I end up doing something I'll regret. "You ready?"

Kevin empties another shot and sets the glass with the rest. Eight. "Yeah, sure." His hand fumbles for his pocket. Finding it, he pulls out some money, and his car keys fall out. I catch them before they hit the floor. Looks like the vodka's finally caught up with him.

Not looking back at Denise or the frat group, I tug Kevin by the arm and we leave. Outside, the rain has stopped and the air is cool. I help him into the passenger's seat, and he manages to buckle himself in. He lays his head back against the headrest and closes his eyes, groaning.

"You good, Kev?" I ask.

He mutters gibberish.

"Don't go and chuck all over your own car, man." I smile crookedly and shut the door.

As I make my way around to the driver's side, I hear the hurried clopping of heels approaching.

"Dominick?"

I pause in mid-reach for the door handle and then turn. "Hi, Denise." Time seems to stop as I take in her beauty from head to toe. She wears a red tank top under a thin, unbuttoned long-sleeved shirt, and dark denim flared jeans. A matching red hairband decorates her cornrows, and her *fleur de lis* necklace hangs vibrantly around her neck.

She smiles, and my body warms. But I'm constantly looking toward the bar's entrance, waiting for William to come out. She follows my gaze, glancing over her shoulder.

"Hey," she says, looking back at me. "I'm sorry about what William said."

I shake my head. "It's cool. You okay?"

"Yeah."

By the way she says that, I know she's definitely *not* okay. "What's wrong?"

She looks at the ground, opens her mouth.

"Denise!" It's William's voice, and Denise instantly clams up.

Damn it.

I glare at the entrance, where William is standing. For a moment, he and I lock eyes. I hope he crosses the street, because I don't intend to hold back my punch this time.

Denise glances at William, then looks back to me apologetically. "I gotta go. I'll call you tomorrow, okay?" she says softly.

I nod and watch her join William.

William wraps his arm around her waist, resting his hand on her ass. "What're you doing out here talking to that punk, baby? You missed me get another bull's-eye."

My fists tighten. I stare at the closed door. *She's gone.*

I hop in the car with a defeated sigh and rest my forehead against the steering wheel. If Denise is worried about something, I want to help her.

But does she want *my* help?

My thoughts are interrupted by Kevin's sudden snoring. Looking sideways at him, I smile, pluck those stupid sunglasses off his face, and drive off into the night.

CHAPTER 15

THURSDAY I LEAVE MY DIGITAL SYSTEMS CLASS WITH TIME to spare, but for the first time ever, I dread having to go to work, knowing William will be there, telling me all about Denise.

Arriving at Frank's, I find William in bay one, tinkering under a wheelless black sedan that's up on a lift. He doesn't seem to notice me. Checking the whiteboard, I discover my name alongside William's with a list of jobs for one car: brake repairs and replacements, struts, and a wheel alignment. Fuck. This looks like Frank's doing.

I can't believe I'm paired up with that asshole again.

Larry walks out of bay two, toward the bathroom. He stops and looks at me.

"'Sup, Larry," I mutter.

Larry does a little double take and lifts an eyebrow. "Hey. Something up?"

I purse my lips. I don't want to come off as a whiny bitch, and I guess I'll have to get over the fact that William's my coworker. Fuck it all. "Nothing, man. Just . . . " I lower my voice. "Girl problems."

Larry guffaws. "Again? Shame. Well, don't bring that drama around me. I've got enough shit to deal with."

"Yeah, yeah." Smiling, I head for bay one. As I approach William, he stops tinkering under the chassis and acknowledges me with a nod. Even that gesture looks fake, creepy. I wanna give him a couple of black eyes and maybe even break some of his fingers for the way he put his hand on Denise's ass last night.

Why the hell should I be mad, anyway? Denise is his girlfriend. And he seems to love her. That's what couples do.

But the more I think about it, the angrier I get. No, jealous. No, angry.

Trinity said I was jealous. Denise would probably think so, too.

Fuck it, then. I'm jealous.

"So what else needs to be done with the brakes?" I ask.

William resumes his work, unscrewing a bolt from one of the front brake calipers. "Needs a line replacement and rotor refacing in the front, and new pads and rotors in the front and rear."

"All right, I'll get started on the pads." I grab a wrench from the toolbox. Since William's working in the front, I go to the rear of the car, as far from him as possible.

We work in silence, other than the sounds of the shop and Nate and Paul shooting the shit with each other under some cars outside.

William, in his usual asshole way, disturbs the peace. "Hey, Dom. About last night . . . "

I sigh. "Don't start."

"No, really, man. I'm sorry. I didn't mean to mess with you like that. It wasn't cool, and Denise didn't have to see that. I should've handled it differently."

I halt mid-crank with the hex wrench. *That motherfucker.* My hand grips the handle, and I slowly resume, pouring every ounce of my anger—jealousy, whatever—into that damn bolt that's being a bitch to get free.

"You know, my Xi Rho Nu brothers are having a party tomorrow night. You're welcome to come . . . *if* you bring a date." There's a hint of a smirk when he says that.

My mouth twitches. "Since when are you in Xi Rho Nu?"

"Since my second semester as a freshman at Chicago State. I've been in touch with the Seattle chapter for a while and got accepted when I transferred to UDub."

"What the hell is a fratboy like you doing working at a place like this?"

He shrugs. "A little extra income. My trust fund pays for tuition fees and living expenses, and the money I make here is for leisure."

I look at him, dumbfounded. *Trust fund? Seriously?* So, he's not only an asshole, but he's a *rich* asshole. "Damn, didn't know you were banking like that."

His face hardens. "I don't go around telling people how much money I have. I have what I have because I had two hardworking parents who taught me the value of a dollar."

"Hey, I'm not mad, man. Just . . . surprised. You never struck me as the rich type."

"Why? 'Cause I don't dress in polo shirts and business suits or sip with my pinky finger out? Seriously, Dom. Don't judge me like that."

I blink. This asshole thinks he knows me? I'll knock his ass out so hard, he'll have dollar signs for eyes like a cartoon character. "What the fuck, man? I'm not judging you. Do whatever the hell you want."

"Yeah, I will. Anyway. About the party. The invitation still stands, if you want to go."

"I probably won't go. No date, and all that." I roll my tongue around in my cheek.

"Shame. Tomorrow night's going to be memorable."

"Andrew's turning twenty-one. I know."

"That's not the only memorable thing happening." His phone suddenly goes off. He pulls it out of his pocket, stares at it a moment, then looks back at me. "Shit. I gotta take this."

With an arched eyebrow, I watch him stride off rather quickly to the bathroom, the phone to his ear. "'Sup, Nick . . . "

I don't think I wanna know what that was all about. But I somehow have this weird feeling in my stomach.

As I'm continuing my work, I hear the office door open. "Dominick, can you check the part number on those new air filters that came in today?" Frank bellows.

I exhale through my lips and toss my wrench in the toolbox. "Yup." I head to the rear of the shop where boxed-up parts are stacked on metal shelves on the wall. Beneath the shelves, next to the bathroom, are opened mail packages, their contents not yet sorted. As I'm searching for the air filters, I hear William's muffled voice.

" . . . whatcha got?"

I locate the air filters and pick out a small box but pretend to go on searching so I can remain within earshot of the bathroom.

" . . . I need some of the hard shit. Got any more G's left?"

G's. Drugs? I blink and stare at the closed bathroom door.

"Dominick! What the fuck's taking so long?" Frank yells from the office.

I'm about to let Frank know I got it, but I stay silent. I don't want William to know how close I am.

" . . . yeah, man," William says. "D's a fucking tease, making me wait so damned long. I'm tired of waiting. I'm poppin' that . . . "

It takes me a moment to fully register that. "D"—Denise. *Holy shit.* I blink several times, and then stand there, dumbfounded. *Virgin.* I can't wrap my head around it. I've never known a twenty-one-year-old virgin. Is she really a diamond in the rough?

" . . . what're you talking about? I'm your best fucking customer. You better give me the hookup."

The office door swings open and slams against the wall. "Just bring me one of those damned boxes," Frank says.

My mouth going dry, I finally head to the office, box in hand, and deliver it to Frank. William leaves the bathroom at the same time I leave the office, and he stops a few steps from the car and looks around nervously, probably for me.

I return to the rear of the car, giving him one of my poker faces. When he sees me, the nervousness in his eyes fades, and he resumes his work.

"Everything okay?" I ask, picking up the wrench from the toolbox.

"Yeah, man. Everything's fine," he replies, not looking up from his work.

My stomach turns. *Bullshit.* The red flags in my mind are way up. Does he intend to take advantage of Denise? But I can't prove anything based on bits and pieces of a bathroom conversation, unfortunately.

"Sweet Lady"—Denise's ringtone—suddenly plays in my back pocket. I hastily take it out. "Hey, hold on a sec," I say into the phone. Covering the screen with my hand, I look over to William. "Be right back."

"Yup." William continues working.

I slip around behind the shop, where my bike is parked. Leaning on the seat, I return to the call. *I hope she's still there.* "Hey, Denise. Sorry about that."

"Hi," she says, and I sigh in relief. "Do you have time to talk?"

Hearing her makes me want to smile, but the concern in her voice keeps me from doing so. "Of course I do. What's up?"

"I'm really sorry again about last night. I feel so terrible that William treated you like that."

I clench my jaw. "I told you, it's fine. No need to dwell on the past."

"I know, but last night got me thinking. I've been . . . feeling hesitant in letting William back in my life after he left for Chicago. It's like he's changed. I really want to love him, but I feel like I can't love him the same way I did back then."

"People change." *Sometimes for the worse, it seems.*

"Yeah, I guess."

"How do you feel like he's changed?"

"Well, like last night, he got all upset about me talking to you outside of Chauncey's. He said he didn't like me talking to you."

I suddenly think about the way Pops isolated Mama from certain people. That was before I realized he was physically abusing her. Before he did what he did to me. My heart races for a moment. "You're a grown woman. You can do whatever the hell you want."

"I know. I told him that. And we got into an argument about it. He also didn't like that Trinity and I are so close, either. I know the two of them don't see eye to eye, but I'm definitely not going to stop talking to my best friend."

"Sounds like he's way too overprotective, if you ask me."

She sighs. "Yeah. He never used to be this way before. I mean, sure, back in high school he'd get upset when boys looked at me wrong, but he never dictated who I could and couldn't talk to. Anyway, I set things straight with him last night."

I want to ask her, to verify that what William said is true about her being a virgin, but it'd be kinda weird asking her something like that outright. So I try a more neutral approach. "So you guys are really close?"

"Yeah, pretty close. I think he's trying to impress me more than anything. He was like that in high school, too. I just wish he'd be himself."

Seems like he's acting like himself to me. A small part of me doesn't like her answer. Because that means what I heard in the bathroom is probably true. "You're an amazing girl, Denise. What guy *wouldn't* want to impress you?"

She chuckles, and I feel all warm inside that I managed to make her laugh. "As much as Trinity can't stand him, she puts on a front around me. I know how uncomfortable he makes her. But she never talked to me about it or anything."

"Have you tried talking to her about it?"

"Yeah, a few times, but she'd always rather talk about something else."

"Maybe she doesn't want to interfere. You know, if you're happy with William and all, then that's all that matters, right?"

"Yeah, you're right."

"Are you happy?"

There's a brief silence. "I don't know. I want to give him another chance. He's really excited about taking me to the Xi party tomorrow, so maybe things will be better then."

My mouth twitches. "Yeah, maybe. Just be careful, okay? Guys like to get stupid at frat parties."

"Yeah, I know how it goes. I probably won't stay too long, anyway. I just want to spend some time with William."

"All right. Just . . . don't do anything you might regret."

"I won't. What about you? Are you going to the party, too? Bringing your girlfriend?"

Has she thought all this time I had a girlfriend? "Are you talking about the girl from last night? That wasn't my girlfriend. She's my roommate's girlfriend. All I did was set the two of them up. You know. Play cupid?"

"Look, you don't need to explain anything. I get it. What you do is your own business."

My teeth pinch my bottom lip. *She sounds frustrated. I bet she's angry, too. Maybe jealous.* "I may or may not be there. We'll see."

"Okay. Well, I should let you get back to work. Bye, Dominick, and thanks for listening."

I say softly, "Anytime, Denise. See you later."

I wait for her to hang up first, and the line goes dead. *She's gone.*

I shut off the phone and stare at the screen until it dims.

CHAPTER 16

FRIDAY MORNING, I LIE IN BED, STARE AT THE FAN, AND listen to the steady downpour outside. *Tonight's the party.* And tonight, William may do something terrible.

I'm still not certain if what I heard is true, but I'm not taking any chances.

Date or not, I'm gonna go.

Later that day at work, while William goes off to talk on the phone in private again, I suddenly feel the urge to call Denise. It wouldn't be too weird to check up on her, right? Searching my contacts, I find her number.

She answers on the second ring.

"Hey, Denise. I hope I'm not calling at a bad time."

"Oh, no. Just having lunch before I head out. What's up?"

What I wouldn't give to try some of her cooking. "I just wanted to see how you were doing today, after the talk yesterday."

"I feel better. Thanks for listening."

"Never be afraid to talk to me, okay? I don't care if I'm at work or sleeping or whatever. Call me whenever there's something on your mind."

There's a brief pause. "I will. Thank you, Dominick. That means a lot."

"You still going to the party tonight?"

"Yeah, I promised William I would."

I sigh. "You know, you don't have to do anything you don't want to."

"Oh, but I do want to go. I really want things to work between us. It's been so long. I'm hoping we can pick up where we left off."

My stomach clenches. "All right. By the way, I think I might be going to the party, too."

"You are? That's great!" Her voice sounds a little too enthusiastic, and I wonder if she really *is* hoping to see me there. "So you have a date tonight, then? You know they won't let you in the party without one."

I roll my tongue around in my cheek while I think. I'll find a way in if I have to. "Yeah, I know," I say, evading her first question. "So what time are you two going to be there?"

"William's picking me up around nine thirty or so. I guess we'll be there sometime after that?"

"Okay, I'll see you then. You take care, okay?"

"I will. Bye, Dominick."

The back of my throat tightens. I hate saying goodbye to her. "Bye, Denise." I listen for the click on her end before I hang up, too. Sighing, I stare at her name and number on the screen until it dims.

At seven o'clock that night, I'm sprawled out on the living room couch eating a B.L.T. with the TV on, but rather than paying attention to the show, I'm figuring out a way to get into that party without a date. I bet the party will be awesome, but Denise is my biggest concern. If William or anyone else takes advantage of her, I swear I will kill them.

I finish the sandwich and chug down a glass of milk.

Chris's door creaks open from down the hall, and I hear his tromping footsteps enter the living room. I don't turn to acknowledge him.

"All right, Dom. How's this?"

I shift my gaze to where he stands, dressed like a male model. I've never seen him go all out like this. With what has to be the twentieth combination he's shown me since I got home, I reluctantly play along to keep my mind from slipping into dark places. "I dunno, man. How about long sleeve instead?"

He looks dumbfounded and does an abrupt about-face. "Dude! Make up your mind. You said short sleeve would be better last time."

"Yeah, but that shirt had a pocket in the front. Made you look like a poindexter."

"Argh! Fine! I'll find another damn shirt." He marches back to his room.

I'm sure my opinion won't matter in the end, anyway. It never does. He's just doing this to calm his nerves, but *damn*, is it annoying. "Why don't you just pick something you like instead of consulting me?" I call. "Do I look like a fucking fashionista to you?"

"Well, yeah? You always dress sharp when you go out. Besides, I got a hot chick to impress. And I'm not about to look like shit in front of all those Xi guys."

I roll my eyes.

Shirtless, he comes out of his room, holding up a short-sleeved, dark green shirt. "How about this one?"

I slam my fists down on the couch cushions. "Damn it! Quit asking me! Do whatever the hell you want!" I spring up. "Just please. Do me a favor. Don't fuck up with Adrienne."

"What? Of course not! Why do you think I'm doing all this? I'm not even sleeping around any more. I mean, seriously, dude, everything about her is amazing."

I raise an eyebrow at him. Chris? Not sleeping around anymore? This has to be some sort of apocalypse. He's never talked like this before. "That's a bold statement, Chris. You really think you'll be able to refrain from sleeping around?"

He nods curtly and lays the shirt on the back of the couch. "I *know* I can. So far, I haven't looked at another girl the same way I look at Adri. She's got the whole package and more. Kinda like how you feel about Denise, you know?"

His mention of Denise makes me tighten my jaw. "Denise is a different story," I say, and leave it at that. "Anyway, this isn't about me or Denise. This is about you."

"Ohhh no." Shaking his head, Chris waggles a finger at me. "You and Denise have *everything* to do with this."

Grumbling, I push my way past him to the kitchen, and he tails me. I rummage in the fridge for more milk.

"You haven't said much about Denise," Chris says, as I pour a glass. "Hell, I don't even think I've seen her before. Does she even exist?"

"Oh, she exists, all right," I say, sticking the carton back inside the fridge. Chris slides his hand past me and grabs a beer before the door closes.

"Okay, then. Show me her picture." He pops open his beer and guzzles it.

"Don't have one."

Chris looks at me stupidly. "No picture? Dude, What the hell?"

I finish the milk and set the glass in the sink with the rest of the dirty dishes. "You need to get on these dishes, Chris. It's your turn."

"I'll get to them when I—hey! Don't change the subject."

I head for the stairs.

"We're not done with Denise!" Chris yells, following me. "So you don't have a picture, but what does she look like?"

I stop at the foot of the stairs and think about her. That smile, her trendy clothes, her ebony eyes, her braided hair. "Words can't describe how beautiful she is, Chris." Leaving it at that, I begin climbing the stairs. Chris keeps following me.

"Measurements?"

I scowl. "I'm not telling you her measurements."

"Dude, come *on*! Not like I'm gonna go after her or something."

I say nothing and head toward my room.

"Just tell me one thing, Dom," Chris says.

I stop at the doorway and spin around as he chugs down the last of his beer.

He gives me a serious look. "*Are* you taking Denise to the party tonight?"

My mouth twitches. He's really pissing me off. "No, all right? *No*, I'm *not* taking her to the fucking party! Now enough with the damn interrogation, understand?"

He shifts his weight, thumps his chest with his fist, and burps. "*Capisce.*"

I slam the door in his face and lie on the sheets of the unmade bed. I don't have a date for the party and consider calling Trinity, but I don't want to use her like that. But she knows I'm into Denise, so maybe it could work.

I dial her number, and she picks up on the second ring.

"Hi, Dominick!" she answers in a bubbly tone.

"How are you, Trinity?"

"I'm good. Don't you have a party to get to or something?"

"Yeah, but I don't have a date. I can't get in without one."

"Oh." Suddenly her bubbly tone dulls.

"You wanna go with me?"

There's a brief pause. "No offense, Dominick, but there will be people there that I don't particularly get along with, and I don't want that to ruin everyone else's night."

"You know, I don't really wanna go, either, but Denise'll be there, and I need to keep an eye on her and William. More so William."

"That's sweet, in a creepy kind of way." She sighs. "Since I can't be there, I hope you can be Denise's wingman instead. I bet you can find a way into the party without a date. In fact, I *know* you can."

I purse my lips. Now I *have* to go no matter what. "All right. I'll talk to you later, Trinity."

"Dominick."

That tone. It's similar to Denise's cry for help. "Yeah?"

"Take care of Denise, okay? Please?"

What does she mean by that? As I'm about to ask, I'm met with a *click* on the other end.

Maybe she's counting on me to make things right. I stare at the phone screen. *I'll make it work somehow.* I run my finger through the contacts and dial Kevin's number. Five rings. Straight to voicemail. Grumbling, I hang up and text him:

Call me ASAP

I call Shane next.

"Hey, Genius!" His voice is always excited and happy—always in a partying mood.

"Hey, Shane. Are you still gonna be manning the door at tonight's party?"

"Sure am. Why?"

"Good. 'Cause I need a favor. I need you to let me in."

He laughs. "That's not really a favor, bro. You're invited to the party. Just come with your girl, and—"

"I'm coming alone."

There's a brief moment of silence. "What?"

"Long story short, my 'date' is going with someone else, and I need to be there tonight to make sure nothing stupid happens."

"I thought you said you had a date?"

"I said it was *complicated*."

"Sorry, man, I can't let you in without a date. It's the number one rule of this party."

"Shane, I wouldn't be calling you like this, asking a favor like this, if it wasn't important. Please do this for me."

He grumbles. "You know you're gonna get me in serious trouble, right? Probably kicked out of the frat?"

"I'll take the heat for you. Please do this for me, bro."

He heaves a huge sigh. "Fine. What time are you coming?"

"Around nine forty-five or so. If you see William there, then I won't be too far behind."

"William?"

I shake my head. "Don't ask. You're doing this for me, right?"

"Yeah, sure," he says, a little less enthused. "See you around nine forty-five."

I hang up and exhale. Sometimes it's great to have friends in high places.

Kevin's ringtone suddenly goes off, and I hastily answer it. "Kev, I need a favor," I say, foregoing the greetings.

"Well, hello to you, too, Dom," Kevin says, sounding annoyed.

I exhale and gather my thoughts. "I'm going to a party, and I need to keep an eye on Denise, but—"

"What's going on?" he says in a low, serious tone.

"To put it simply: frat party, drugs, and virgin."

"Holy shit."

"I can't let whatever stupid shit William intends to do with Denise happen."

"Understood."

"Can you take me to the party tonight? I don't know what's gonna happen, and I probably shouldn't be taking my bike."

"Naw, don't ride. I'll come and get you. I'll call one of my buddies to fill in for me at the club tonight."

I smile. I can always count on Kevin for anything. "Thanks, bro, you're the best."

"I know." I can imagine him smirking at that.

CHAPTER 17

KEVIN HONKS HIS HORN AROUND NINE THIRTY AND I RUSH out the door, all dressed to impress. I hop in the passenger's side of Kevin's car, and he and I exchange our secret handshake.

Kevin looks me up and down and then raises his eyebrows. "Damn! Looking good, li'l bro."

"Thanks," I say, though my mind is still too scattered to really appreciate his compliment.

Kevin puts the car in gear. "So where we goin'?"

"Windermere, east of campus. Just drive."

Kevin pulls out of the complex. We ride along in silence, and I stare out the window at the passing streetlights as we head toward the 513 overpass.

Crossing the Montlake Cut, Kevin asks, "So what do you intend to do, anyway?"

I look to my brother. "About what?"

"About the situation." Kevin keeps his eyes on the road. "I'm gonna watch him. And her. But mainly him."

"And what if shit goes down?"

"Then I kick his ass."

"In front of everyone? That I gotta see."

"They're not gonna let you in without a date," I say flatly. "I was barely able to get one of my club brothers to help me out."

"So you're saying they'll turn even DJ Kevitron away?"

I raise an eyebrow. Was he really going to intentionally show himself like that? "Uh, I dunno. They might. Even if they don't, it'll be pretty boring there without a date. I mean, c'mon, it's a frat party."

"I don't care about the party, man. I'm worried about you."

My lips tug into a smile. "I'll be fine, Kev." I point ahead. "Turn right on 58th."

We weave around the winding residential street of the upscale neighborhood toward a dead-end street, where a bunch of cars are parked. I notice William's car in front of a blue one that looks just as decked out as his. The only house at the end of the street is lit up like a Christmas tree with multicolored lights and paper lanterns extending from the front door down the length of the walkway. Music thrums from the direction of the house, but it's not loud enough for neighbors to be calling the cops. Groups of college kids are hanging out around the yard. Kevin manages to squeeze into a spot along the curb, not far from Adrienne's car, which is parked three cars ahead.

As we get out, Kevin tips down his sunglasses at a group of girls standing near the walkway, talking. "Holy shit, Dom. You did *not* tell me there would be some beautiful honeys here."

I roll my eyes. "What do you expect at a frat party? Anyway, I thought you were done with relationships?"

"Who said anything about relationships? I'm simply enjoying the view."

"Okay, well, you do that while I take care of business inside. I'll call or text if I need you."

"Mmhmm." He seems too fixed on the group of curves to listen to anything I have to say, so I leave him.

I brush past the girls, not even stopping to acknowledge them. Arriving at the doorstep, I tilt my head to Shane, who stands with his arms folded over his chest like a bouncer.

"'Sup," I say.

Shane returns the nod, glances over his shoulder, and then glares back at me. "You owe me big time for this, Genius," he whispers.

"Only if I get you in trouble."

"They're gonna find out."

"Not if you keep your fucking mouth shut. Now, are William and Denise here?"

Frowning, he thumbs behind him. "They got here about five minutes ago." He steps to the side to let me though. "You better know what you're doing."

"Don't worry, I do." I pat his shoulder as I walk past. "Thanks, by the way."

People are everywhere, drinking, smoking, dancing, socializing. Techno music blares from unseen speakers, and the floors and walls vibrate to the thump of the bass. Christmas lights and paper lanterns strung about the walls and ceiling keep the room dim, colorful, and inviting. Weaving my way through the living room, I notice all the furniture has been shoved against the walls, leaving a wide enough space in the center for people to dance. Couples laze around on the sofas and chairs, either making out, or looking pretty damn close to doing so. I try to act casual and not make eye contact with anyone. But my focus is on Denise and William, who are mingling in the crowded kitchen and bar area, where the drinks flow.

They stand among a growing crowd, waiting for their drinks to be prepared by the two Xi guys manning the bar.

"What's happenin', Nick?" William says to one of the guys, and they do a special handshake.

Nick. The guy who called William yesterday.

William asks for a margarita and a Long Island iced tea. As Nick prepares the drinks, William turns to Denise and kisses her intimately on the lips. William blocks my line of sight to Nick, and I crane my neck, but a group of people push past me and crowd the bar. Breaking the kiss, William turns and grabs the prepared drinks. I stare at Denise's drink as William hands it to her, making sure he doesn't discreetly drop something in it. Keeping my head lowered, I blend in with the crowd and make my way to the bar just as they leave. Denise and William wander out to the back patio, where they mingle with more people, some of them frat guys.

William gets into some intense conversations with them and shows off Denise.

Standing at the patio doorway, I continue observing as I down my rum 'n Coke.

Someone suddenly slaps me on the shoulder, and I nearly choke.

"Dude! You made it!"

I turn my head and widen my eyes at Chris. "Shit!" I hiss and grab his arm and pull him along with me. "Follow. Now." I knew Chris and Adrienne were going to be here, but I figured they'd be too caught up with the party to notice me.

Chris gives me a curious look, but tails me. I head down to the basement, where people are pouring drinks from giant steel beer kegs and playing beer pong in the center of the room. The popcorn ceiling vibrates from the music above.

I hate letting Denise and William out of my sight, even for a moment, but I can't risk being seen—and possibly ratted out—by Adrienne, wherever she is.

I spot two empty lawn chairs and make a beeline for them. Sitting down, I finish my drink.

Chris sits and slides his chair closer to mine. "Dude, you look like you just seen a ghost. What's up?"

I stare toward the beer pong game and lower my voice. "Chris, I need you to do me a big favor. Keep away from me, William, and Denise. And Adri needs to do the same."

He blinks. "What?"

I look at him, more serious this time. "I mean it, Chris. This is important. I don't want either of you talking to any of us. I need to keep an eye on Denise, and I can't get kicked out of here."

"But I thought—"

"No." I shake my head. "She came with William. I had to sneak in. And if you tell anyone that, I swear I will kick your ass."

"Okay, I promise I won't tell. But what's going on with Denise? You need any help?"

"Naw, I got this. Just keep Adri away from me. She hates my guts right now after the other night. It would be nothing for her to call me out."

"Eh, she was drunk. She gets a little crazy sometimes when she's drunk, but damn, I love the hell out of her." He finishes his drink and sets the red plastic cup down with several others that litter the floor. "Speaking of which," he says, getting up. "I better go make sure she's behaving."

I arch an eyebrow, watching him leave. "Adrienne? Behaving?"

Chris grins. "Well, you know. She can't be letting a bunch of drunk frat guys grope her. Only I do the groping. And man, do I ever!"

I raise my other eyebrow. "Uh, all right, see you later."

The beer pong game ends not long after Chris leaves, and one guy who was playing lays out on the floor, too piss-drunk to even move. I head back upstairs. There's laughing and cheering from the patio. Curious, I wander out the back door. A crowd has formed around the man of the hour, Andrew, who's sitting on his knees at a table covered with shot glasses. My eyes scan the shot glasses sitting before the pale-skinned, lanky guy—twenty-one.

I survey the rest of the crowd and spot Denise and William standing together on the other side of the circle. Thankfully, they both seem focused on what's going on and don't notice me. I remain at the back of the crowd and peer between people. William stands behind Denise, his chin resting on her shoulder with his arms wrapped around her, and his hands slowly rub her midsection. Denise brings a red cup to her lips, and her eyelids flutter as she drinks.

I frown. *How many has she had already? Or did he . . .*

A Xi guy, who looks like he's already had a few too many, steps up on a plastic patio chair. A few people in the crowd laugh and try to steady the chair, though they look equally buzzed.

"Twenty-one shots! Twenty-one questions for our birth-day brother!" The crowd cheers, some raising their red cups.

"Question one! Go!" Chair-guy points to a random person in the crowd—a short, blonde-haired girl wearing a black, strapless dress.

"Have you ever done a threesome?" she asks, and the crowd responds with hollers.

Andrew picks up his first shot. "Nope, but the night's not over yet." He downs the shot in a single gulp and slams the empty glass on the table. Cheers and whistles erupt from the crowd.

"Question two!" Chair-guy points to another random person.

I look across the circle to see William whisper something in Denise's ear, and she grins, looking back at him. William leads her away from the crowd and they head back into the house. I watch until I can no longer see them, and then I follow after them. They snake through the dancers and drunks and head toward a set of stairs. I wait for them to reach the top of the stairs and disappear around a corner before I slowly follow. Halfway upstairs, I hear a door slam.

The hallway is lit up with more Christmas lights and lanterns. The doors to the three bedrooms are all closed, a couple is making out on the floor next to the railing, and a girl is sprawled out near one of the doors, drink in hand, her other hand clutching her side. She's nodding off. Maybe she saw which room they went in.

I wander over to the girl, kneel down, and gently pat the side of her cheek to rouse her from her drunken stupor. "Hey. Did you just see two people come up here?"

The girl looks up at me with half-opened green eyes, her frazzled brown hair sweeping across her cute face.

"Hey," I say again, now that I seem to have her attention.

"Ohh shiiiit. DJ Kevitron's here!" Her speech is slurred.

I cringe. *Do he and I really look that much alike?* "Uh, yeah, that's right. Think you can help me, sweetie?"

"Mhmm." She downs the last swallow of her amber drink. Her body jerks, and she groans, her face contorting in pain.

She hasn't let go of her side. "Hey, what's wrong? Are you hurt?"

She grunts. "Just some stupid asshole that don't know how to treat a lady. Pretty face, but feet like fucking lead, telling me to 'get out the fucking way.' Who the hell does he think he is? Eh?" She elbows the door behind her and yells, "That's right, fuck you, asshole!"

I blink. Did William kick this girl? That son of a bitch. Now that I know what room he's in, I'm gonna fuck his ass up for this.

But first, I need to get rid of her before making my move. Things might get violent, and I don't want innocent bystanders getting hurt. I grab her arm and lift her up from the floor.

"C'mon, sweetie. Can you stand? I'll get you away from that asshole."

She stumbles and staggers as she gets to her high-heeled feet. *Damn*, she's drunk. "I can take care of myself." She wraps her other arm around me and hangs on for dear life. "But I don't mind being rescued by DJ Kevitron. Ha! My musical prince came for me."

Keeping her steady, I pull her away from the door. Her face gets close to mine, the strong smell of whiskey making me wrinkle my nose.

"Hey, I gotta pee. Wait for me, 'kay?" she murmurs.

I wince, her hot, alcohol-tinged breath hitting my ear. "Yeah, sure. Take your time." I drag her to the only bathroom up here and turn the light on for her. Shoving her inside, I shut the door.

Now, Denise.

I return to the door at the end of the hallway. I try it once and discover it's locked, not to my surprise. Pressing my ear to it, I try to make out any sort of sound, but it's a little hard with all the party stuff going on below.

I scowl when I finally make out William's voice.

"You don't know how sexy you look right now, D."

"Can we go now? I'm not feeling well," Denise says.

"We just got started. It's time, D."

I grit my teeth. The music downstairs ramps up a notch, and it gets even harder to hear what's happening on the other side of the door. William says something about wanting to make the night memorable for her, and then Denise groans. I catch the words "home" and "headache," then nothing. But a moment later the sounds of Denise's moans filter through.

The music cuts out, and in the sudden silence, their conversation is horribly clear.

"No . . . Not tonight," she says.

"Not tonight, not tomorrow night, not next week, then when?"

"I don't know . . . "

"Stop being scared."

"I'm not, but . . . wait!"

My hand falls away from the doorknob, and I rest my forehead against the door and close my eyes. That panicked voice, the uncertainty, calling out for help.

That was me.

"No, William!"

You're not going to win, you son of a bitch.

There's a scream, but it's so brief, it most likely went unheard.

By everyone but me.

I open my eyes.

I tried screaming, once, too. But he covered my mouth to muffle my screams, nearly suffocating me with his massive hand that smelled like ass and alcohol. I was so scrawny then, and no match for my old man.

"You need this."

"No!"

"Shut the fuck up!"

Downstairs, the music has started up again, and it pounds in my head. Red is all I see. Dark crimson that turns me blind with rage. I slam into the door, attempting to plow through it with my shoulder. The door holds, despite my efforts, though there's a small splinter in the wood where my shoulder hit. The couple in the hallway seem too involved with each other to care about the commotion I'm causing.

"Keep it down out there!" William yells.

I step back and try again, using every ounce of my strength. The door swings open, splintering at the hinges and lock. High school football has finally paid off.

I discover William on the bed, his shirt off, jeans halfway down his ass. He's straddling Denise, whose blouse is open, revealing her white lace bra. Her pants are off, and her arms and legs are pinned by his.

William's head snaps in my direction. His eyes widen and he gawks. "What the fuck are you doing, Dominick?"

Denise moans, but I don't sense any sexual feeling in her voice.

William tightens his hold on her. "I said shut the fuck up!"

My left eye twitches. I see the way my father hit me. The way he yelled at me. The way he choked Kevin. That pain. That suffering. That near-death experience. It all becomes an endless ball of rage packed into my hands, which snatch one of William's arms and yank him off the bed. Off Denise. He grunts as he falls to the floor and hits his head on the wooden dresser.

He gets up awkwardly, nearly tripping over his pants. He pulls them up. Gritting his teeth, he grabs a table lamp sitting on one end of the dresser and holds it up, the cord ripping out of the socket. "Get the fuck out this room, now!"

I clench my fists. "I will, once I deal with your sorry punk ass."

He charges at me with the lamp, and I try to block the incoming blow, but he's much too strong. I shut my eyes and turn my head as the lamp shatters against my right forearm. It stings like all hell and then goes numb. Shit. I hope it's not broken. Thankfully, my left side is my fighting side. I see the blur of his fist coming at me, but I land one right on his nose before he has a chance to connect.

He grunts and stumbles backward, his head snapping back. "Oof!" A line of blood flows from his nose down to his upper lip. He teeters a moment, then comes at me again like a raging bull. "Son of a bitch!" he spits, cocking his hand back.

I dodge his incoming punch and meet him force for force with my left elbow across his face. His head snaps to one side and blood flies out of his mouth.

He grabs a handful of my shirt and slams me against the wall. The back of my head hits the drywall hard enough to daze me a moment. I headbutt him, the impact making my own forehead sting, but it's just enough to break his hold. As he stands there holding his head, I shove him backward. I get some feeling back into my right arm, thank God. Must be the adrenaline.

"You motherfucking piece of shit!" I say, landing a punch in his solar plexus. I have a headache like all hell, but I'm so pumped, I ignore it.

He doubles over, and I knee him in the face. A few teeth fly out when the blow connects. He tumbles backward, slamming his head to the floor. I straddle him on my knees and punch him repeatedly across the face. Left. Right. Left. Right. His head whips back and forth. God, this feels good. It's invigorating to let all this shit out now. Those fucking demons—every bit of my anger is being branded on his body. He's gonna remember me for a long time. And I won't hesitate to kick his ass again. And again. Adrenaline overtakes me, and I breathe heavily. My fists are covered in his blood.

He's out cold, nose broken, two black and blue eyes, and mouth full of blood and broken teeth. I wipe blood from my hands, get off him, and pull my foot back, ready to deliver a good hard kick to break some of his ribs, when I hear Denise's weak moan.

The sound of her voice calms me. Lowering my foot, I turn around. She looks back at me with half-open eyes. She seems to be fighting her own consciousness. I rush to the bedside and sit her upright. Her head bobs around, and her body seems lifeless.

My God.

"Denise, can you hear me?"

She stares blankly, her pupils dilated.

"I'm getting you out of here and to some help." I fix her clothes and pull her out of bed, wrapping her arm around me to keep her steady.

As I head for the door, I look back at William's unconscious body. As much as I want to finish him off, I decide against it. Killing him will just help him take the easy way out, like Pops.

We head downstairs to the front door, where Shane is still standing.

"Leaving already, Genius?" he asks, looking at both of us oddly.

"Yeah," I say, my voice emotionless. "I'm taking Denise home."

"Where's William?"

"Napping." I harden my gaze, hoping he won't ask any more about William.

His brow furrows, but thankfully, he takes the hint and steps aside. "Okay. Take it easy, man."

Kevin is still in his same spot, holding a conversation with a different group of girls. "Kevin!" I yell firmly, letting him know that this shit is serious.

Kevin glances up from the girls, then tells them all goodbye. The girls leave, disappointed. Kevin looks me and Denise over and scowls. "Did you do it?"

I nod. "I did."

"Good job, li'l bro." Kevin opens the driver-side back door. "What's wrong with her?"

"She's drugged, man. Bad." I set her in the backseat and climb in next to her.

"Damn, I'll get to the hospital as fast as I can."

I look at her face and run my hand along her cheek. Her eyes are shut, but she's still warm. I wrap my arms around her, feeling the warmth of her body, the softness of her skin. I inhale her pear scent, which I can still smell beneath the alcohol and William's stink. I feel her heart beating. It's weak, but there.

Mine, however, beats fast. *Way* too fast.

CHAPTER 18

THE RIDE TO THE HOSPITAL SEEMS TO TAKE FOREVER. Denise still hasn't woken up, but she's still conscious and warm. I trace my hand down her arm to her hand and gently interlock my fingers with hers. The passing streetlights outside reveal her pale face, and I frown.

"Hang in there," I murmur. But I'm not sure she can hear me.

I glance at the rearview mirror, and Kevin's eyes meet mine. Then he looks back to the road.

We arrive at the emergency entrance of the university hospital, and I hop out of the car with Denise. She can barely stand, so I carry her inside. Kevin goes to find a place to park. I hate hospitals. The smells, the dreariness, the cold feeling of death and sickness everywhere. It reminds me of the first time I came here as a kid. I swore I'd never return to a hospital again.

Well, here I am, but this time, I'm not the unfortunate patient.

I stand at the receptionist's desk, Denise in my arms as I try to sign her in. Her body is limp, and her head is tilted to the side like she's sleeping.

As I explain Denise's condition, and what happened to her, the receptionist's eyes settle on her, and the woman's face pales. She buzzes a nurse, and moments later, the double doors that lead further into the emergency room swing open. A nurse wearing blue scrubs wheels out a stretcher. She's young, wears glasses, and her dirty blonde hair is tied in a ponytail.

"Sir, we need to get her to immediate treatment. Please lay her down here," the nurse says, patting the sheet-covered padded cushion of the stretcher.

I do so carefully. Denise's head leans to the side, and her eyes are still closed. She looks peaceful in that state. "Where are we going?" I ask the nurse.

She sighs and shakes her head. "I'm sorry, but I can't allow you to be with her at this time. I will take it from here."

"What? But, Denise—"

"We will take good care of her, sir. For now, though, you must wait out here until a nurse or doctor gives the okay."

"How long will that be?"

"I'm not sure. Perhaps several hours, at the very least. Now, please . . . " She steps in front of the stretcher and pushes it through the double doors.

Denise . . .

I stand at the closed double doors, staring helplessly. Finally, I slump my shoulders and make my way to the waiting room. It isn't too crowded in here, and I settle in a vacant chair in the back.

The pain and numbness in my right arm returns as my adrenaline high subsides. Now that I know it's not broken, I'll just ice it up when I get home.

My phone vibrates in my back pocket, and I pull it out. *Chris.* I frown and reluctantly answer it. "What's up?"

"Dom? Did you leave already?"

"Yeah. I'm at the hospital right now."

"What? What the hell's going on? Are you okay?"

"Yeah, Chris, I'm fine. Look, I gotta go. I'll be home later and we can talk."

"Dom! Wait, why haven't you—"

I end the call and stuff the phone back in my pocket. I look up in time to see Kevin come into the waiting room. He sits in an empty chair beside me.

"How's she doing?" He asks with concerned eyes.

"The nurse just took her in," I say. "Denise was conscious, but I don't know what kind of damage William may have done to her." I crack my knuckles. I swear, if William infected her with an STD or worse, I *will* make him pay.

Kevin rubs his hand over his hair, looking distraught. "Damn. I never thought this would happen again. That we'd be in a hospital again, y'know?"

I purse my lips. I know what he's getting at, and it sucks that we're both thinking about it. I remember that day at the children's hospital, where I had to go through so many tests I felt like some science experiment.

"Pops didn't win this round, by the way," Kevin says, breaking me from my thoughts. "So don't you start thinking he did."

I grit my teeth. I'm sure Pops is happy that I'm feeling miserable right now. This whole night has been emotionally exhausting. How could he have *not* won? Someone valuable to me has been hurt, and I can't do a damn thing about it right now.

I wake up to the sound of Kevin's voice. "We need to go to the cops about this, man." Yawning, I check the clock and realize I slept in the same position in a waiting room chair for six hours. I stretch and turn to my brother, who still looks whipped.

Cops. Oh yeah. That *shit happened.* And still no one has given us any updates on Denise's condition. "Yeah, we definitely need to. Whether or not the cops do anything about it is a different story."

"I'm sure they will. They've been taking rape cases seriously, especially this time of year near the end of the spring semester with all the parties."

"Yeah, but won't Denise have to say something to the cops, too? What if she doesn't remember anything?"

"It's worth taking the chance that she will, li'l bro. Now come on."

Before leaving, I give the receptionist my number, telling her to call me as soon as there is news on Denise's condition.

We're at the police station for what seems like hours reporting the incident and filling out tons of paperwork. It's almost noon Saturday, and while we're getting a bite to eat, I get a call from the hospital about us being allowed to see Denise. We haul ass back to the hospital. I make a quick stop at the gift shop to buy some roses and a teddy bear.

The receptionist allows us through the emergency room's double doors. Inside, we pass by the nurse's station and one of them looks up at us cheerily. "Good afternoon, sirs, may I help you?"

"Hi, I'm looking for Denise Ramsey," I say.

She gets up from her chair and comes out from behind the desk. "This way."

We head down a long hallway of curtained-off rooms. The lights are dim, and my skin still tingles from all the sickness and despair everywhere. The muted sounds of coughing, talking, and groaning fill my ears.

The nurse leads us to Denise's room and peeks through the curtain. "Miss Ramsey, you have some visitors."

"Okay, thanks."

I smile, noting the life that's returned to Denise's beautiful voice.

The nurse steps out of the way. "Go right in."

"Thank you," I whisper.

"No problem. If you need anything, let me know. My name is Paulette." She leaves.

For a moment, Kevin and I stand before the closed curtain. My heart pounds.

Kevin nudges me with his elbow. "You go first," he whispers.

I nod, open the curtain, and slowly head inside. The room is big enough for a bed, a small table, and a chair. Denise is there in bed, wide awake. Her face is no longer pale, and her eyes are bright and cheery.

She looks great.

My throat tightens. "Denise."

She smiles. God, I missed that beautiful smile. "Dominick!" She moves to get up from the bed, but I sweep in beside her, presenting her the flowers and stuffed animal.

"No, don't get up," I say, setting the vase atop her bedside table. "You need to get as much rest as you can."

She eyes the flowers and cuddles the bear. "Those are beautiful. Thank you."

Kevin pokes his head from behind the curtain. "Hey." He waves and approaches the foot of the bed.

Her face softens. "Hi, Kevin. Or do you prefer 'Kevitron'?"

"Ah, 'Kevin' when I'm not on stage."

I gently run my hand over her arm, my mind going over last night's events. "How are you doing?"

She looks down at her lap. "I'm okay."

The curtain opens again, and a woman enters the room, clipboard in hand. She wears a stethoscope around her neck.

A plastic nametag hangs from the front pocket of her white overcoat—Dr. Cindy Bannerman. She adjusts her tortoise-shell glasses as she looks over the three of us cheerily. Her gaze settles on Denise. "Hello, young lady. How are you doing?"

"Great, Cindy. Thank you. Will I finally be leaving now?"

"You definitely will. And it looks like you have two handsome princes here to take you home." She nods to Kevin and me.

Denise chuckles, and Kevin and I grin. I like this doc. Reminds me a lot of my nurse when I was in the hospital, Shevonne Holsen. She always made her young patients laugh and gave them a lollipop before they left.

"All right," Cindy says. She scribbles something down on her clipboard, then clicks the pen and sticks it in her front pocket. "What I recommend for you is lots of rest and to make an appointment to speak with a counselor." She pulls out a sheet of paper from her clipboard and hands it to Denise. "Here's a list of counselors in the area. If you're looking for someone close to the campus, this one has an office only a few blocks away."

I glance at the name she points to and recognize it as the same counselor Kevin and I had. On her right hand, Cindy wears a silver ring with a teddy bear symbol on the inset. I recognize that symbol as one some of the doctors and nurses at the children's hospital used to wear on lapel pins or on their name tags. I look up at Kevin, and we lock gazes for a moment. He must've seen the ring, too. Perhaps he's thinking the same thing I am about the doc.

"And these,"—Cindy pulls out two business cards from one of her coat pockets—"are numbers to the rape and sexual assault hotline and the crisis center that's not far from here. Please don't be afraid to call them. I know it's never easy to talk about this kind of thing, but please remember that help is only a phone call away."

"Thank you." Denise takes the cards.

Cindy smiles warmly. "You are very welcome, Miss Ramsey. Now, then. I will get your discharge papers ready, and you will be all set to go." She turns to leave.

"Ah, Cindy?" I call.

She looks over her shoulder. "Yes?"

I lick my dry lips. I'm so curious about her now. "Did you use to work at the children's hospital?"

She nods. "Yes, a long time ago. That's where I started. I still go there from time to time to see old friends and colleagues."

"You wouldn't happen to know a nurse named Shevonne Holsen?"

Cindy's eyebrows raise. "Shevonne? I know her very well. She still works at the children's hospital. We used to work very close together. A very sweet lady, she is."

"Yeah." I feel a little choked up. "If you ever see her again, can you tell her 'Dom-Dom' said hi?" Even now, I still haven't forgotten the ridiculous nickname she'd given me, like she had done for all her patients.

"'Dom-Dom'?" Cindy chuckles. "That definitely sounds like her doing. All right, I will be sure to let her know if I see her again." Cindy leaves, closing the curtain behind her.

Denise gives me an amused look, and I shake my head. "It's a long story."

"A long, but cute story, considering the circumstances," Kevin says. "Man, I swear, that woman knew how to turn any bad situation good."

"I'd love to hear it sometime," Denise says.

I smile. "Maybe one day I'll tell you."

Kevin turns to leave. "All right. I guess I should give you two some privacy. I'm gonna go wait in the car."

I nod and watch him leave. The curtain closes, and I return my attention to Denise. Sadness begins to fill her eyes. Just seeing this makes my eyes start to burn, too.

There's so much I want to ask her. I don't know where to begin.

"Please say it was all just a dream," she whispers, hugging the bear to her chest.

I purse my lips to stave off tears. *So she remembers?* "I wish it were. Then we could move on with our lives. But unfortunately, that's not the case." I take one of her hands, interlocking my fingers with hers. "Do you remember anything?"

She nods slowly. "He was so forceful. He looked so dangerous. So scary. Like a changed man. I've never seen him like that before." A tear rolls down her cheek. "I don't remember anything after that."

There is one question still floating in my mind. An important one, because it would mean an even greater trauma for her—and for me—if I was too late to stop it. But I'm not sure how to ask her. "Denise, did he, that is . . . I . . . um . . . "

She squeezes my hand. "No, he didn't get that far, thank goodness. The doctors who checked me out said they saw no signs of intercourse." She stares deep into my eyes. "Dominick, I owe you my life for saving me. You're like . . . a guardian angel. I can't believe you were there. I looked for you at the party but didn't see you. How did you even know where I was?"

I manage to smile. *Her guardian angel.* I like the sound of that. "How? Well, I, uh, kind of shamelessly stalked you. I hated William the first time I met the bastard. Even Kevin agreed that you two didn't look right together."

She wipes away her tears. "I really should've insisted Trinity talk to me when I sensed something was bothering her."

"I think you might've been drugged. I'm not sure."

She averts her gaze. "Yeah, Cindy said I had GHB in my system. I don't understand how. I mean, I didn't put my drink down or anything. Do you think William really drugged me?"

"Well, the other day at work, I overheard William talking on the phone to someone named Nick about buying some G's. Nick was one of the guys manning the bar, so it could've been him that put something in your drink."

"Nick. God, I know him. He's such an ass. He had a thing for me, but I wouldn't give him the time of day. I can't believe he would do that to me."

My blood boils. "I'll find him and give him a piece of my mind. And my fist."

"No, he's not worth it."

I sigh. "Well, I at least reported the incident to the cops. You may have to go down there and give your report, too."

"All right." She frowns and lowers her gaze. "How could I have ever loved him?"

I kneel at her bedside and tilt her chin over so that she looks at me. "Hey. It's not your fault. You deserve a better guy than William. And when you find that guy, he better treat you right, or else I'll kick his ass, too."

She looks amused. "I think I've already met a guy who's a million times better than William."

I blink. "Have you?"

Her eyelids flutter downward again, and she leans her face closer to mine, her lips parting. "Yes."

My lips slowly part as well, but I don't advance. *Holy shit. This is real. Is this what she wants?* I stare at her full lips. *I don't want her to feel obligated to me, but . . .* I lean in to her, our lips meeting halfway. Her soft lips touch mine, and I taste her. Beneath the remnants of salty tears, she tastes better than any candy in the world. So sweet. So innocent.

No. This is wrong. I have to stop.

But I can't bring myself to pull away—I don't, and neither does she.

CHAPTER 19

IT'S ALMOST THREE O'CLOCK IN THE AFTERNOON BY THE time we finally leave the hospital. Denise is in scrubs, as her old clothes were confiscated by the hospital staff to be sent to the police. We head to where Kevin's car is parked. Denise walks close to me, never letting go of my hand.

Kevin's laid back in the driver's seat, fast asleep. Poor guy. I reluctantly rap on the window, and Kevin jerks awake. He rubs his eyes, fixes his ball cap, and opens the door for us.

"About damn time," he says groggily.

"Sorry, we had to wait on the doc to finish all the paperwork. Need me to drive?"

"Naw, I'm good."

I climb into the backseat with Denise.

Kevin's keys jingle as he takes them out of his pocket. "So, Denise, you gonna be okay if we take you back to your place?"

Denise looks ahead toward my brother and bites her bottom lip. "Um . . . "

I give her hand a small, reassuring squeeze. I know she's probably still feeling scared. Scared that William might come back. Scared of the dreams—*nightmares*—she'll have playing over and over of that horrifying moment. "I understand if you don't want to go back right now. Being alone there, and such," I say.

"Well," she says. "Lauren will be there, though she might start asking questions. I really don't want to talk about that with her right now. Especially with how uptight she can get sometimes." She looks at me hesitantly. "Would it be okay to stay with you tonight?"

I blink. The question comes as a great surprise. But she needs me to be strong for her. She needs me to be her guardian angel.

Before heading to my place, we stop by the police station so Denise can give her report. She's hesitant about it at first, but decides it is probably best to get it over with. I'm there with her for almost an hour while she gives her statement and fills out paperwork.

By five thirty, we pull up to my duplex, and I notice Adrienne's car parked out front. *Fuck.* I don't feel like dealing with her drama. I only hope that she and Chris are too busy with each other to notice Denise and I come in.

We get out of Kevin's car, and I tap on the driver-side window. Rolling it down, Kevin gives me one of those "concerned big brother" looks.

"Thanks, man, for all this," I say.

"You sure you two will be okay?" Kevin asks.

I nod. "Yeah, man." I glance over my shoulder at her, and she smiles.

"All right." He stares ahead, out the windshield. "I got a call while I was waiting at the hospital for you guys. Got this huge gig at a radio station down in Portland next Wednesday, so I'll be gone. But I'll be back by Friday."

"Wow, Kev, that's great! I'm happy for you, man."

"Thanks." He looks back at me. "Take it easy, li'l bro, okay?"

I nod again, slowly. While I'm happy that he's got more work, it sucks that he'll be gone again. "You, too."

We do our secret handshake, and I watch him drive off.

"Kevin seems really nice," Denise says, resting her head on my shoulder.

I wrap my arm around her waist. "Yeah, he's cool."

I lead Denise around the side to the backdoor leading into the kitchen.

Denise pulls out from under my arm and sighs. "All I want to do is take a nice long shower and lay down."

"I hear ya. Well, the bathroom with the shower is this way." I lead her out of the kitchen and down the hall, stopping before the bathroom door across from Chris's room. His door is closed.

I turn the bathroom light on for Denise. She scrutinizes the small space and then nods.

"It's not much," I say, "but it's got a shower."

"This is fine, thank you."

I look her over thoughtfully. "I'll try and find some spare clothes you can wear. There's a clean towel and washcloth under the sink you can use."

She smiles graciously. "Thank you, Dominick."

I leave her to do her thing and rush upstairs to my room. I set the flowers and teddy bear on the night table, and then turn my closet upside down looking through the smallest shirts I own. I find a pair of basketball shorts and an old football jersey that actually used to be Chris's. When he decided he didn't like the player any more, he gave it to me. Go figure.

Bounding down the stairs, I hear the shower going. I go to the kitchen and fill up a small baggie with ice from the freezer. Holding the makeshift ice pack to my sore arm, I head to the living room and flip on the TV. I sprawl out on the couch, kicking off my shoes and propping my feet on one of the armrests, and stare idly at a home gym infomercial that's showing. My mind continuously goes over last night's events. The more I think about what might've been, the angrier I get. Now with William out of the picture, things are definitely going to be different. And what am I going to tell the guys at work when William doesn't show up?

Chris's door creaks open, and I snap out of my thoughts. I peek over the couch toward the hall, and Chris trudges in looking worn, his long hair unkempt. "Dom?"

"'Sup." I turn back to the TV.

Chris moves my feet aside and sits on the armrest. "Dude. We need to talk. Seriously."

I sigh and look at him. "Yeah, I guess we do."

"Why the hell did you leave so early? The party was just getting started."

"I had things to do," I say simply.

Chris scowls. "That's bullshit. You told me you were at the damn hospital. And then you go and leave me hangin' and not even say *which* hospital! Seriously, dude. I thought we were like *this*." He crosses his middle finger over his index.

"I know, man. I'm sorry. So much shit went down tonight, and I'm still rattled from it."

"So enlighten me." He glances toward the bathroom. "Who's in the shower?"

"Denise."

Chris's eyes widen. "Seriously? Wait. Doesn't she have a boyfriend?"

"She did. Long story."

"And you brought her here?"

"Yeah, and I'd appreciate it if you and Adri left her alone right now. And tell Adri to leave *me* alone, too."

"Adrienne's so over you. She was drunk that night at Chauncey's and was feeling in a feisty mood—at least that's what she told me."

"Right."

"So, yeah, back to Denise."

I mute the TV.

"What the fuck's going on, dude?" He looks at me with a serious expression. It's rare that he ever gets like this with me. So yeah, it's definitely for real.

I exhale through my nose. "What I'm about to tell you can't leave this room, got it? I mean, seriously, Chris. This is personal shit. Promise me."

"I swear. My lips are sealed." Chris nods curtly. "What happened?"

As I gather my thoughts, I stare at the TV. Some toned woman in spandex demonstrates a freestyle exercise machine. "Denise's boyfriend, William, assaulted and tried to rape her."

Chris's jaw drops. "Holy fucking shit. *What*?"

I nod in agreement. "I went to the party alone to keep an eye on the two of them."

"Well, damn! Glad you did. That's some serious shit."

"Yeah . . . "

"How's Denise?"

I look in the general direction of the bathroom. I still hear the shower going. "She's better, I think. But still shaken. She's going to spend the night here."

Chris nods and shifts his weight on the armrest. "I'm glad you're okay. And Denise, too, even if I still haven't formally met her yet."

"Don't worry, you will. But for now, don't ask about her. Hell, don't even tell Adri about her. I don't want her getting all up in Denise's business."

"Noted. So what happened to William?"

I scowl. "I fucked him up good, so he's gonna remember me for a very long time."

"Oh, so is that why you're icing your arm?" He points.

My fingers tingle, and parts of my arm starts to grow numb, so I remove the ice pack. "Something like that."

"Heh, I would've loved to see—"

"That's the longest-ass piss you're taking, Chris!" Adrienne yells from his room.

I freeze. Chris slides off the armrest. "Don't worry, man. I got this. Adri and I are going to the club tonight, so you can relax." He heads back to his room. "Sorry, babe. Got hungry. Now where were we?" Chris's door slams shut.

I leave the TV muted and stare at the announcers silently showing off another overpriced exercise machine.

The shower stops, and I bolt up from the couch. Clothes in hand, I hurry to the bathroom door and knock softly.

"Denise?"

She opens the door, and a cloud of steam escapes. She has a towel wrapped and secured around her still-wet body. She smells fresh and clean, like my soap. My eyes can't help but trace down her towel-covered body. *Damn it. I shouldn't do that. I won't.* Swallowing, I force myself to look into her eyes.

She smiles sweetly at me. "Thanks for letting me use the shower."

My eyes absently drift to her neck, down to the subtle swell of her breasts accentuated by the way the towel presses against them. She shifts a little, and my eyes instantly snap back to her face. "You're welcome. Here, you can sleep in these." I hand her the clothes.

"Thanks." She holds up the jersey, checking it out. "Oh wow, my dad loves this team."

"You can keep it if you want. Throw your scrubs in the laundry. I'll wash them tomorrow, okay?"

She looks slightly surprised. "Oh, you don't have to do that. I'll do the laundry tomorrow. They're just scrubs, anyway."

I don't argue with her, but I plan to get up early enough tomorrow to do them before she can. Even if they are just scrubs. "Okay. Well, I'll let you get dressed, and I'll show you where you can sleep."

"Okay."

She shuts the door, and I stare at it. The image of her in that towel remains etched in my mind. *Why does she have to be so damn beautiful?*

Returning to the couch, I sit, fidgeting with my hands. The images on the TV are a blur.

The bathroom door opens, and I hop up from the couch again. Denise holds her scrubs in a bundle. The jersey she wears is a bit oversized on her small, lithe frame, and the hem of the shorts falls just below her knees. *God, I won't be able to sleep tonight.*

"So where should I sleep?" she asks, and I snap my gaze to her face.

I blink a few times, trying to regain my composure. "Oh yeah, you can sleep upstairs, and I'll sleep down here." I tilt my head, gesturing for her to follow. I don't really consider myself a messy person, though I'm not sure what she thinks when I show her to my room, which has a few clothes scattered around as a result of my earlier search for clothes for her. Damn, I should've cleaned all that up before I brought her up here. I clear my throat and hastily gather the stray clothing. "Yeah, so . . . uh, you can sleep in here if you like. There's a half-bath across the hall that you can use, too." I toss the clothes haphazardly in the closet.

She looks around my room, apparently intrigued. A few posters of some of my favorite hip-hop artists hang by thumbtacks on the drab walls. A framed picture of Kevin and me taken at my high school graduation hangs on the wall by the door.

Denise sits on the edge of the unmade bed, which bounces and creaks under her. I need to remember to fix that later. "Hey, Dominick," she says.

Something's on her mind, I can tell. I have to be careful. Gentle. I can't send the wrong signals. Smiling softly, I approach her. "What's up?"

She reaches out and takes my hands in hers, closes her eyes, and brings them to her soft lips.

Whoa.

"I don't want to be up here alone," she whispers, her warm breath caressing my hands. But there's a little hint of fear in that whisper, and I can't ignore it.

I lick my lips. *Well this is . . . I don't know what it is.* I remember a time as a kid when I'd frequently sneak into Kevin's bed and sleep with him because I was so scared of sleeping alone, that our dead father would come back to do bad things to me again. I trusted that Kevin would protect me, just like he'd tried to before. "I'll stay if you want me to."

She nods slowly, and her eyelids flutter.

She's thinking about it again. I don't want to see her cry again. I pull one of my hands from hers and touch her chin, tilting it up. "Hey. I told you—I *promised* you—no one will hurt you ever again."

She wipes a stray tear away. "Stay, please . . . please." Another tear falls, and I wipe it away with my thumb.

My throat tightens. "I will."

She wraps her arms around me, resting her head on my chest.

I slowly embrace her as well, my arms encircling her waist, my hands settling just above her tailbone. Inhaling her scent, I catch a whiff of pears among the soapy smell. Maybe she has pear body spray in her purse or something. "It's okay," I whisper. "Everything's okay." I walk her to the bedside, and she lies down. She nestles under the covers and huddles into a fetal position.

I could use a good shower myself. Especially if I'm going to be in the same bed with her. I hand her the teddy bear. "Hey, I really need a shower. Are you going to be okay for like, five minutes?"

She swallows and nods slowly, cuddling the bear close to her.

"Okay. I'll be right back, I promise." I set her purse by the bed and hand her my phone. "If anything happens, use my phone and call 9-1-1. Okay?"

She remains silent, and I don't say anything more.

I jump in and out of the shower in record time, foregoing a shave, even though I'm desperately in need of one.

It's nine o'clock by the time I'm back upstairs and in bed with her. I drape one arm across her body. She's so warm, her skin silky soft. Her ass presses against my groin, and it's too damn difficult to resist getting hard from it. I bunch the sheets up between my groin and her ass so she doesn't feel it as much, rest my chin on her shoulder and listen to her breathe.

"Are you comfortable?" I ask.

She holds my hand, brushing her lips across my fingers. "Mmm."

I sigh. "You're a brave girl, you know that? Really brave."

Her body shudders, and I hear her sniffle. Is she crying again?

"Denise?"

"Why me, Dominick? Why did this have to happen to me?"

"I'm sorry. I really am. I know it's none of my business what went on between you two."

"But I'm glad you made it your business. I'm glad you were there. I'm glad you . . . you . . . " She presses my hand to her lips and sobs.

Hearing her cry is just too much. She's too beautiful—too strong—to be sad. My vision blurs as my own tears well up, but I fight them back to keep them from falling. *I should tell her. Let her know how much I understand what she's going through.* "Denise, I . . . I have something to tell you. Please don't freak out afterward."

Her sobs are reduced to small sniffles. "What is it?"

I swallow as I carefully go over my words. It's now or never. These demons have to come out. Licking my lips, I stare into her ebony eyes. "When I was twelve, I was raped. By my father."

Denise sits up in bed and faces me, staring wide-eyed. "Oh my God. I'm so sorry," she says in short breaths, and another tear falls down her cheek.

I sit up as well and take her hands in mine. Images of my past flood my mind. "It was the most terrifying experience of my entire life."

"Where is your father now?" Denise asks.

I scowl. "Dead. He committed suicide after we called the cops on him. He took the easy way out. That coward. I still can't find peace from it."

"What about Kevin? Did he—"

"No. He was there when it happened, though. Tried to save me, but our father hit him and then tried to cut his neck open with a box cutter. Kevin fought hard, but Pops was too strong and ended up choking him out." I think about all the tattoos Kevin has. The ones that go along the left side of his neck hide the permanent scars from that box cutter.

Denise grimaces. "What about your mother?"

"She lives down in Renton. She and Michael had gone out grocery shopping earlier that day."

"Who's Michael?"

"My oldest brother," I say through clenched teeth.

She places her hand to her mouth. "Oh." She blinks away more tears and then wraps her arms around me and hugs tight. "Dominick, I'm sorry. I'm so sorry."

My body tenses at her touch. I want to enjoy it, but the demons won't let me. Fucking demons. "You didn't do anything, so stop apologizing. I wanted to tell you this because I want you to know that I understand what you're going through right now. It'd be great if we could just forget about it. But things like this are etched in your mind forever. It's something not even a counselor can help you get over." I purse my lips and think about all those damned sessions Kevin and I had to go through while we were in middle and high school. We both hated it so much and were glad when we weren't required to go to them any more. "We can't let the demons run our life, though. We have to be stronger. We have to continue living our lives, finding that happiness, that peace, that balance that will suppress those demons. I guess for me, the only way I can find peace is to not let what happened to me happen to other people—like you."

"I understand, Dominick. I really do. Thank you so much for being there for me. I owe you my life."

I shake my head. "No, you don't owe me anything, and I'm not gonna ask for anything in return. I want you to live your life and be happy. I miss your smile."

And just like that, her smile returns. I can't help but smile back.

"Thank you, Dominick." She leans over and kisses me on the cheek. It's soft and brief, but it still sends electric jolts of happiness throughout my body.

She lies back down in a fetal position, and I fall in behind her. "Try to get some sleep, okay?" I say. "I'll be right here. You're safe, I promise."

She says nothing, and I continue to listen to her breathing. It soon becomes slower and more relaxed. Everything is so quiet, so peaceful, compared to last night that my ears ring. And there's no greater sound than Denise's breathing with my own heartbeat pounding steadily against her back.

CHAPTER 20

I WAKE UP TO THE SOUND OF MY PHONE VIBRATING AND realize we are still lying in the same position, my arm still around her. My body's so stiff, I can barely move. Thank God it's Sunday. Thoughts of Friday night's party still haunt me, and I don't know what I'm going to tell Larry. The sound of Denise's steady breathing shakes me from my thoughts. I stare toward the window. The first signs of daylight are starting to show between the blinds, casting a dim, dark blue glow about the room.

With Denise still asleep, I carefully slide my arm from around her and roll onto my back. Bones pop and crack, and I groan. One of my arms is asleep for having lain on it for so long. I fish for my phone on the floor and shut off the vibrating alarm, catching a glimpse of the time. 7:30. *Oh yeah, I was gonna do her laundry.*

I slowly get out of bed, taking care not to wake her. I stretch, cracking more bones. Retrieving my old clothes and Denise's scrubs, I trudge out of the room and downstairs to the laundry closet, which is adjacent to the kitchen. With everyone still asleep, there's a pleasant silence in the duplex as I toss the clothes into the front-loader.

While the clothes are going, I raid the fridge for eggs, bread, and the last of the oranges. I frown, realizing it's Chris's turn to go grocery shopping again.

I crack open two eggs in a frying pan and scramble them. I hope she doesn't mind scrambled eggs. Hell, I hope she even *likes* eggs. But it's the thought that counts, right?

I hear Chris's door creak open but ignore it. I grab a plate from the pile of clean dishes in the sink—thank God Chris *finally* did them—and dump the eggs onto it.

"Wow, something smells good," Chris says from the hall.

Footsteps draw closer, and I spot a figure leaning against the doorframe of the kitchen.

"Dude! Are you *cooking* now?"

I give Chris a look. "You act like I've never cooked before."

"Okay, okay. So I *rarely* see you cook. Can't deny that you make a wicked chicken florentine."

Maybe one night I'll invite Denise over and cook that for her. "By the way," I say, "it's your turn to do the grocery shopping. Is Adri still here?"

"Yeah? Why?"

"Good. Then she can drive your sorry ass to the store."

Chris groans and carefully bangs the back of his head against the doorframe. "Fucking A."

I rinse the orange and begin cutting it up into small slices. Denise would at least eat the orange if she hates everything else, right? I mean, I haven't met a girl who didn't like fruit.

"Hey," Chris says in a more serious tone, which makes me pause in my cutting. "So is everything cool from last night? You know . . . "

"Yeah," I say quickly. "Everything's cool. She's fine."

"Good." Chris nods then pushes off the doorframe. "Okay, I'm going back to bed. It's too damn early. I don't even know how you're up this early. You're weird, man."

I smirk. "I'm the best kind of weird."

Returning to my room, I find Denise sitting up in bed, flipping the pages of one of my old issues of *Street Throttle Racer*. Smiling, I sweep around to her bedside. She looks up at me with a start.

"Morning," I say. Then, skillfully holding the tray of breakfast on one palm like the waiters do, I open the blinds with my other hand. Morning sunlight filters through the window and casts over Denise's squinty face.

"What time is it?" she mumbles, shoving the magazine aside.

"It's early," I say, then present the tray. "Made you breakfast."

She stares at the tray, her eyes slowly becoming less squinty, and she scoots further back in bed until her back rests against the headboard. "You made this for me?"

"Yup." I set the tray on her lap. "I hope it's okay."

She beams. "'Okay'? It's amazing! I've never had a guy cook me breakfast in bed before. It's very sweet. Thank you."

Yes! I do a small fist-pump, and she gives me an odd look, then breaks into laughter.

"You know, you don't have to try so hard to impress me."

I scratch the back of my head. "I'm not. I just felt like cooking something for you. You know . . . since I went ahead and washed your clothes and stuff."

"What! But I told you I would do it."

"Yeah, I know. But it's done now, and I cooked you breakfast as an apology." I avert my eyes.

She snickers then bursts into laughter. "Oh my God, Dominick. Listen to us argue over washing a pair of hospital scrubs."

I have a hard time keeping a straight face, too. "It's the principle of the thing."

Rolling her eyes, she skewers some eggs with her fork and then pops them in her mouth. "Wow. You not only know *how* to cook, you cook *well*! Definitely a one-of-a-kind guy. Thank you again, Dominick."

I exhale, relieved. "Anytime. I'm glad you like it." I sit on the edge of the bed and watch her gobble more eggs and break off small pieces of toast. She looks so cute when she eats. "So when did you want me to take you home today?"

Her face falls. "I . . . I don't know. I guess I should go back soon. Lauren's probably wondering what happened to me. I'll call her later. It's about time I tell her what happened."

I swallow. *She doesn't want to leave?* "All right. Well, there's no pressure, you know."

There's an amused twinkle in her eye. "You're not trying to kick me out, are you?"

"What? No! Of course not. You can stay as long as you like." *Forever, I hope.*

She chuckles and finishes her breakfast. She gulps down the glass of milk and slides out of bed, tray in hand. "I'll take this downstairs."

I swipe the tray from her. "Naw. I'll do it. Go shower. Or go back to sleep. Or simply laze around up here. You can find another shirt in my closet to change into, if you want."

She gapes, and before I give her a chance to retort, I leave. Returning to the kitchen, I wash the dishes, then transfer the wet laundry to the dryer. The smell of the cooked eggs and toast still lingers in the kitchen, making me hungry, so I whip up a plate of my own. I return to the living room with it and plop down on the couch. Turning on the TV, I flip to the sports channel and indulge in last night's scores and highlights while I finish my breakfast. My mind drifts. Tomorrow's Monday, and if William ends up not coming to work, I know I'm going to be the first person Frank and Larry ask.

I take out my phone from my pocket and scroll through my contacts. Stopping at Larry's name, I stare at the number.

Maybe I should just get it over with and tell him about Friday night.

It's after nine in the morning, and I figure the old man's already up by now. Punching the dial button, I get up from the couch and head out the kitchen back door to talk in private.

CHAPTER 21

THREE WEEKS HAVE PASSED SINCE THE INCIDENT. THREE weeks of pain, confusion, and worry. Rumors of the party floated around campus, and I made sure Denise's name was not associated with them. It was bad enough that her friends were asking her about it, but I wasn't about to have mere strangers talk about her like that. I had to protect her.

We hadn't seen or heard from William since that night. He didn't even show up at work that Monday. According to Shane, Nick was kicked out of the fraternity after they found a load of drugs—that hard, crazy shit that can kill faster than rat poison—in his car. But that was all Shane said about it. Not long after, I'd found out William was also kicked out and got arrested on drug possession charges. That, coupled with Denise's and my reports on her attempted rape and assault, gave him quite a long rap sheet.

We'd gone on with our lives as best we could in those weeks. Finals week was upon us, so we tried staying focused in our classes. But memories of that night never went away. I did everything I could to help ease the pain: took her to the movies, took her out riding around Cougar Mountain, let her cry on my shoulder, lent her my ear—anything and everything to make her feel special. Because she was very special to me.

I can't deny that I think I love her.

Denise set up sessions with my old counselor. To be honest, I wasn't happy to go back there. But I did it for her. She needed it. She eventually told Lauren what was going on, and, at first, Lauren went crazy, but her knowing that I was the one who saved Denise made her a little nicer to me. Just a little. I really think she just has a problem with trusting guys. Can't blame her. She's probably met too many Williams in her life.

I was hesitant about telling Frank what happened. But I knew I had to tell him at some point. To my surprise and relief, he didn't go off on me. But that didn't mean he wasn't pissed. Our workload went back to being crazy again. Larry didn't say much to me after I told him. In fact, he acted as though nothing happened. It was weird.

It's another Sunday afternoon, and Denise and I laze on the couch, studying for finals tomorrow. She's been coming over more often, sometimes spending the night. It's been cool. This time, she's spending the entire weekend over. Curled up next to me, Denise wears another one of my pro-football jerseys that fits her like a nightshirt.

I'm anxious for Chris and Adrienne to get back from grocery shopping. I have plans to make that chicken florentine tonight. It's been on my mind since Chris mentioned it last month, and I've been waiting for the right opportunity to make it for her.

The muffled sounds of car doors slamming makes me start. Chris and Adrienne are back. I want this dinner to be a surprise for Denise, so I have to be careful and work fast. The front door swings open, and Chris and Adrienne trudge inside carrying armfuls of grocery bags and disappear into the kitchen. Denise shifts on the couch, but I stop her before she decides to get up.

"No, stay here. I'll help them unpack. Why don't we take a break and watch a movie? You pick."

Denise furrows her brow, and then nods. "Okay."

I get up from the couch and hand the movie binder to her. Her eyes go wide as she flips through the pages. "Holy . . . This one came out last week! I can't believe you have it already."

I idly scratch my after-five-o'clock stubble. "Yeah, Chris got the hookup."

She slides the disc out of the sleeve and hands it to me. "Let's watch it."

I take it and pop it into the player. I don't really know which movie she chose, as my mind is mulling over dinner. I should get started. But I don't want her to know what I'm up to. "Okay, get comfy. I'll be right back."

Reaching the kitchen, I find Chris and Adrienne unloading the bags of groceries sitting on the table. Adrienne wiggles her eyebrows as she pulls out the Chardonnay bottle from one of the bags.

"Planning a hot night, are you?" she says.

I swipe the bottle and stuff a wad of cash in her hand. "Just dinner," I say, sliding it in the fridge.

"It's never 'just dinner' when there's wine involved." She flashes a grin, sticking the money down her shirt.

I manage to fight down a smile. Adrienne's been more tolerable since she learned of the incident. She's actually pretty cool once I got to know her a little more. Quite the flirt and likes to have a good time. And she's head over heels for Chris. No wonder he likes her so much.

"I don't have any plans," I say.

As Chris is reaching up to place a box of cereal in a cabinet, Adrienne nudges him in the ribs, making him start. "Babe, your roommate is all sorts of weird. What kind of guy buys expensive wine if he doesn't intend to make a night out of it?"

Chris looks over to me, and then laughs. "Guys like Dom, that's who."

"What a flake," she mutters, but I can hear the amusement in her voice.

"Yeah, he's a flake, but he's my best friend. Had to put up with his sorry ass since high school, after all." He smirks at me.

I shake my head. "I don't know how the hell I haven't gone insane by now, having you for a roommate all these years."

Adrienne stifles a giggle.

Chris rolls his eyes. "Whatever, dude."

We finish unpacking the groceries, and I set aside the ingredients for dinner. Chris and Adrienne leave the kitchen, and I get started. As I boil pasta on the stove and chop up the chicken breast and place it on the electric grill, I suddenly realize I've left Denise in the living room for far too long. Fearful of her coming in the kitchen, I fill up a glass of water and take it to her. She looks up from the couch's armrest as I approach.

"Well, there you are," she says.

"Sorry," I say sheepishly. "I was . . . uh . . . looking around to see if we had any more packs of popcorn, but I couldn't find any." I hand her the water. "Here's some water, though."

"Thank you." She sniffs. "Is something cooking?"

Shit. The chicken. "Oh yeah, I think Chris is making something. Let me make sure he's not about to burn the place down." I give a small chuckle. "Be right back."

"Okay."

Returning to the kitchen, I tend to the chicken, adding the seasonings, and start on the spinach sauce. I want this dinner—this night—to be absolutely perfect, because tomorrow is Monday, finals week, and once we get to campus, Denise and I will be going our separate ways.

Chris's door opens, and I ignore the sound. I rush to and from the stove and the grill, finalizing the meal.

"Just dinner, huh?"

Cringing, I spin around and see Adrienne and Chris standing at the kitchen doorway.

"Now *that's* what I'm talking about!" Chris says.

"What are you two doing? Get outta here before Denise sees you both!" I say in a loud whisper.

"Dominick? Is everything okay?" Denise calls from the living room.

My heart pounds. "Uh, y-yeah. Just fine. I'll be right there."

Adrienne walks into the kitchen, scrutinizing the food. "Wow. That looks and smells good. Okay, so any guy who knows how to cook *this* good gets cool points in my book."

Her compliment flusters me—if that was, indeed, a compliment. "Thanks," I say, and then gently shoo her toward the exit. "Please, you guys, I really want this to be a surprise."

Adrienne scoffs and brushes my hand away. "Yeah, yeah." She links her elbow in Chris's. "Why don't you ever cook something for me, babe?"

Chris clears his throat, and I snort. Chris would probably burn ice cream, and he knows it.

"What are you doing in here?" Denise appears behind them, and I freeze.

"Oooh, busted," Chris says.

Fuck! I shake my fists. "Damn it, you guys."

Denise peeks around them. "What's going on?"

I sigh. "Everything's okay, Denise."

"Your man cooked you dinner," Adrienne says, nudging Denise in the arm. "Isn't that sweet?"

"What?" Denise blinks.

I throw my hands up. "Damn it, Adri!"

Adrienne chuckles and wraps her arms around Chris. "Just playin'." Smiling at him, she gives him a tug back to his room.

Chris licks his lips. "Damn. Round two?" He follows her and gives me a quick wink.

His bedroom door slams, and I exhale a long sigh. Denise still stands at the kitchen doorway looking dumbfounded.

"So what's all this about dinner?" Denise asks, narrowing her eyes. "Did I hear that right?"

I glance at the floor. "Yeah. I wanted to cook you dinner tonight. Do you like chicken florentine?"

Her expression slowly morphs into absolute amusement. She strides into the kitchen and stands before me, hands on her hips. "Are you serious? Did you really cook me dinner?"

Rubbing the back of my head, I nod. I'm not sure what to make of her actions. Is she offended that I cooked for her?

"Seriously, Dominick. What's up with that?"

"Well, uh, nothing. I like you. A lot." I close my eyes. *I love you.*

She exhales, and I open my eyes. She smiles softly, her cheeks awash with hints of red. She draws closer and wraps her arms around my waist. I inhale the scent of her hair. Her skin. Relish her warmth and the softness of her beautiful body against mine. My cock stiffens as she tightens her embrace.

"You are the most amazing guy I've ever met," she says in almost a whisper. She leans up and plants a soft kiss on my cheek.

Those lips. My God, those lips. They're soft and feather-like, sending prickles of pleasure down my spine and to my groin. "Denise . . . " My voice cracks. Words can't describe how fucking amazing she is.

She slowly unwraps her arms. "Is the food ready?" she asks, peering around me at the pots on the stove.

I nod slowly. "Yeah. Let me set the table first and—" Before I can continue, she's searching the cabinets. She finds the one containing the plates and glasses and takes two of each.

"Nuh-uh. I can't let you do everything," she says. "Where are the forks?"

I can't help but smile at her willingness to help. I give in to her insistence and point to a drawer near the sink. "There."

While she sets the table, I bring the pot of pasta over and fill both plates with a modest amount. Then I pour the chicken and spinach sauce on top from the other pot.

I notice she's gotten out water glasses, so I snatch them up and replace them with wine glasses.

She scrunches her face. "What? Those glasses weren't good enough?"

I shake my head. "Nope. Because . . . " I retrieve the Chardonnay from the fridge. "We need special glasses to drink this."

Grinning, she watches as I pop the cork and fill the glasses halfway.

I pull a chair out for her before seating myself.

I lift my glass. "We should do a toast."

She raises her eyebrows. "To what, this time?" She picks up her glass. "Not ballet again, I hope."

I chuckle. "No, not ballet." I gaze into her eyes—deep into her eyes. "To the most beautiful and amazing girl I've ever met."

She bites her bottom lip. The red in her cheeks is a little more prominent. "Dominick . . . "

Smiling, I shake my head. "Don't say anything. Just toast."

We clink glasses, and I take a long sip, while hers is very brief. We take a few moments to enjoy dinner, which turns out great. Nothing is overcooked and everything is seasoned just right.

Denise looks like she's having an orgasm when she samples a forkful of pasta. "Holy—! This is the *best* thing I've ever tasted. *Ever!*"

I grin. "I take it you like it?"

"Are you kidding? I don't even think my own mother can cook this good. You should totally be on one of those network cooking shows or something."

My grin broadens. I always followed my mother around the kitchen when I was little but never considered getting into culinary arts. "Well, I don't think I'm *that* good, but thank you." I smear some pasta into a puddle of sauce and pop it in my mouth.

We finish our first helpings and end up having seconds. We don't leave so much as a piece of pasta or a drop of sauce in the pots.

I clear the table and wash the dishes. Denise helps out by drying them. It's a little cute how we do dishes together. Like the way I've seen it done in the movies.

She's happy right now. And so am I.

Our bellies full, we're ready to laze around on the couch. It's dark outside, but I have no idea what time it is, and I don't want to know. I don't care. I pop in another movie—an action-packed one—and we curl up on the couch. I nestle against the back and armrest, and she lies between my legs, her ass rubbing against my groin. My cock twitches from the contact. I wrap my arms around her, my hands resting on her taut belly. She smells so good. Hell, she *always* smells good. I inhale her warmth, her scent. The movie starts, but I'm not paying attention to it. I have a beautiful girl in my arms.

I gently rub her belly with my hands. I can't help it. I have to keep my hands working. Damn mechanics' twitches.

She closes her eyes and exhales. She's obviously not paying attention to the movie, either. "Dominick, when are you gonna stop spoiling me?"

I pause my gentle massage. "Never. You're a very special girl. You deserve only the best."

Her smile broadens. "You've done so much in these past weeks to help heal my pain. I thought I could never love again. That I would be too scared to be with anyone again. Then you came along. You've always been there."

I blink. *What is she saying?*

"Maybe it was the initial attraction I had for you when we first met," she says. "Then you fixed my car, took me to dinner, did all those nice things for me in between . . . "

" . . . And then William came along and ruined everything."

She frowns. "I was stupid to think I could love him again like I did before. You've been nothing but sweet to me, and I took it for granted. But when I needed you the most, you were there. Oh God, were you there."

I kiss the back of her head. "I will always be there. If you want me to be."

"Yeah, I do . . . because I like you, too. A lot."

I smile. She shifts in my lap and faces me. Light flashes across our faces from a car explosion in the movie. At this point, I think we're too fixated on each other to pay attention to it. She cradles my face in her hands and leans in closer, slowly. She touches my lips with a feather-soft kiss. Her taste is amazing. I don't want it to end. But much to my dismay, she slowly pulls away. She runs her fingers down my cheek, brushes them over my lips. I try to kiss every one of those slender fingers.

I want her. Right now.

But I know I can't have her. She'll save herself for someone special. And I'm glad.

CHAPTER 22

DENISE SLIDES OFF ME, TAKING MY HAND, AND STANDS. Curious, I get up from the couch. The movie still going, she leads me out of the living room and upstairs. My throat tightens in anticipation and slight worry.

"Denise?" I say when we reach the doorway to my bedroom. "Wait, we should—" She places her index finger to my lips, pulls me inside, and shuts the door.

Removing her finger, she says, "You know."

I blink. "I know? I know what?"

"That I'm a virgin," she says matter-of-factly.

I swallow and nod. "Uh, yeah. But I'm not bothered by that. And you shouldn't be, either. I'm glad you're waiting. Not many girls do that these days." *That's why I love you.*

She wraps her arms around my neck. "Dominick, no guy has done the things you've done for me. Said the sweetest things. Cared so much. Thank you."

I grin, and she kisses me.

My heart thumps, and I return the kiss. *She's delicate. Maybe I shouldn't.* Part of me wants to pull away, but I can't. I can't hold back how much I care about her.

How much I love her.

I wrap my arms around her waist and rest my forehead against hers. "Denise."

She looks up at me with those enticing ebony eyes. Our gazes fix on each other for a moment, then she meets her lips to mine, this time, deeper, more passionate than before. My mental dam breaks. I kiss those beautiful lips, tasting every drop of her sweet, addicting taste. My hands caress her waist and up her back. Kissing along her jawline and down her neck, I taste her sweet, flawless skin. She breathes short, ragged breaths, but her body is relaxed. I slide my hands down her back again and stop just shy of her tailbone. What I wouldn't give to grope her ass right now. Would she mind?

Then she buries her hands beneath my shirt, her slightly cool touch caressing the skin of my abs. Oh God, she has such wonderful hands. Every spot she touches is electrified. *No, I have to stop or else*— I take a deep breath and reluctantly pull away. She looks at me, confused and flustered.

"Denise." My voice is husky from the moment. "Th-think about what you want." I swallow, savoring the remnants of her taste on my tongue. "Think about it before—"

She places her index finger to my lips again. "It's been you all along, Dominick. I see it now." She removes her finger, and, before I can respond, her lips are on mine.

Her hands are on my abs again, and my hands are on her tailbone, then slide lower to her ass. A small moan escapes me as I grope her cheeks. So soft. So round. So amazing. I pull her against me, my manhood rock-hard in my pants.

I exhale and look into her eyes. "Denise, it's getting hotter and, well, I don't want you to do something you might regret."

She looks back at me, her expression mirroring that of a drunk's, only she's drunk on pleasure. "My only regret is that we didn't meet sooner. I want you, Dominick Anderson."

Shit. She's serious.

I'm speechless.

She wants me. She wants me!

And yet, there is still one question that lingers in my mind.

I pepper her lips with gentle kisses. "Do you love me?"

Smiling, she stops me and places her hands on either side of my face. "I love you."

There is no hesitation in her eyes, her voice, when she says this, so I say, "I love you, too."

We kiss, sealing that confirmation. Sealing our love.

I sweep my hands around to her hips, hiking her oversized shirt up slightly. She shivers as I run my thumbs along the tops of her thighs. She grips my T-shirt collar and tugs. I pull back slightly and shrug out of the shirt.

I look to her with need, my eyelids heavy. She leans in and feathers my torso with her soft lips, kissing over my pecs and down my sternum. I watch her, feeling like I'm half-drunk myself. Running her tongue over my abs, she moves her hands skillfully over my chest.

Sweet Jesus.

"Are you sure you're a virgin?" I ask between breaths.

She pauses, looks at me, and smirks. "Why? You think virgins suck at foreplay?"

"Hell no. Then again, you're the first virgin I've been with."

She chuckles and resumes licking my chest, trailing that wonderful tongue across my pecs. Her lips pepper new spots on my skin—new *sensitive* spots—and the strain in my groin becomes unbearable.

I pull her shirt up off her, and we break the kiss. I pull back and admire her body—her beautiful, perfect body. She's lean and built like a dancer all over. I run my hands down her shoulders and arms, relishing the feel of her soft, flawless skin. I move to her chest and cup her small, perky tits. She moans as I use my thumbs to rub her nipples, which harden at my touch. My lips ravaging her goose-bumped skin, I slide down to her midsection. My fingers graze along the contour of her waist, down to her hips. I lick and kiss her navel, and she whimpers.

"Dominick . . . "

The way she utters my name makes me feel like my dick's about to burst out of my jeans. *I want her. I need her. Now.* I lift her into my arms and settle her onto the bed, laying her back onto the pillows and disheveled bedding. Crawling on top of her, I kiss every inch of her passionately. When I reach her lips, she moans. Positioning myself between her legs, I indulge in her flawless, caramel-toned body, starting with her neck and running down to her chest. I gently massage one of her tits with my hand, going in small circles. She whimpers and moans, and her whole body shudders. Her nipple is harder than a pebble beneath my palm. I draw my kisses to her other soft, beautiful mound, and flick her nipple with my tongue. Then I take it into my mouth and suckle until she moans again. She runs her fingers along my scalp, her tiny nails scratching it. Releasing her breast from my mouth, I continue my tour of her body. I get a good look at her abs, and realize just how tight and defined they are, like she's been on some sort of workout regimen. I've never seen a girl this fit.

"God, Denise," I whisper, my breath hitting the contours of her musculature. "You are so fucking hot, I can't stand it."

She mutters something in response that I can't understand, and I'm too aroused to try and make sense of it.

I kiss every inch of her tight muscles, taste every bit of salt from the small beads of sweat that form a sheen over her skin. My tongue slides lower, between her legs, and she squirms and takes hurried breaths.

I kiss her inner thighs while I draw one hand down between her legs. The smell of her sex is driving me insane. My fingers graze her warm center, massaging it, the touch of her wetness utterly amazing.

Her body tenses, and she sucks in her breath. I kiss down the length of her long, beautiful legs.

"Oh God! D-Dom, please . . . " she says through an exhaled breath.

I lift my lips from her skin only briefly to shift to the edge of the bed and reach under it for the box. With two fingers, I pull out a foil packet. Palming it for now, I lay on top of her and shower her lips with kisses. I want her badly, but I want to make absolutely certain this is what she wants, too.

I plant one last kiss and pull back. "Look at me, Denise."

Her eyelids flutter open, and she gazes at me with aroused, ebony eyes.

"Do you trust me? Do you . . . truly love me?"

Beaming, she replies breathily, "Yes, Dominick. I trust you. I . . . I truly love you."

I sit up and undo my jeans and wiggle out of them and my boxers. Relief spreads through me when my hard, pulsing erection is freed from its tight confines. Her eyes widen in awe at the sight.

Smiling at her reaction, I tear open the foil packet and sheathe myself. Returning to my position atop her, I rest the lower half of my body between her legs. "I'll go slow. I promise." My lips returning to hers, I run my hand down the side of her thigh, lifting her leg slightly as I slide inside her in a careful, gentle push. I let out a long, slow groan against her mouth. She's so damn tight. She breaks the kiss and cries out, and I refrain from pushing further. I kiss the side of her neck reassuringly.

"I know," I whisper. Even though she's scared and in pain, she trusts me. She *loves* me. And I love her. Maybe one day I'll marry her. I'll be a better man to my wife than my father could have ever been to his and his children.

Denise digs her fingernails in my back, and I push further, little by little. Her tightness clenches around my pulsating length, causing me to breathe a little harder. If this is what a virgin truly feels like, then my God, nothing can ever compare to this perfect moment.

Slowly, gently, I grind my hips against her, and our bodies rock in a steady rhythm. Louder, she moans, and her hips press against mine, meeting force for force. I bury my face in her chest as I go a little faster. Harder. Our bodies are sweaty and slick. She reaches down and grabs my ass, her nails digging into my cheeks. *Fuck, those nails.* It drives me closer to release. The pain makes me plunge deeper into her tight depth.

She lets out a painful cry, but one that's also tinged with pleasure. I kiss her mouth, and she wraps her arms around my back, pulling me into her. Faster, we move, with hurried breaths and loud cries. Then, her body twitches, and I feel her heat rush over my dick. To feel her reach that point of pleasure—that point of absolute bliss—makes me shudder and let out a low groan. We ride out our orgasms until we finally collapse from sheer exhaustion.

CHAPTER 23

I OPEN MY EYES TO MUTED SUNLIGHT THAT FILLS THE ROOM.

Is it morning already? Did I really sleep away that wonderful night?

I look at the beautiful girl sleeping peacefully in my arms, a hint of a smile upon her lips.

My girl.

I kiss her forehead, and her eyelids flutter slightly, but she doesn't awaken. I watch her as I mull over last night. The night she became mine. The thoughts make me kiss her more, run my fingers across her shoulder and down her arm. I caress her cheek, her face, run my thumb over her lips. I can't stop touching her. I love her so much that it hurts. I close my eyes for a moment, only to open them again when my bliss is interrupted by the urge to piss.

Damn it.

Carefully peeling myself away, I gently wriggle my arm from around her, replacing the spot where my arm touched her skin with more of the blanket, and my head with another pillow. Finally free, I slip on my boxers and hustle to the half-bath. Finished with my business, I open the bathroom door to find Chris standing there in his Magic Touch Auto Detail polo work shirt and jeans.

Fuck! It's Monday?

"Dom? You still here?" Chris asks, eyeing me curiously.

I widen my eyes. It *is* Monday. "Holy shit! It's finals week. What time is it?"

"Uhh . . . 9:20?"

I slap my forehead. "Shit! Shit! Shit!" I missed my circuits final. I gotta make it up somehow.

Chris furrows his brow. "What the hell's wrong with you?"

I look at him and exhale. He hadn't heard us last night? Maybe he and Adrienne were too busy doing their thing to notice. "Is Adri still here?"

"Nope. Left about an hour ago. Wait, is Denise still here?"

I shift my gaze to anywhere but him. "Yeah, man."

His mouth makes a very refined O.

Not wanting to risk waking Denise, I head for the stairs, motioning him with my head to follow.

"Duuuuude!" Chris exclaims in just above a whisper when we reach the kitchen. "So I *wasn't* hearing things last night!"

I reach for the fridge's door handle, pause, and stare at Chris, horrified. "You heard us?"

Chris nods, smirking. "So did Adri. These walls are thin, after all."

I grimace.

"It's about damn time you finally put those condoms to use again."

"Not a word," I say.

Chris shrugs innocently. "Yeah, yeah. My lips are sealed. But I can't deny what I heard up there, and it sounded pretty damn good."

Grinning slightly, I open the fridge and grab the milk. "Yeah, it was good. Real good."

Chris exits the kitchen. "All right, man, the bus'll be here any minute. See you later."

"Later."

I pour myself a glass while I try to plan out the day. At the rate I'm going, I'll end up missing my physics final. Doesn't Denise have finals, too? I shouldn't miss work, though. We're still short-staffed. I chug my milk and head back upstairs.

Denise is still sleeping, and I don't want to wake her, but I must. Kneeling at her bedside, I gently nudge her arm. She moans and shifts but doesn't wake up. Amused, I resort to kissing her closed eyelids and soft lips again.

"Wake up, sleepyhead," I whisper in her ear.

Her eyelids flutter open. She stares at me sleepily.

"Hey," I say, taking her hand in mine. I bring her hand up to my lips and gently kiss it.

"Hey," she mumbles.

Not taking my eyes off her, I rub my stubbly cheek against her hands. "It's Monday, you know."

Her brow wrinkles slightly, as though it's taking her time to process this, then her eyes widen. "Oh no." She rips her hand away and sits up in bed, wrapping the blanket around her.

"Yeah." I frown when I can no longer touch her. "I missed the two finals I have today so I'm just going to go straight to work."

She bites her bottom lip and fidgets with a loose thread on the blanket. "I'm sorry."

I stare at her. "For what? It's not your fault. I overslept."

"Yeah, but last night, we—"

"—had the most wonderful night ever. And I wouldn't trade it for the world. I love you, Denise."

She smiles, but it's brief. She slides out of bed, letting the blanket and sheets fall away from her naked body, and retrieves the discarded shirt from the floor near the foot of the bed. "I need to get to campus. I told Lauren yesterday that I would catch a ride with you today, and she'll pick me up around twelve thirty after my world literature final."

I nod. Of course, I don't want her to leave, but she has a life, too. Maybe one day when I get my own place, I can convince her to live with me. "Let me hop in the shower."

By eleven o'clock, I'm zipping through the busy streets on my bike with Denise on the back, hugging my midsection so tightly I have to gasp for air. But I don't complain. I'll never complain about anything she does.

I park in the lot near Padelford, and Denise gets off. Remaining mounted on the bike, I slip off the helmet. I don't want my voice to be muffled when I say goodbye to her this time.

"Thanks for the ride," she says.

"No problem. Good luck on your test."

She smiles. "Thanks."

I trace my finger around the chrome trim of the speedometer. "You wanna do something tonight?"

She tilts her head to the side, her gaze fixed somewhere on my bike. "I do, but I promised Lauren we'd have a girls' night out tonight. Maybe tomorrow?"

I nod, frowning. I can't be mad about that. After all, Denise has known Lauren way longer than me.

I glance at the passing students, who pay us no mind. My stomach twists from a strange feeling I have—fear of the rumors about the Xi party that might still be floating around. But then I see Trinity running our way, and I relax. The two of them meet each other halfway in an embrace.

Denise breaks their hug and walks over to me. "Go to work. I'll call you later, okay?"

She leans in and kisses me deeply. But as quick as the kiss comes it's over, and I exhale.

"Get going," she says.

I cast a glance at Trinity, who smiles at us both. I look back at Denise. "I love you," I say, then slip on my helmet.

From now on, that is what I will say to her instead of "good-bye."

"I love you too," she says, and my heart flutters.

I rev the engine and leave campus. But the farther I get from Denise, the more dread I feel rising in the pit of my stomach.

Arriving at Frank's nearly an hour earlier than usual garners me surprised looks from Paul and Nate. Larry, however, continues tinkering under a car that's up on a lift and doesn't so much as acknowledge me. I wave to Nate and Paul, who resume working under the hoods of two cars parked outside, and make my way to the whiteboard. The office side door creaks open, and Frank pokes his head out.

I give Frank a small salute. "'Sup."

"The hell you doing here, kid?" he asks.

"I got out of class early."

He scowls. "Well, don't expect to be getting paid overtime for it."

I shrug, scowling back. "Never expected to be." *Though it'd be nice for a change, asshole.*

Frank slams the office door shut, causing the whiteboard on the wall to shake. Glancing at the tasks, I can immediately recognize Larry's handwriting, but the job he has assigned to me isn't small and simple. I have to do a timing gear and chain replacement. And the truck he has me working on is the very same one *he's* working on. *Wow, that's a first,* I think, heading over to him. We almost never work on the same vehicle together. The truck is tireless in the front, and its radiator has been taken out and set aside. Larry's at the front of the car on the driver's side, repairing the ball joint suspensions.

"So are you gonna just stand there and admire my ass all day or are you gonna get to work?" Larry lowers his hands from inside the chassis and grins. A small towel is draped around the back of his neck.

I laugh. "Yeah, yeah. What the hell's wrong with you, man? This shit's gonna take all night."

"Good." Larry pulls a wrench from his pocket and tosses it to me. "More time to talk."

I catch the wrench with one hand, look at it briefly and then back at him. "Talk? About what?"

"You know," he says in a low tone, his expression hardening.

It takes me a moment to process this, and then I frown. *He must mean that talk we had about Denise weeks ago.* I didn't think he'd given it another thought. He acted so nonchalant about it at the time. Maybe Larry just needed time to process everything about that night. But after all that, I'd neglected to tell him about my own demons.

Larry comes out from under the truck and presses a green button on the wall. The truck slowly lowers to the ground.

"You finished the ball joints already?" I ask, furrowing my brow.

"Nope," he says, rounding the front of the truck.

I follow and peer under the hood. Much of the engine has been stripped away, allowing me to easily spot the timing cover. Only one of the bolts has been removed. "Holy shit, Larry. How long have you been at this?"

"All fucking morning." Larry points to the cover. "The air wrench was too big to get to the bolts, so they'll need to come out manually."

I nod and begin unhinging the first bolt while Larry inspects the camshaft and valves.

"Glad someone around here has hands and arms small enough to get to some of those hard-to-reach places." Larry's eyes cut to mine, and he lowers his voice. "How are you two doing?"

I pause and look up at him. The concern in his voice makes me smile a little. The man actually cares. "Denise is doing much better. She talks to a counselor twice a week, and I think it's helping. As for me, well . . . I'm just taking it one day at a time, making sure she's safe and all that."

"It's all you can do."

I swallow a lump in my throat. "I still worry about Denise, though. I still get scared about leaving her alone. Like, she might need me again and this time I might not be around."

"You can't be with her all the time. It's not healthy to smother her like that. She's not a kid."

"I know, man, but it's hard." I sigh. "I love her."

A hint of a smile brushes over his lips, and he refocuses on one of the valves. "Ah, young love," he mumbles, reaching for a can of lubricant. He sprays a small amount around the valve stem. "Just be there for her when you can."

"I try, but I feel like I can do more." I remove another bolt from the cover and set it in a growing pile with several others. These things are as tough as shit to unhinge, as they've probably never been removed from this decades-old truck.

"I've said all I can say on the matter, Dominick, but if you really insist on always keeping her around, well . . . I guess you could bring her to work."

My hand slips from the wrench. "Wait, can I do that?"

He shrugs. "Why couldn't you?"

"No. I won't do that. I don't want the guys harassing her and making her uncomfortable."

Larry grunts. "If anyone here does that shit, you let me know, and I'll kick their asses."

"What about Frank?"

"What *about* Frank? I'll kick his ass, too, and not look back if he fires me afterward."

I gawk at him. "You'd risk your job?"

"I won't work for any asshole who mistreats women," he says flatly.

My smile returns. Larry's one of the few people in my life who can make me genuinely smile. "Hey, Larry, why don't you join me tonight for some drinks at Chauncey's?" I ask, removing the last remaining bolts.

Larry whips the towel from around his neck and slings it over his shoulder. "Sorry, kid. I gotta work. These cars won't fix themselves."

"Take a break, man."

"Can't afford to take a break. Not when there's so much to do—especially now that William's gone."

I meet his eyes briefly, then shift my attention back to the timing chain cover, which I remove and set aside. "You're a workaholic, Larry, but you're also human. Even *you* need a break sometime. Just take one night off. That's all I ask. If Frank gives you any flack, well, then blame me."

"I'm the senior employee. If I slack off, we'll have an even longer backlog of work to do—more than what just the four of us can deal with."

"But it's only a few hours tonight. That's all. Not like you're taking the whole day off. What're a few hours going to hurt?"

He sighs and grumbles under his breath. "I'll think about it. Now finish changing that damn chain."

I remove the filthy, damaged chain from the gears and set it aside. Larry hands me a new chain, and I meticulously line it up in the gears. My dirt-smeared hands start to sweat from focusing so hard.

It feels like it's taken hours when I finally finish aligning the chain properly, matching up the timing notches. I lift up from the hood and sigh, my fingers cramped and hurting from handling the small parts.

Larry tosses me the towel. I take it and wipe my hands. The more I notice the way he looks out for me, the more I think he knows when something's up. *I should tell him.* He has a right to know, putting up with me for this long. Being concerned about me when he doesn't need to be. I'll tell him, but not here.

"Hey, Larry, it would really mean a lot to me if you joined me for a drink. It would just be my way of saying thanks for always having my back. You've been a good friend." *And I wish you could've been my father instead.*

Larry turns back to the hood, staring idly at the stripped engine. "Nothing special about me, kid."

"Whatever, man. Sometimes I wish you were my father." I freeze. *Oh shit. Did I just say that aloud?*

With an eyebrow arched, he stares. "What?"

I purse my lips. Damn it. He knows. I guess I have no choice now. But not here. "Nothing, man. I'm sorry. That was way outta line."

"No shit. You have a father."

That statement hurts. If only he knew. "Trust me, Larry. You are a much better father than that sick son of a bitch could ever have been." I clench my jaw. I don't want to talk about it here.

Larry sighs. "Look, I'm gonna finish those ball joints. Thanks for the help here. Now go give Nate and Paul a hand outside, eh?" He thumbs over his shoulder.

Pursing my lips, I step back from the truck and watch as Larry pushes the button on the wall again and lifts the truck high off the ground. He remains silent, and I head out the open bay door.

"I'll see you tonight," Larry says.

CHAPTER 24

GOD MUST REALLY BE IN A GOOD MOOD, BECAUSE TODAY just keeps getting better. I can't believe I'm actually going to manage to drag Larry to Chauncey's for the first time in . . . well, since I first started working at the shop.

Refreshed after a long shower, I step out the bathroom, steam billowing out into the hall. Chris went over to Adrienne's tonight, so I have the place to myself. With a towel wrapped around my waist, I head upstairs. My phone is on the bed, the green notification light blinking.

It's a missed call—from Denise.

Shit! I redial her number, hoping and praying that she answers.

"Hello?"

I plop down on the bed, consumed by her beautiful voice. "Hey. Sorry I missed your call before. I was in the shower."

"It's okay. You're not in trouble. *This* time."

I suppress a grin. "Oh yeah? Well I don't mind being in trouble with you."

She chuckles. "You're crazy."

"So whatcha doing tonight?"

"Lauren and I are just leaving the movies. I think we're going to get some food next."

"That's good. I hope you're having fun."

"I am." She pauses. "I gotta go now. Lauren says hi."

I raise my eyebrows. "Really?"

She laughs. "Yeah. She doesn't think you're such a deadbeat anymore."

I laugh at that.

"I'll see you tomorrow, okay? Bye, Dominick. I love you."

Those three words uttered from her lips send a wave of happiness all the way to my groin. "I love you too, Denise." I leave it at that.

She hangs up first, and I sigh, missing her already.

My phone rings again and Larry's number appears on the screen. *Larry?* I have to do a double take. He almost never calls me. *He better not be canceling tonight.* I answer it with a frown. "'Sup, Larry?"

"Hey. You still home?" Larry asks, his voice gruff. He sounds like he's driving.

"Yeah. 'Bout to head out in a few."

"Give me about . . . " Larry's quiet for a moment, then says, "five minutes." *Click.*

I stare at the screen. *The hell?* I hold it back to my ear. "Hello? Larry?"

Silence.

Is he coming over? Larry has only come over once, and that was last year to give me my wallet that I'd left at work that day. I quickly dress in a black and yellow hoodie over a gray T-shirt, a pair of faded, loose-fitting jeans, and black sports shoes. I race down the stairs to the living room and peek out the blinds. The streets are dark and empty.

Maybe I just misunderstood what he said. He can be weird like that sometimes. I grab my keys and helmet from the kitchen and head out the back door. As I'm walking my bike out from around the side of the duplex, I hear the low rumble of a truck approaching. A pair of headlights shine in the street. I swallow. *Larry?* I hustle to the front and see Larry's blue and white pickup truck parked at the curb. I stand there in the walkway, open-mouthed, my helmet in one hand, my keys in the other.

Holy shit.

The passenger-side window lowers, and Larry peers at me. "Didn't I tell you to give me five minutes?" he calls.

I smile. "Sorry, guess I misunderstood."

"Whatever, boy. Get your ass in this truck."

I gesture for him to hold on and put my bike and helmet away. Afterward, I hustle to the truck and hop in. Larry's dressed pretty sharp, like he's ready to have some fun at a club. I almost don't recognize him. I've never seen him dressed in anything other than jeans and his blue work shirt that's always smeared with oil and dirt by the end of the day.

"Damn, well, this is a surprise," I say, buckling up.

"What can I say, I'm full of surprises." He sounds so serious when he says that, it makes me laugh.

As usual for this time on a Monday night, the streets aren't very busy, and we make it to the interstate in mere minutes.

"Thanks again for doing this with me, man," I say. "It really means a lot."

"Eh."

I chuckle. "You'll thank me that you took some time off for yourself for a change."

"I already take enough time off for myself to eat, sleep, and shit. I'm considering this as doing a favor for a friend."

"And *I'm* considering this a sign of the fucking apocalypse. I actually managed to get your ass out of the shop."

He looks over at me, amusement in his eyes, says nothing, and returns his attention to the road.

We pull up to Chauncey's, which is crowded as usual, no matter what day it is. We head inside and find two seats at the bar. Ironically, these are the same seats that Kevin and I sat in last time. A guy is working the bar tonight instead of Olivia. He looks new. A group of guys are playing darts nearby, and a mixed crowd is gathered at the foosball table in the back.

"I'm buyin'," I say, reaching in my back pocket for my wallet.

Larry puts his hand on my shoulder, and I freeze. "No. *I'm* buyin'."

I blink. "C'mon, man. You drove. I'll buy."

He gives me one of those hard stares. The kind a parent gives a kid when they're acting up. The kind that says, "if you argue with me, I'll knock the shit out of you." And coming from Larry, I've no doubt he'd smash me open with one of those steel fists of his. Swallowing, I hold my hands up in surrender. "Okay, okay, you're buyin'."

He orders some beer on tap. I get my usual.

"I didn't *just* come here to do a favor for a friend, you know," Larry says, tipping back his drink.

I stop in mid-swig and look over the glass at him.

"Thought it might be a good time to talk," he says. "Get whatever's on your mind out."

I lower the glass and stare at the bobbing ice cubes inside. "She's the only thing on my mind right now," I say, just loud enough for him to hear. "Nothing else matters."

"Why didn't you do something with her tonight, then?"

"She had some stuff to do with her friend."

"So you're stuck with me, eh?" He looks amused and takes another gulp.

"I do worry about her. All the time. I know what it's like to—" I bite off my words. "Sorry. I shouldn't be rambling about that."

"Rambling about what? Out with it, kid."

I purse my lips. I never really told Larry about my past, and I'm not sure why. I can trust him, like Kevin. I down the rest of my drink.

"Well?" He gives me that look again, and it makes me cringe. I bet he was a great parent, keeping his kids in line with that look alone.

I rub the back of my neck. "It's not easy to say."

He finishes his beer and then shifts on his stool, one elbow resting on the counter. He looks at me and lowers his voice. "I'm listening."

I pause as I try to find the right words. "What almost happened to Denise"—I close my eyes—"actually happened to me.

Even over all the noise in the bar, I can hear him hiss. My skin tingles with goose bumps from his tension. I open my eyes and stare at him. Sadly. The way he looks back at me is genuine concern. Pity. Guilt.

Leaning his head closer to mine, he mutters, "You were raped?"

I look back at the melting ice in my drink and give him the slightest of nods. "By my father."

He leans back on his stool and sighs then turns back to the bar and orders another beer. He seems to be thinking hard on something. Perhaps wondering how to respond to something like that. But no response is required. It is what it is. Clenching my jaw, I signal to the bartender for a refill, as well. A mug and a glass slide our way, and I don't hesitate to bring my drink to my lips.

"Sorry to hear that, kid," he says. "I really am."

My eyes burn, and I know it's not from the rum. "I'm dealing with it," I say, holding back my tears. "The memory's still there, of course."

"It'll always be there, unfortunately." His grip tightens around the mug's handle, and his knuckles whiten. "Where's your father now?"

The way he asks that, I think he's going to hunt him down and kill him. I wish he had. I wish he could. "He's dead. Committed suicide before the cops could arrest him, the coward." I try to laugh it off. "God, I have such a fucked up life." I gulp down the rum-infused Coke, and chew on an ice cube afterward.

"No," Larry says, placing his hand on my shoulder. His touch—his voice—soothes my emotions. Kind of like what hearing Denise's voice did to me that night at the party. "You have a better life without him around. If there's one thing I believe in, that's destiny. Things happen for a reason, even the darkest things. Maybe experiencing that dark point in your life was needed for you to save another's—like Denise."

What? I narrow my eyes and shrug off his hand. "Are you shitting me, Larry? You're saying that I *should* have gotten raped?" I say that a little louder than I should, but luckily no one around us seems to be paying attention to our conversation.

Larry shakes his head. "No! Of course not. No one deserves that."

I sigh and lower my head.

Larry orders his third beer. "You know the saying 'love conquers all'?"

"What about it?"

"That was my motto when I used to box. Still is. Everyone fights for what they believe in. Everyone fights for what they love the most, no matter how bad it gets. You're in a dark tunnel right now, Dominick. Been stuck in that dark tunnel for a while. But you can't give up what you believe in, what you love. Because what you love the most will be waiting for you at the end of that tunnel."

Speechless, I lean my elbows on the countertop and rub my hands over my face. I think I'm having déjà vu here. *That's pretty much what Uncle Adam told me.* The rum burns my stomach. I'm already feeling a buzz after three drinks. God, I'm such a lightweight compared to Kevin.

"You okay?" Larry asks.

I rub my eyes, nodding. "Yeah, man. I'm good. Just thinking."

Larry nurses his beer. "If I could've adopted you as my son after that shit happened, I totally would have."

I blink, my buzz suddenly going away. *Is he for real?* I would have taken him in a heartbeat if only to get back some sliver of the childhood that had been ripped from me. "That's deep, man," I finally say, running my finger around the brim of my ice-filled glass. "You've always been like a father to me, since I met you."

Larry pauses in mid-gulp and looks sidelong at me.

"Besides Kevin, and maybe my uncle, you're the only man I've ever looked up to."

A hint of a smile appears on his lips. "Jesus Christ, Dominick. Does it matter whether or not you call me 'Dad'? I'm still the same person either way."

"Yeah, I guess you're right. Man, your kids are lucky to have someone like you."

He guffaws. "What kids?"

I blink. "Oh, sorry. I just assumed you had kids."

He finishes his beer, then sets the empty mug on the counter. "Nope. And no family, either, though I was once told I had an aunt somewhere in Philadelphia."

"No family? You mean you've lived alone your whole life?"

"I was left abandoned outside a hospital not long after I was born. Went through the system and all that. I was glad when I was finally old enough to get out on my own."

Who the fuck wouldn't have wanted to adopt someone like Larry? I bet he was probably the best kid a family could ever ask for. Why do good people always have to be shitted on? "I'm sorry that happened to you."

Larry scowls. "Those agencies were a joke. Felt like a puppy in a pet shop. I hated it. Anyway." He looks at me. "You're not alone, Dominick. You ever need anything, I got your back."

And just like that, my anger ebbs. Larry's such a good man. He needs more friends. Maybe even a girlfriend or wife. A family. All these years, he's been alone. Fixing cars or doing whatever he does. Hopefully, he at least knows how much I appreciate him.

Larry slaps down some money on the counter and stands. "It's getting late. And as much as I'd like to stay here and drink some more, I have work to do back at the shop."

Sighing, I stand as well. I guess good things don't last forever. "All right. Well, I'm glad you came here with me."

"No problem." He reaches in his back pocket for his keys. Then his body suddenly goes still. He stands there, hand stuffed in his back pocket, staring toward the entrance.

His surprised expression confuses me, so I nudge him in the arm. "You okay? Need me to drive tonight?"

"Fuck no," he says in a long, drawn-out whisper.

I scrunch my face and follow his gaze. I freeze as well.

It's Lauren.

And Denise.

CHAPTER 25

THE TWO WOMEN MAKE THEIR WAY TO A VACANT TABLE. My jaw drops at the sight of Denise. She looks like she just stepped out of a fashion magazine. Her hair's done up in a new cornrowed design in the front and falls away in a thick, curly, twist-out ponytail in the back, secured with a yellow ribbon. She wears a black-and-white-striped tank top under a yellow short jacket and denim capri pants. Her open-toed platform shoes reveal yellow painted toenails.

Lauren's dressed just as stylishly in a red halter top and black, loose-fitting pants, making her look twenty years younger. Around her neck hangs a ruby red gem. Both arms are decorated in an array of wristlets and bangles. The makeup on her face is done just right, and her dreadlocks are tied back in a ponytail.

I exhale, taking them both in. *Holy shit. Is this girls' night out, or are they trying to snag dates?* I cringe at the thought.

I go to nudge Larry, but he's not there. He's headed to their table. I chase after him.

Lauren whispers something to Denise and then rises from her chair, but Larry closes in on her. I swoop in behind him to Denise. The two women look at us with a start.

"Dominick?" Denise says, eyes wide. "What are you doing here?"

I plant a kiss on her cheek. Unlike Lauren, she's wearing no makeup other than that peach lip gloss, just the way I like it. "I should be asking *you* that. I thought you two were getting food?"

Denise shows off that contagious smile of hers. "We did, and then Lauren wanted to get a drink afterward." She looks to her roommate, and I follow her gaze. Lauren and Larry practically ogle each other.

I smirk. "Hey, Larry, don't you have some work to do at the shop?

Larry cuts his eyes to me. "I think I have a little time to spare."

"Shop?" Lauren asks, penciled eyebrows raised.

"He's a mechanic, too. But don't worry, he doesn't have a motorcycle," I say.

Denise laughs, and so does Lauren.

Larry coughs, clearly uncomfortable with having all the attention on him. "Can I get you a drink?" he asks Lauren.

Lauren's smile broadens, and she nods. "Sure, thanks. Margarita on the rocks."

Larry nods and looks over to Denise. "How about you?"

"Long Island iced tea, please."

"Wait, Larry, I can get Denise's—" I fall silent when he gives me one of those looks, and I hold my hands up in surrender. "Never mind."

His face softens, and he leaves.

I pull up a chair beside Denise and sit. "So what are you two all dressed up for tonight?"

"It's girls' night out," Lauren says. "We went out shopping at the mall all afternoon and got one of those free makeovers."

"Oh, I see. So you two aren't looking all hot and sexy tonight to pick up guys." I grin.

Denise playfully punches me in the arm. "And what if we are? Are you jealous?"

"Nope. 'Cause I'll fuck up the idiot who dares to try and touch you."

Denise rolls her eyes. "Don't worry. You're the only guy for me, and that's that." She plants a kiss on my lips, and I melt.

Lauren clears her throat, and we break the kiss. "So who's your friend, Dominick?"

"That's Larry, a coworker. He's cool."

"And damn fine," Lauren mumbles, eyeing him from afar.

I try not to smile. "Also single, as far as I know." *God, am I playing matchmaker again?*

Denise giggles. "And here I thought you swore you'd never get involved in another relationship, Lauren."

"Yeah, well. I think I might have to give that one a try. You did say he was single, Dominick?"

I nod. "Yep."

"Hmph. A fine piece of ass like him's probably got kids though. They all got kids."

Denise arches an eyebrow. "What's wrong with that? You don't like kids?"

"It's not that, D. I just want to deal with a man first before I start involving myself with his kids."

I rub my chin. "Well, actually, Larry doesn't have any kids."

Lauren's eyes widen. "You shittin' me? A man his age? No kids? He's a diamond in the rough!"

Larry returns with the drinks and sits beside Lauren. His eyes scan her up and down, and he grins. "I suddenly realized I didn't catch your name."

Lauren traces a finger along her smiling lips. "Lauren."

My gaze bounces between them, and then I lean over to Denise and whisper, "Wanna hang out back?"

Denise nods, as if she had the same idea. She stands and takes her drink. "Hey, Lauren. Call me when you're ready to go, okay?"

"Yeah, okay," Lauren says absently, not taking her eyes off Larry.

"Larry?" I say, but he doesn't acknowledge me. "Don't leave without me, please."

"Uh-huh," Larry says.

The back door leads outside into a fenced-in area with more places to sit. It's lit up by white lights and hanging lanterns strung through the trees and across the top of the wooden fence. The sky is clear, revealing the bright stars and quarter-moon. Among the few people that linger out here, there are plenty of places to sit. I zero in on a small table for two and pull out a chair for Denise.

Not wanting to sit across from her, I slide my chair around next to hers. I wrap my arm around her and pull her close. She rests her head on my shoulder. I inhale her scent and my mind goes wild.

"That was unexpected," she says, breaking the silence.

"What? Larry and Lauren?" I ask.

"Yeah, I mean, Lauren went through a really bad divorce last year. She swore she was done. Whenever she puts her mind to something, she always follows through."

"She seems to like him." I stare at her Long Island iced tea, and now I'm craving another drink, too. "If it's not too personal, what happened?"

She sips her drink. "Don't say anything about it, okay?"

"My lips are sealed."

"Her husband of seven years ended up cheating on her. She came home one night and caught him and another woman in their bed. The guy had no shame whatsoever. Apparently, he'd been secretly seeing that woman for over a year and Lauren didn't know. After that, Lauren washed her hands of it and swore she was never going to get into another relationship again."

I frown. "I'm sorry to hear that. A shame that she wouldn't give it another chance because of one bad one. It sounds like she just doesn't trust guys."

"Can you blame her?"

"I'll tell you this: I've known Larry a long time, and I know he'd never try to hurt her. He hates guys who mistreat women."

Denise nods. "I know Lauren still hurts, even though she tries to hide it from me. It's hard getting over a bad relationship."

"It really is." I stroke the side of her cheek with my finger. "How are you doing?"

Her smile slowly returns, as she seems to be enjoying my gentle caress. "I'm okay. I can't believe it's almost been a month."

"Yeah," I say, almost in a whisper. "But each day, you heal." I lift her head from my shoulder and turn her chin so she looks at me. I can never get enough of her ebony eyes. "Can you stay with me tonight?"

She leans in and kisses me on the lips. "Okay, but I can't afford to miss tomorrow morning's final."

"Don't worry, neither can I."

She finishes the rest of her drink. "Guess what I bought at the mall today?"

"What?"

"A new motorcycle jacket. Red." She smirks.

I widen my eyes. "No shit?"

She nods, and the thought of her in her own motorcycle jacket gives me a hard-on. I can't believe she's really serious about this riding business. "Now I don't have to borrow yours all the time. It's in the car. I'll show you later."

Fuck, I wanna see it *now*. "We should probably go check on those two."

She chuckles. "Yeah, I guess. Though I'd hate to break them up. I haven't seen Lauren this happy in a long time."

"Yeah, same with Larry." I get up.

Back inside, we discover Lauren and Larry are gone.

"Shit! Larry left me? I can't believe this!" I say through clenched teeth.

Denise looks worried. "I hope Lauren didn't take off, either." She takes my hand and leads me to the front door. "C'mon."

We hurry outside and look up and down the street for Larry's truck or Denise's car. I exhale when I spot the familiar mounted rooftop lights on a blue and white truck parked along the curb, three cars down. "There." I point.

As we draw nearer to the truck, I can't tell if anyone is inside or not. Rounding the passenger side, I fling open the door.

Lauren and Larry freeze in the middle of a make-out session. Like two damn high schoolers. Lauren quickly smoothes out her wrinkled top and looks daggers at me. "You're shittin' me now, right?"

Larry's eyes pierce through me, and I have to take a step back. Holy shit. This is insane. "Uh, sorry, Larry," I say. "I thought you left without me. How long are you—"

"Boy, close that fucking door!" Larry growls.

Lauren gives Denise a brief smile. "I'll call you later, dear. Have fun." She grabs the door handle and pulls the door shut. I hear the locks activate.

Denise and I exchange glances. Well fuck me.

Denise covers her mouth and snickers. Her laughter is contagious, and I take her hand and lead her away from Larry's truck before they hear us.

"Oh. My. God." She wipes tears from her eyes, her body still spasming with laughter. "It's so adorable, it's funny."

I shake my head, still smiling. "I'll probably get an earful at work tomorrow."

As we're walking to Denise's car, a blue car creeps slowly along past us. It looks like it's had some custom work done on it, but the windows are tinted far too dark for me to see the driver. Squeezing Denise's hand, I keep my eye on the car. It stops at a light on the corner, sits there several seconds after the light turns green, then speeds up and disappears further down the street.

I get this strange feeling that I've seen that car somewhere before.

Taking Denise's car, we drive by her place so she can pack some clothes for the night. It's eleven o'clock by the time we get to my place. I don't hesitate getting her inside and up-stairs. I just want to relax with her in my arms. Lying in bed in just my boxers, I scroll through the emails on my phone while I wait for Denise to come out the bathroom. I don't understand why girls have to take such long-ass showers.

I hear the tromping of footsteps coming up the stairs, and Denise enters my room, wearing a cute purple-and-black-plaid tank top and matching short-shorts. She carries a bundle of discarded clothing in her arms and sets it in her duffel bag.

Tossing my phone aside, I sit up in bed, gawking at her. Those short-shorts barely cover the bottom of her ass and show off every bit of her beautiful legs. My hard-on tents my boxers. "Fuck, you did that on purpose," I say breathily.

She wanders over to the bed and sits on the edge near me. "Did what?" she asks, a hint of a smirk on her lips.

Oh, she knows. She fucking knows. That little tease.

"Wear *that*." I gesture to her choice of sleepwear.

She chuckles. "It's what I always wear to bed."

I moan. "You know, you still never showed me that new jacket you got." I reach out to touch the sides of her bare arms, but she gets up.

"Okay." She returns to her duffel bag and pulls out a red and black jacket. She puts it on over that sexy sleepwear and zips it up. The words "Ride for Speed" are embroidered in large red script across the front.

Ho-ly shit.

"So what do you think?" she asks, turning around and modeling it.

I think I'm going to have a serious orgasm right here, right now. My dick is so stiff. I'm practically numb. "Stay. Right. There," I say with short, ragged breaths. I scramble off the bed and lumber to her despite my painful hard-on. I put my arms around her waist and pull her to me.

She squeals. "I take it you like it."

"You have no idea," I say in almost a whisper, my lips close to hers. "*No* idea."

She laughs and braces herself, trying not to fall backward.

Oh, I want her so bad right now. *So* bad.

Our lips lock. Hard. That intensity, that need—we both know we want it. At this point, I want her out of that jacket. Out of that sexy sleepwear. Moaning against her lips, I unzip her jacket and push it back from her shoulders until it slides off her arms and onto the floor at her feet. My lips not leaving hers, I walk backward toward the bed, pulling her with me.

I brush my lips across the side of her neck, down to her collarbone. I run my hands under her tank top, massaging her tits with both hands, her hardened nipples vised between my fingers, which entices a small moan from her. Straddled over my lap, she shifts and squirms her ass atop my erection, and I moan as my dick throbs from her weight. My hands run down her abs and trace along the elastic waistband of her shorts. She exhales deeply, and I slip my hand down her shorts. She's so hot down there, so wet. I know she wants me. My fingers wander down toward her center, and she gasps. I kiss her jawline as I rub her—tease her—with two fingers. Her whole body shakes, and she cries out.

"Please . . . "

Enough of this damn foreplay. Whipping my hand out of her shorts, I gently push her off me and onto the bed. I strip off the boxers, and while she pulls off her shorts, I seize a condom from under the bed and sheathe my erection. I turn off the bedside lamp, lie back in bed and pull her on top.

"Take that off, too," I say, tugging the tank top once my eyes get adjusted to the darkness.

I hear the sounds of clothing rubbing against skin and see her silhouette moving against the dim light from the window. Her warmth hovers over me, and I wrap my arms around her, pulling her close. Our lips touch. Her skin is so soft, so hot—just like the rest of her. My hands rub down to her ass while I draw my kisses from her lips down to her neck.

I grind my hips against hers, and she does the same, shifting her lower half, inch by inch over my dick. I make contact with her tightness, and a low groan escapes me. Kissing down her chest, I thrust inside, grasping her ass cheeks and pushing her against me, forcing my dick to drive deeper. She cries out, almost screams a mix of pain and pleasure. Sucking on her tits, I feel my dick get clamped. Hard. Moaning, I thrust into her in a steady rhythm. My tongue flicking over rock-hard nipples, I'm in absolute bliss. Her body melts into mine. With each thrust, we meet somewhere in the middle, force for force. The bed squeaks and shakes the faster we move. Between each breathy moan and cry, we try to kiss, but damn, it's hard. I want to give her everything I have. Everything she deserves. Her ass bounces up and down against my hands, and I'm practically done for.

"God, I love you so much, Denise," I manage to say before my body suddenly spasms and I'm seeing sparks.

"Dom—I . . . ahh!" Screaming, she trembles, her warmth spreading over me.

I kiss her lips tenderly, slowly rolling my hips against hers to ease the afterglow.

As our bodies collapse, my eyes grow heavy with sleep. But before I give in to sleep, I wrap her in my arms and kiss the crown of her head.

CHAPTER 26

DENISE'S PHONE RINGS IN THE MIDDLE OF THE NIGHT, AND she shifts in my arms. I slowly let her free, though I'm still half asleep. *Probably Lauren,* I figure, rolling over on my side. I reach down and activate my phone, glimpsing the time that lights up on the screen. Four fucking thirty. Groaning, I roll back onto my back and drift off to sleep again.

I awaken again, this time to my phone alarm music. I shut it off and sit up in bed. The sun hasn't risen yet, and, as I yawn and stretch, I realize something's not right. I pat the sheets next to me.

No Denise.

No way is she still talking on the phone after two hours. Springing out of bed, I flick on the light and see that Denise's duffel bag is gone.

Did she really leave?

Concern stings my throat. *Why did she leave so early? Did she go back home? Did she not want to stay with me any more?* As the questions bombard my mind, I try to recall the last thing that happened. But I'm still fuzzy with sleep. She had a phone call, but that was it. I assume it was from Lauren, or maybe Trinity or one of her other friends. I mean, who else would be calling her that early in the morning? Running my hands over my hair, I head out of the room and downstairs.

"Denise?" I call, but there's no answer. "Denise!"

Chris's door is wide open, and when I flick on his room light, I discover it empty. He must still be at Adrienne's.

I peek out the living room window. Denise's car is gone, and I frown.

She really is gone. What the hell happened? I rush back to my room and check my phone. She'd left a text two hours ago.

Needed to go home & see Lauren. Call u later. gl on finals. <3

I exhale, a little relieved, but still curious about what happened. I text her back.

is everything ok? i was worried. gl on finals, too. Love you.

I wait for her to respond as I get ready for class, but she doesn't, and the tightness in my throat never leaves.

Even though Denise's text sounded like she was okay, I can't help but worry about her, and it affects my concentration on my systems analysis final. I'm scheduled to retake my circuits final later this morning. It's been a rough few days cramming, and I'll be glad when the semester's finally over.

By afternoon, I'm on my way to work. I don't feel like talking to anyone but Denise today. Not even Larry.

Arriving at the shop, I find Larry under a car on a lift, fixing a muffler. Paul is in bay two, working on brakes on another car. Nate's sorting through a new shipment of parts. I scan the whiteboard, and I'm tasked with a head gasket replacement on a mid-sized car that's parked outside. Looks like Frank's handwriting again, damn it.

Outside, I pop the hood and get to work. But I still can't get this morning out of my head. *Maybe Larry knows what's up.* I pull up from the hood and wipe my hands on a towel. I'm heading toward bay one when I hear a car behind me, crunching sand and loose gravel beneath its tires. I glance over my shoulder just in time to see that blue car from the other night creeping past along the street. Then it quickly speeds up and rounds a corner.

I still have this feeling I've seen that car before, a long time ago, but I can't remember where. But with it being the second time this week I've seen it, it's obvious that whoever it is is watching me.

And I don't like being watched like that.

I wait a few moments to see if the car returns, but it doesn't, so I head to bay one. Larry's still under the lift, small sparks showering down around him while he welds a muffler pipe.

"Larry, did Lauren talk to you today?" I ask.

Larry stops welding and lifts the iron mask up from his face. "No, why?"

"Denise left at four thirty this morning to see Lauren. It's not like her to just up and leave like that, so I thought maybe something happened to Lauren."

"I talked to Lauren just last night, kid. She was fine."

"But—"

Larry's nostrils flare. "Look, if it'll make you happy, I'll call her after I finish this. Now just calm the fuck down, will you?"

I open my mouth to argue again, but close it instead and look to the floor. "Yeah, sure."

"Good. Now get back to work."

As I'm walking back to my car, Denise's ringtone goes off, and I quickly pull the phone from my pocket. "Hey, Denise."

"Hi." She huffs a little, and sounds like she's outside, maybe walking.

"Where are you?" I ask, my heart pounding nervously.

"I'm just leaving my life science final, my last one of the day. On my way home."

The pounding in my chest still doesn't let up. "Everything okay with Lauren? You left early this morning."

"Yeah, I know, and I'm sorry. Lauren had a severe migraine and needed me to get some more painkillers."

"Damn, what were she and Larry doing last night?"

She chuckles softly. "Nothing that I know of. Sometimes she gets these really bad migraines during her monthly."

It takes a moment for me to process that. "Oh."

"Hey, can you come over today? I got three unknown missed calls on my phone. I have this weird feeling. I'd rather stay with you, but I should stay with Lauren in case she needs me."

My skin prickles. "Okay. I'll be over there after work."

"Thanks, Dominick. I love you."

Quittin' time. Thank God. I clock out not a minute later.

"Hey," Larry calls as I'm mounting my bike. He looks at me with concern. "I called Lauren, but she didn't pick up."

"She's probably asleep, man," I say. "All drugged up on painkillers."

Larry blinks. "What?"

"Eh, female problems, according to Denise. Might wanna stay away from her today."

"Damn. We had a date tonight. Guess it's another night of overtime at the shop for me."

I gear up and start the bike. "Take it easy, man." I ride cautiously through the streets, anticipating seeing that car again. Rather than going my usual route to Denise's place, I take a lot of side streets. It takes longer, but if someone really *is* watching me, hopefully I'll throw them off.

I ride through the winding streets of Denise's neighbor-hood. It's still rush hour, and many of the neighbors haven't gotten home yet, so the neighborhood seems pretty quiet. When Denise's white house comes into view, I speed up. I have no stop signs on this road, so it's a straight shot. That eerie feeling in my gut returns, and I grip the handlebars tighter. I see Denise's car parked out front, but that doesn't make me any more relaxed.

Only a block away from her house, as I cross an intersection, a large blue object pulls out in front of me. A car, perhaps, or maybe a truck. It's there and gone, so I have no idea. I try to stop—at least I think I do. My ears ring and patches of blue sky spin in my vision. My heart drops into my gut like I'm on a rollercoaster, falling, falling. I slam into something solid, the inner cushions of the helmet yielding to the back of my head. Sliding to a stop across the hard surface, I let out a groan. My body goes numb, and the sky darkens until all I see is black.

CHAPTER 27

THE DARKNESS SLOWLY LIFTS, AND MY VISION BLURS AND clears as I regain consciousness. How long have I been out? I can feel my body being pulled somewhere. Who the fuck's touching me? I try opening my mouth to yell, but no sound comes out.

I glimpse my motorcycle helmet on the ground nearby, scuffed and the plastic face shield cracked. My jacket lays next to it in a heap of torn material.

"Jesus, Nick, hurry up before someone sees us!" says a male voice. It's distant, but my mind is too jumbled to try and recognize it.

"He's fine," Nick says, his voice much closer.

Nick. Oh, hell.

My mind starts to piece things together. But before I can think any more, I feel soft cushions beneath me. The scent of pine trees hit my nose, further rousing me. I'm in the backseat of a car. A Christmas tree air freshener hangs from the rearview mirror, and the tops of two heads are visible over the two front seats.

Fuck, no.

Grunting, I will the rest of my body awake. "Let me out," I say through a loud groan.

"Shit, he's coming to," the guy in the passenger seat says. "Hurry up and get us outta here."

The engine starts, and adrenaline pumps through me. I'm still winded, but I'm strong enough to push myself up. "No," I groan. I get a good look at the two guys. William's in the passenger seat, and Nick's driving. "You," I say, eyeing William. My mind is fuzzy. "The cops arrested you."

"He's got friends in high places. Unlike you, man," Nick says, putting the car in gear. "Now shut the fuck up."

I lurch for the driver's seat and grab Nick in a headlock as his foot hits the gas. He gasps and lets go of the wheel, and the car jolts forward out of control. His foot desperately searches for the brake.

"Shit!" William reaches for the wheel with one hand and under the front seat with the other. I catch a glimpse of a shiny object.

No! No, No, No, No. I thought that shit only happens in the movies.

"Let him go, or I'll blow your fucking head off!" William growls, pressing the gun into my temple.

For a moment, I can't breathe. The cold steel of the gun barrel sends shivers through me. The smell of gunpowder is strong. *So this is what it's like to have a gun pulled on you.*

But I'll be damned if I let these motherfuckers drive me off to
hell knows where.

And Denise is so close.

I slowly unwrap my arms from Nick's neck and lower
myself into the backseat. Nick quickly stops the car then goes
into a coughing fit before gathering himself. Out of one of
the back windows, I see a woman, half a block away, jogging
along the sidewalk in our direction with a small dog on a
leash. She stops short of the intersection and notices my motorcycle laying in the street. Then she looks in our direction.

I need to keep them here as long as I can. I turn to William, who's more focused on Nick. I notice a missing tooth
on the side of William's mouth, and a few scars on his face
from where I'd pummeled him that night. "What the fuck,
man?" I say. "Why are you kidnapping me?"

William points the gun at me. "Shut up. Just shut. The
fuck. Up. You ruined me, you know that? Ruined my fucking
life!"

"Why? Because I saved a girl from getting raped by you?"

"It was *not* rape. She wanted it."

"Yeah, once you got her all drugged up." I watch the
woman in my peripheral vision. She starts jogging a little
faster in our direction, and the little dog barks crazily.

Ignoring me, William shoves Nick. "Hurry the fuck up
and get us out of here!" He peers out the driver-side window.
"Shit! Someone's coming!"

While William's distracted, I lunge between the two front
seats for the gun. Grabbing William's wrist, I twist it and the
gun toward the passenger-side window. Bones break in his

wrist, and William screams. A loud bang drowns out the sound of window glass shattering, and then my right ear rings like a motherfucker. The smell of gunpowder assaults my nose.

Nick reaches for me, and I slam my left elbow into the side of his head. He grunts, his head snapping to the side and smashing into the driver-side door.

I deactivate the locks and scramble out of the backseat. As soon as my feet hit the asphalt, my knees buckle and I collapse. Crawling away from the car, I see William lumber out of the passenger side, aiming the gun at me with his uninjured hand.

"Get the fuck back here!" I hear him yell through the ringing that still lingers in my ears.

The lady runs across the street, away from the danger, her phone to her ear. Her tiny dog is barking madly, tugging on the leash in our direction.

A car turns down our street and stops. A man gets out and looks in our direction, phone in hand.

"Shit, man," Nick says nervously. "You're on your own. I'm not gonna get arrested over this shit."

William locks and loads the gun with a single click. "Don't you leave me, man," he says, not looking at Nick. "You promised you wouldn't." His hand shakes dangerously.

More cars stop in the street, people coming home from work and school. All of them are on their phones. Nick runs away, and some people yell and point.

"It's over, William," I say. "You gonna kill me? Then do it, man. Get it over with. But Denise still won't love you."

His gaze tears into me like he's looking into my very soul. And I stare back, ready and waiting for him to pull that trigger. This is not the way I thought I'd die, but at least I'll die knowing that he'll never have Denise's heart.

He sneers. I wish he'd just shoot me already and get it over with.

His shaky hand lowers the gun. He sinks to his knees and shudders. "You stole her from me."

Sirens echo down the street, and I exhale. Thank God.

Two houses down, the front door to Denise's house swings open, and there she is, standing on the stoop, looking in my direction.

I want to yell for her to stay away, but I know she wouldn't hear me, and it's too late to stop her. I watch her run toward me, her jean shorts showing off those sexy legs.

Two police cars pull up before us. Officers jump out and move in on William, disarming him, then hefting him up in handcuffs. A third police car zooms past, in the general direction Nick had run.

Denise stops short of the scene, her face pale as she watches William being escorted into one of the cruisers.

Another officer kneels down before me, his radio blaring with voices and static. "You okay, buddy?"

I manage to nod and then look in Denise's direction. She bites her nails as she watches.

"There's an ambulance on the way," the officer says. Then he stands and talks into his radio.

Ugh, no hospitals!

The adrenaline has subsided and weariness overtakes me. Drawing my eyes back to Denise, I stare until my eyelids grow heavy and all I see is darkness.

We leave the hospital a few hours later. Thankfully, the doctors said I only have some minor bruises. Denise drives me to her place, and the neighborhood's quiet once again. Larry's truck is parked along the curb as we pull into the driveway.

Denise shuts off the engine and traces her finger along the steering wheel.

I reach over and caress her cheek. "Hey, what's wrong?"

She looks at me sadly and then shakes her head. "I just can't believe it. Everything. I mean—"

"The motherfucker must've gotten bailed out or something. I doubt he'll get out so easily this time."

"He was in my neighborhood, Dominick!" Denise says, her voice cracking. Her eyes become glassy. "If you weren't here, he might have—" She covers her mouth with her hand and shudders. Tears begin to fall.

I exhale through my nose and pull her toward me. "Well, he didn't, and he won't. I told you I'm not gonna let anyone hurt you again, understand?" I kiss the top of her head.

She pulls back and manages to smile beneath those tears.

We get out of the car and make our way up the walkway, but Larry answers the door before we reach the stoop. His eyes full of concern, he lets go of the doorknob.

"Shit, Dominick, are you okay?" Larry asks. "I heard there was a shooting around here."

I nod. "I'm fine, man. Had another run-in with William."

His gaze hardens, and he steps aside to let us in.

"How is Lauren?" Denise asks.

"She's all right. We were just having coffee."

Denise's face brightens. "So she's finally up? That's great!"

Denise leaves, and I plop on the couch with a sigh. "Man, what a day. What time is it, anyway?"

"Ten thirty," Larry says, sitting next to me. "You sure you're all right, son?"

I freeze. *Son. He called me "son."* My eyes sting. Maybe he doesn't realize what he said, but I know exactly what I heard. "Y—yeah, man, I'm good. Never thought something like that would ever happen to me."

"Scary shit, ain't it? I worked as a bouncer when I was your age, and I saw my share of scary shit."

"The docs said I shouldn't have survived that motorcycle accident the way I impacted. I don't even know what happened, but apparently it was pretty bad."

"You're one lucky kid. Don't blow that luck on something shitty." He grins.

I almost laugh at that. *Man, this "guardian angel" business is some tough shit.*

CHAPTER 28

It's Friday night, and the semester is over. Kevin's back from Portland, and he's spinning tonight at Club Wildfire downtown.

The doors to the club are just opening by the time Denise and I arrive. I'd gotten my bike repaired and returned as good as new. As I park in a lot across the street, I spot Larry's truck nearby. *Larry's clubbing tonight, too?* This I have to see.

We head across the street and stand on the long line that's practically out the door. It's moving fairly quickly, but I drape my arm around Denise's bare shoulders, holding her close and admiring her sparkly, silver-sequined strappy dress and matching heels.

The sound of Kevin's music begins to filter outside. I smile. It'll be good to see my brother again.

We're nearing the front of the line when I feel a hand on my shoulder. I jerk and turn around. "Larry? I thought I saw your truck. What are you doing here?"

Larry nods, grinning slightly. Lauren is next to him, her arm hooked with his. "What? You think this old man don't know how to dance?" he says.

I clear my throat. "Well, I didn't say *that*."

Denise snickers.

Lauren smirks. "I'm sure he's got more rhythm than you."

I roll my eyes at her, then turn back to Larry, getting a good look at him. He's dressed sharp, looking a good ten years younger in his white blazer over a blue button-down shirt and black pants. "Damn, Larry, you've really outdone yourself this time."

"Didn't he?" Lauren beams, nestling herself closer to Larry.

Denise nudges me in the arm. "And you don't look half bad yourself, Dominick." She leans up and kisses my cheek, and I grin stupidly.

At the front of the line, we show our IDs to the bouncer and head inside. Strobe lights and fog surround us, and Kevin's house music vibrates the floor as we walk. People are everywhere dancing and drinking. Neon spotlights rain down on the stage over Kevin, who's hard at work on the mixer. Dressed in one of his many colorful button-down shirts and a black backwards baseball cap, Kevin's body bobs, as if he's caught up in his own music. Sometimes he can get really deep into his own little world like that. I guess that's why his music always sounds so amazing. Girls surround the foot of the stage, swooning and moving to the beat.

Larry and Lauren separate from us, and they head toward the bar, where the two of them get lost in the sea of dancing bodies. Denise holds my hand, and I snake through the tight crowd, leading her as close to the stage as I can get. She lets go of my hand and breaks out in a sexy dance, every movement graceful and smooth like the natural dancer that she is. I move in time with her, then reach out and pull her against me. Our bodies together, her back to my chest, we rock and grind to the bass beat. The crowd all around us roars and screams at the stage in their rowdy, drunken fashion, moving, dancing, getting possessed by the music. Colorful sparkling lights from the mirror balls and neon strobe lights above engulf us, and I feel like I've entered a fantasy world with the most wonderful girl in my arms. Her body is so hot, her pear scent mixed with her sweat, it arouses all of my senses. I close my eyes for a moment and savor the intoxicating bliss of our dance, the music, the atmosphere. Pure freedom.

Then I feel her lips touch mine, and I open my eyes. It's like waking up from a dream.

The music's still going, though the melody and drumbeat has shifted. People around us are still dancing, but Denise has stopped and is breathing hard. She leans her face close to mine. "I need a drink."

I nod, huffing, my heart pounding. We squeeze our way through the throng of sweaty bodies toward the bar, and I flag down a scantily clad bartender.

When we get our drinks, I pull Denise off to the side, away from the oncoming bar traffic. "Looks like we won't be seeing Lauren and Larry any more tonight," I say as I scan the crowd.

Denise winks. "And they won't be seeing *us* tonight, either."

I raise my eyebrows at her. "Huh?"

She places the cup to her lips, tips her head back, and downs her entire drink in a few gulps.

Damn! Never seen her drink like that *before.*

She grabs my arm and pulls me across the main room toward another, smaller, black-lit room full of couches, padded benches, and beanbag chairs. A few couples occupy the neon-glowing couches, while others lounge around in the other seats. I manage to finish my drink before Denise swipes the ice-filled cup from my hands and tosses it in the garbage. She pushes me backwards onto an oversized beanbag chair and plops on top of me. She plants her lips onto mine and kisses me hard. My hands fall to her hips as I welcome her forcefulness. Her dress gives off neon sparkles under the overhead black light. The music shifts again and the thumping, possessive beat returns, making the room vibrate. She cups my face with her hands, kissing me deeper, and I feel her tongue prod my lips.

Oh, fuck yes.

I touch my tongue to hers, tasting her sweet, natural taste infused with Long Island iced tea. My hands move around to her middle, caressing those firm abs. Moaning, she kisses over my cheek, down to my neck. Her amazing pear scent drives me insane. Holy shit, she's horny. I want to take her right here in this comfortable chair. She moves back up to my lips, and we share an intimate kiss. I pull out my phone and glance at the time. Almost one o'clock. As much as I want to see Kevin tonight, I feel more inclined to tend to this wonderful girl in my arms. I reluctantly break the kiss and sit her up in my lap.

"Let's get out of here," I mutter in her ear.

She grins and dismounts me, taking my hand. We leave the club and return to the bike. She climbs on behind me and wraps her arms around my waist. My diaphragm contracts as her hands are dangerously close to my groin. God, I have a serious hard-on right now. I bet she's doing that on purpose, damn it. I fumble with the key and eventually start up the bike. I take every shortcut I know to get home quick. Entering through the kitchen, I hear Chris and Adrienne's voices coming from the living room. Hard breathing and moaning.

Neither Denise nor I seem to give a fuck right now as we make our way to the stairs. Chris and Adrienne don't seem to stop, either. I pull Denise into my room and shut the door. She kicks off her shoes and sits on the edge of the bed. Smiling, I sweep over her and indulge in a deep, passionate kiss. Returning the kiss, she begins undoing the buttons of my shirt. Before I know it, both of us are shrugging out of our clothes and tossing them to the floor. I lay her back in bed. Her sexy scent is strong, tantalizing. Everything about her is truly amazing. I've had my share of girls, but before Denise, I'd almost given up on moments like these—moments of happiness when you truly love someone.

I have no idea how much time has passed as we lay naked in bed together, with her in my arms. Despite my exhaustion, I can't sleep. I keep replaying our lovemaking in my mind. She was beautiful, amazing. So gentle, yet so forceful.

My phone reads 4:30 when I reach over to check it. In several hours, my M/C club's benefit cookout will begin. A month ago, I didn't imagine I'd be going with Denise, but here we are. I slide out of bed, slip on my boxers, and tiptoe off to the bathroom, tossing the used condom in the garbage along the way. After doing my business, I return to bed and cradle her back into my arms. Smiling broadly, I close my eyes and drift off to sleep, dreaming about the most wonderful girl in the world.

CHAPTER 29

"**W**AKE UP, LAZY-BUTT!"

A pear-scented pillow hits me in the face. I jerk myself awake, the cool air of the room whisking over my bare chest. Denise is at my bedside, pillow at the ready for another assault. Dressed in a gray cut-off shirt and flared denim jeans, she looks incredibly sexy, which agitates my morning wood.

Her eyes glance down toward my groin, and she smirks. "You better get up before we're late for the cookout."

I rub my eyes and yawn. *Oh yeah, the cookout.* "Yeah, yeah. I'm getting up. What time is it?"

"Nine o'clock. It starts at eleven thirty, right? So get up!" She smacks me in the head with the pillow again and laughs.

I wince. "Ooh, should *not* have done that." Grabbing the pillow, I give it a good tug and pull her atop me. She squeals in laughter. Our faces come close, and I steal a kiss. A small moan escaping her, she returns the kiss, then slowly pulls away.

"We're never going to get there in time at this rate," she says, rolling off me.

I grin. "Well, I'm not complaining."

"Oh, come on. What about that poor little girl you're supposed to be raising money for?"

I rub the back of my head. "All right, all right." Yawning again, I slide out of bed and sort through my clothes, also grabbing my denim, patch-riddled M/C club vest, then head downstairs.

Leaving the bathroom, showered and dressed, I catch a whiff of cooked eggs and toast. Following my nose to the kitchen, I spot a plate of scrambled eggs and french toast sitting on the counter next to my bike helmet.

I smile. *Did Denise make this for me?*

"If you don't eat it, I will, because *damn*, that toast was good!"

I snap my attention toward the kitchen doorway, where Chris, dressed in a black T-shirt, a pair of camo cargo shorts, and his favorite black all-star sneakers, is leaning against the frame with his arms crossed.

"And yes, Denise made that for you," he says, as if reading my mind.

"Wow, man. This is unreal. I've never had a girl cook for me before. Well, except my mother."

"Moms don't count."

I pick up the plate and brush past him, muttering, "I'm sure this tastes as good as it looks."

"Dude, are you kidding me? Denise makes your awesome chicken florentine taste like shit!" Chris laughs.

Frowning, I head to the living room. Denise and Adrienne are sitting on the couch watching Saturday-morning cartoons.

"Morning, ladies," I say, plopping down on the armrest. I finally take my first bite of the toast, which is still warm.

Holy fucking shit!

My eyes widen as the bread practically melts on my tongue. There's a hint of sweetness to the toast, and I realize it's been sprinkled with sugar.

It's only breakfast, but Chris is right, it *does* make my chicken florentine—which I've been quite proud of—taste like shit.

This girl is amazing.

Denise beams at me, perhaps noticing my look of pure bliss that I just can't hide.

"There, you see, Denise?" Adrienne says, gesturing toward me, mirroring Denise's smile. "You have him practically wrapped around your pinky now. He'll do anything you say to get more of that awesome french toast." She looks at me. "Won't you, Dominick?"

I swallow a mouthful of toast. "Uh, sure," I say absently, even though Denise has had me wrapped around her pinky since I first met her.

"But I still like his chicken florentine," Denise says, grazing the jawline of my five o'clock shadow with her finger.

Her brief electrifying touch almost makes me choke on the eggs, which also taste awesome. "I'll—I'll cook some for you tonight if you want."

She just smiles. Hell, she has me practically wrapped around her pretty little finger with just that damned smile alone.

"Thanks for the breakfast, by the way," I say, realizing I've cleaned the plate of every bit of food. "You've completely put my cooking skills to shame."

"What cooking skills?" Chris says, then laughs.

I flip him off. "Fuck you, man."

Denise giggles. "I figured you'd be too busy working at the cookout, so you won't really have time to eat until later. Besides, I wanted to pay you back for the breakfast in bed."

"I think this more than pays for that." I glance at the TV. "Gotta say, you two are the first girls I've met who actually like watching cartoons."

The girls raise their eyebrows in unison.

"You're kidding, right?" Adrienne says. "Who the hell doesn't like cartoons?"

"The dull girls, apparently." I laugh.

"Dom's right," Chris says. "I mean, I've had tons of girls think cartoons were too childish and immature."

Adrienne rolls her eyes. "Well the hell with them. They don't know good quality TV when they see it."

I'm liking Adrienne more and more. She's turning out to be cool people. No wonder she and Chris hit it off so well.

I check my phone. "It's ten thirty, guys. I need to head out and help set up." I slide off the armrest. "Denise, if you wanna ride with Chris and Adri, that's cool."

Denise scrunches her face and stands with me. "Whatever. I'm going with you."

I'm a little taken aback, then eye Chris and Adrienne, who both wink at us.

I love this girl.

CHAPTER 30

COLORFUL POP-UP TENTS AND THE SMELL OF BURNING charcoal greet us as we arrive at Cal Anderson Park around eleven. I park my bike with the rest of my club brothers' and, taking Denise's hand, make my way to the big main tent where rows of tables and chairs are set up. Shane and Marco are manning the grills, while Jason is setting up the cash table. Gregg, Darryl, and Alonzo are setting up the last row of folding tables and chairs. Charles is putting the finishing touches on a huge sign of a blown-up photograph of Troy's little girl, Ashley, with a handmade cut-out of her name sprinkled in glitter underneath it. Plastered beside the photograph is a hand-drawn goal meter. Troy is talking with some vendors, who are setting up their tables and tents along the walkways surrounding the main area, and Matt is helping a group of workers do a sound check on a small raised platform near the big tent.

It's hard to believe that the few of us can organize something so huge. But Troy has a lot of connections, one of the reasons he's the club's president.

Troy spots me and waves. Like me, he's wearing his motorcycle vest, which is also covered in various patches with our club's colors and emblem on the back. I wave back and walk over to him with Denise in tow.

"What's up, Genius?" he says. We do our special handshake.

"Yo, Wolf."

His eyes scan Denise, who looks amused. "And who's this pretty lady?"

I let go of her hand and wrap my arm around her waist. "This is my girlfriend, Denise." I pause, realizing it's the first time I've ever referred to her as my girlfriend. But the word just came natural to me. I look sideways at her, and she doesn't look the least bit offended by it. "Denise, this is Troy, but we call him Lone Wolf. He's the club's president."

"Hi, nice to meet you." She smiles and extends her hand.

Troy shakes it, grinning broadly. "Oh, the pleasure is all mine."

"So are we pretty much set up now?" I ask, looking around the rest of the park. People already start trickling in our direction. It's almost eleven thirty.

Troy rubs his chin. "Yep, just waiting on the deejay. He's running a little late. That's my fault for calling him on such short notice."

I look to the platform, where Matt and the workers are running wires to four speakers set up around it. "Damn, a deejay, too? You went all out."

"What's a cookout without some good music, eh?" He pats me on the shoulder. "All right. Looks like the crowd's coming. Better get to your station."

I give him a thumbs-up.

He turns and hustles toward the big tent.

I look to Denise. "Hey, you should walk around and check out the vendors before the crowd comes."

She scans the various tents and tables and looks thoughtful for a moment. "All right. I'll be back, okay?"

"I'll be manning the raffle table." I point out the table set next to a vendor's tent.

We kiss, and I watch her wander off. I rush to the unmanned raffle table and pull out the rolls of red and blue tickets and a locked tin cash box from under it. As I pop up a sign on the table, I notice the vendor next to me. It's an older lady. Another one of Troy's many connections. Dozens of different types of jewelry decorate her cloth-covered table.

She looks back at me and smiles. "Hi." She cranes her neck and squints, perhaps trying to get a glimpse of the name patch on my vest. "Genius?"

"Hello," I say politely, nodding.

"I'm Marcy. Looks like we're tablemates today, hmm?"

"Looks like it." I scan the jewelry. Each piece is unique, and they're not something I'd find in one of those expensive stores in the malls.

"I made all these," Marcy says, as though reading my mind.

"They look nice. Different."

Marcy beams. She picks up a handful of pieces and shuffles in the narrow space between our two tables. "These are my newly made ones. What do you think?" She holds them in her hands.

I really don't care to look at jewelry, with the crowd starting to filter our way as they peruse the vendors. People are already lining up under the big tent, and I notice movement at the platform, but the crowd blocks my view. But I try to be polite and look at her works of art, which she's obviously proud of. One piece catches my eye. It's a pair of silver-studded earrings in the shape of the *fleur de lis*.

"How much are those?" I ask, pointing to the earrings.

"Forty." The corners of Marcy's eyes wrinkle as her smile widens.

I fish in my back pocket for my wallet and purchase the earrings. Marcy wraps them up in tissue paper and places them in a cute little box, securing it with a coily red ribbon. I hide the box under my table for now. I haven't gotten Denise a gift like this before. It's about time I did.

By four o'clock, the club ends up raising close to twenty thousand dollars. Kevin even surprised us all by making an appearance and providing musical entertainment. The crowd thins as the club and volunteers start breaking down tents, stacking chairs, and cleaning up garbage. Denise helps me fold up the raffle table. I swipe her present from under the table and hide it in my pocket for now. We tote the table and raffle items toward the main setup area. With most of the crowd finally gone, I spot Kevin on stage packing up his dee-jay equipment. I turn to Denise. "C'mon. Let's go see my brother."

Denise and I run to the stage and surprise Kevin as he's slipping a record in an unused sleeve.

"Yo, Kev! I can't believe you made it out here," I say, slapping him on the back.

Kevin looks up and grins. "You know I wouldn't miss this for nothin', li'l bro." He sets the record in a crate, and we do our secret handshake. Then he nods to Denise. "Hey, what's up, Denise?"

"Hey," she says, smiling. "Loved the music. I think my crazy girlfriends loved it more."

Kevin laughs. "I aim to please."

I begin to help him pack away his equipment, but he stops me. "No, Dom. You've worked enough today. Take a break and go somewhere with your girl."

I furrow my brow. "But I don't mind—"

Kevin gives me a stern look. "Go. Get outta here. I'll call you tomorrow."

Denise tugs my arm, and I turn to her. With a tilt of her head, she gestures for me to follow.

It's almost five o'clock by the time the club finishes cleaning and packing up. After I say my goodbyes, I return to my bike with Denise in tow.

"Let's ride somewhere," she says.

I beam. "Cougar Mountain again?"

Her eyes light up. "Ooh! Yes! I love those winding roads."

"Me too." I stop in mid-reach for my helmet, and slip my hand in my pocket for the box. "Before we leave, I wanna give you this."

She carefully takes the tiny box and looks at it curiously. "Dominick? What did you—"

"Just open it," I say, shaking my head.

Slowly, she tugs the ribbon free and opens the box. She peeks inside and gasps. "Oh! Dominick, they're beautiful. Thank you." She hugs me tight.

I return the hug and indulge in a deep, loving kiss. "Just a little something to say that I love you." I take the earrings from her and help her put them on. Afterward, I stand back and admire her. "They look perfect on you."

She grins and then kisses me again. "I have something for you, too."

I raise my eyebrows. "Oh?"

"I know it's a little late, but . . . " She fishes through her purse and pulls out a quarter.

Laughing, I take it. "I can't believe you remembered that," I say, pocketing the coin.

"How can I possibly forget the first time I met you?"

I lean in and kiss her deeply. *Yeah, I'll never forget, either.*

We gear up and leave the park. Denise's arms are wrapped tightly around me. No piece of jewelry in the world can ever express my true love for this girl. It's crazy how fate can bring two people together. Or was it destiny?

Maybe that's why Denise is so special to me, and I will cherish it forever.

There *was* a light at the end of that tunnel, and that light was her.

Kevin Anderson lives the high life as a deejay and prospective pro-basketball player. But it's timeout for that life of fame when he meets Trinity Brown. Upon learning her secrets, Kevin must decide if it is worth risking his career—and his life—to help the woman he loves.

Please see the next page for a preview of

Scratched

CHAPTER 1

I PULL UP TO THE DRIVEWAY OF DOMINICK'S DUPLEX AND wait while he and Denise get out. I'm mad about what went down last night. But fortunately, Dom was there to save her from that shit. If I see that guy William again, I'll kill him for Denise *and* for my baby brother, who had to experience the mental trauma all over again. I know Dom. As tough as he thinks he is, his mind is still fragile. He must've suffered one of his recurring flashbacks when he rescued Denise at the party.

Where she was almost raped.

I wish I could have taken a good, clean shot at William, too, that fucking bastard. But it was Dom's fight.

Dom taps the driver-side window, shaking me out of my thoughts. Rolling down the window, I'm met with a light breeze of the mild Seattle night that kisses my face. I stare at my brother, concerned and hoping tonight's ordeal doesn't send him off the deep end. He's got a lot of anger boiling inside after putting up with our father's abuse for all those years. It's a miracle I've been able to help him keep it under control for this long.

But still, he's like a ticking time bomb, and it worries me, especially with Denise there. She's been through enough, and she doesn't need his "issues" on top of what she already has to deal with. I know Dom likes her—*loves her*—but I don't think she knows what he's gone through.

"Thanks, man, for all this," Dom says.

I scrutinize the two of them. "You sure you two will be okay?"

Dom nods. "Yeah, man." He looks over his shoulder at Denise, who smiles in return.

She's got a beautiful smile. There's a glow about her that brings out the best in my brother. I hope she can help him quell his demons.

"All right," I say then stare out the windshield at nothing in particular. "I got a call while I was waiting at the hospital for you guys. Got this huge gig at a radio station down in Portland next Wednesday, so I'll be gone. But I'll be back by Friday."

Dom grins. "Wow, Kev, that's great! I'm happy for you, man."

"Thanks." I look back at him. "Take it easy, li'l bro, okay?"

He nods, his smile fading. "You, too."

I reach out the window, and we do our secret handshake that we've been doing since we were kids. Back then, it reminded us that we were inseparable no matter how bad it got.

I drive off into the night, glancing in my mirror to see Dom and Denise head inside the house. I won't see my little brother for a few days, but that doesn't mean I'm not going to call and check up on him.

Sunday night, I pack and head south on the interstate toward Portland. It's less than a three-hour drive, and I could've just left early on Tuesday, but I want to meet up with some of my deejay friends on Monday, some of whom I'll most likely crash with.

And there are other things that I need to take care of as well.

Twenty minutes into my drive, I detour east to Renton to a place I hate going back to. It's been a little over six months since I last visited, and the guilt inside me says I should stop in and at least say hello. I pull into the driveway of a little blue house that sits back among a cluster of trees. My headlights shine on the back of a white SUV parked in front of me. *Uncle Adam's here.*

Getting out the car, I slip on my earbuds and start up the music player in my back pocket. House music fills my ears, calming my nerves. A narrow, pebbled, flower-lined walkway leads up to the front door of the decades-old home. The scent of azaleas—Mama's scent—fills my nose, and I pluck a blossom and twirl it between my fingers. Each time I return, this place seems so new to me. So foreign. Maybe it's because I've been trying hard to forget the past. All that's left of "home" is pain. And my mother.

Warm light from the living room's curtained window casts a dim glow over the outside bushes. The small white light of a TV flickers. I ring the doorbell, and moments later, the door swings open. Uncle Adam's giant six-foot-six frame fills the doorway. A broad smile parts his dark, haggard face.

The music still going, I pull the earbuds out, and they hang down the front of my shirt.

"Kevin!" Unc steps out and embraces me in a big bear hug.

I tense up for a moment then relax and return the hug. Having worked on cars and construction all his life, Unc is strong and his body feels like a brick wall.

"'Sup, Unc," I say, pulling out of his arms.

He peers past me and frowns. "Still no Dominick, huh?"

I shake my head. "Naw, he's got some things going on, but he's handling it."

Unc heads back inside, leaving the door open for me. "Your mother had an accident in the garden yesterday. Sprained her ankle."

"Damn. Is she okay?"

"Yeah, it's just a minor strain. But the doctor told her to take it easy. I'm taking care of her for the weekend."

After our father—that coward—committed suicide, Mama was left alone and scared. That was when Uncle Adam stepped in. It's hard to imagine, even now, that this man is my father's brother. Unc is nothing like my father. Many times I've wondered if Uncle Adam was really my father instead of that other son of a bitch.

He's your dad, like it or not, Unc had said. *But don't think for a moment that I am like him. You three might as well be my sons, and I love you all very much.*

Uncle Adam really did love us, still does, and I don't think I ever heard those words uttered from my real father's mouth.

Unc leads me through the living room, where the TV is tuned in to an old sci-fi movie. My throat tightens as the familiar sights, smells, and sounds of my childhood fill my senses. The tail of the cat clock hanging on the drab grey wall in the kitchen still grinds steadily back and forth. Framed photos from family trips line the narrow hallway leading to the master bedroom, along with ones of Dominick, Michael, and me as babies and schoolchildren. At the end of the hall, a large family portrait hangs prominently. We seem happy, with Mama holding baby Dom and smiling, but that happiness was all a front. At the sight of it, I choke back angry tears.

I sneer at the way Pops appears in that portrait. His smile looks fake, plastered on, as if he knew exactly what he was going to do to his family.

"Kevin," Unc calls, pulling me back to the present. I didn't realize I'd been standing and staring for so long.

I snap my head to him. "Sorry. I just . . . "

He stands at the door to the master bedroom, his hand on the knob. "No, son. Don't you dare apologize. This is your home. Now, go see your mother." He opens the door.

I swallow then moisten my lips. The room has changed since I first left home. The old white draperies have been switched for teal ones. The once-drab white walls are re-painted to a sea blue with white trim. The furniture has been rearranged, and some new furniture added. The twin walk-in closets have been reconstructed into a single big one. I helped Uncle Adam with the painting and construction on that job. It was a fun project and helped ease the pain a little.

The bedside lamp sheds its warm glow over Mama's bronze face. She's sitting up in bed, her bandaged foot propped up on a pillow, her eyes focused on the thick, dog-eared Bible open in her lap. She got serious with the religion stuff after Pops died.

Her big brown eyes meet mine, over the top of her read-ing glasses, as I approach her bedside. Beaming, she book-marks her Bible and sets it aside. "Kevin? Oh, honey, you're back!"

"Hi, Mama," I mumble, hugging her and kissing her on the cheek. She's almost fifty, but the only wrinkles on her face are around her eyes and are probably due to all the cry-ing she's done over the years. She still smells like Mama—all flowery and sweet. I close my eyes and feel them start to burn as memories take over. How could that son of a bitch of a father hurt this beautiful woman? And how could Dominick and I ever be mad at her for what she did? I forgave her, but Dom . . . well, his demons still run rampant.

I look at her swollen foot and ankle. "Uncle Adam said you had an accident. Are you okay?"

"Yes, baby. I was planting some new flowers and stepped on a spade. Carelessness on my part." She holds my hands and takes me in fully. "How are you doing?"

Sitting on the edge of the bed, I stare at her small, calloused hands over mine. "I'm fine. I'm on my way to Portland, so I thought I'd stop in and say hi."

"What's happening in Portland?"

"I've got a radio gig down there on Wednesday."

"Oh." The excitement on her face dulls. "Still doing that deejay stuff, I see."

"Yeah, and this upcoming gig could be my big break."

"So you're not going to finish college?"

I purse my lips. I really didn't want to drop out in the first place, but I had a personal obligation to Dom. Since *that day,* I've swore on my life to protect him, and to always be there for him whenever he needed me. I can't concentrate on school while worrying about him all the time. "I don't know yet," I finally reply.

"Kevin, you're twenty-four years old. It's not too late to finish. Maybe you can try out for the team again, get your basketball scholarship back, and—"

"Mama . . . "

"Baby, I don't want to see you throw your life away. You have so much going for you. The Lord blessed you with a talent, and you're not using it."

I scowl. "I'm not throwing my life away, Mama. I'm happy doing what I'm doing. I'm living comfortably with what I earn from my deejaying."

"But you need a college education. You're not going to get a decent job at a high school level. What happens when you get tired of deejaying? Then what? Going to get some dead-end job, living paycheck-to-paycheck for the rest of your life? How will you support yourself and your wife? Your children?"

"Whoa." I pull my hands from hers. "Wife and kids? You're thinking a little too far into the future, Mama. How about we think about the here and now?"

She smiles softly. "I want grandbabies someday, Kevin. Is there a special someone that's caught your eye?"

"Uhh, not really." It's partly true. I meet tons of girls every time I work, but most of them become a blur. Except this one girl named Trinity Brown. She's cute, deliciously chubby, follows me to my downtown gigs, and is always the first in line to get into a club I'm spinning at. She's someone I can never forget.

"Well," Mama says, "one day you will meet that special person, and you'll need to find a better way to support the both of you once deejaying is no longer your passion."

I stiffen. *Fuck that.* "I'll never get tired of deejaying. Music is my life. It's the only thing that keeps me sane right now. You should be happy for me."

She clasps her hands together on her lap. "Baby, I don't want you or your brothers to be satisfied with just getting by in life."

I clench my jaw. Being a deejay isn't "just getting by in life." It's a fun and exciting life for me, and I wouldn't want any other kind of job.

But then I think maybe it's *not* too late to try out for the team. And I only need seven more credits to graduate. "I'll think about going back. I'll talk to Coach Langley about trying out again."

The smile returns to her face. "Oh, baby, that's all I ask. Please don't throw your talent away. Maybe one day I'll see you on TV playing pro."

I laugh. "I'm not *that* good, Mama. The pro guys are no joke. Anyway, I can't rely on basketball my whole life. I'll eventually get too old to play, or I might get injured. Either way, my career would only be temporary."

"That's why you need to finish school—so you can get a good job to fall back on. That business degree will go a long way, Kevin."

"Mama." I exhale slowly. "I know what I wanna do with my life. It may or may not be what you intend, but I promise I'll use my God-given talents to go as far as I can."

"Thank you, baby." She leans over and kisses my forehead. "How's Dominick?"

I avert my gaze and look anywhere but at her. I can't tell her about what happened to Dom and his girl the other night. "He's fine."

"He hasn't come to see me since he graduated from high school," Mama says. "He's only called a handful of times. I try calling, but he doesn't answer. I miss my baby boy."

"He's still mad, Mama."

"At me?" Her eyes start to get glassy.

I don't reply.

"He thinks I don't care about him, doesn't he?" She covers her mouth, and a tear rolls down her cheek. "I tried. I really tried. I just wanted my family back. Lord Jesus, I just wanted my family back." She closes her eyes and sniffles, more and more tears falling.

My vision wavers and blurs, and I pull her into an embrace. She cries on my shoulder. "Mama." My voice quivers, and I blink away some tears welling up in my burning eyes. *No, damn it, I have to be strong for her, since Pops couldn't be.* But hearing her sobs and feeling her warm tears causes some of my own to fall. I quickly wipe them away with the back of my hand. "You'll get your family back one day. It's just . . . these things take time. A long time. I'll try talking to Dom more. I'll try to get him to come see you." *But not now. God, not now.*

I pull her away and wipe the tears from her cheeks with my fingers. A small smile touches her lips.

I cup her face in my hands. "No more, tears, Mama. I hate it when you cry. You've gotta be strong, okay? Be strong for all of us."

She nods and sniffs.

I release her then get up from the bed. "I should go."

"Kevin." She grabs my hand, and I look back. "Stay the night, please."

I draw my hand away firmly. "I can't, Mama. I'm meeting some friends in Portland tomorrow afternoon."

"But it's late. I don't want you driving on that interstate alone at night. Please, baby."

I look up at the ceiling and sigh. She always knows how to get to my heart when she uses that *needy mom* tone. "All right. But I gotta leave by nine tomorrow morning."

She beams. "Oh, that's fine, Kevin. Thank you."

I smile halfheartedly and leave the room. Returning to the living room, I discover Uncle Adam asleep on the couch with the TV still on. I quietly head toward the kitchen. *Might as well find something to eat before I go to sleep.* When I reach the breakfast nook, I halt. My eyes zero in on a spot on the wall near the baseboard. The paint in that spot is a shade lighter than the rest of the wall.

I remember that spot all too well. It's the same spot the back of my head hit after Pops grabbed me, choked me, cut me, and threw me against the wallboard. I blacked out from the impact and thought I'd died.

I place my hand to that spot on my head then move it down to the side of my neck, where my father sliced me with a box cutter. Even though I've covered up the scars with tattoos, they remain visible in my mind.

I raid the fridge and wolf down a plate of chicken and rice. Uncle Adam's still asleep by the time I finish, so as I head to bed, I turn off all the lights and the TV. The hallway leading to our bedrooms seems like an endless dark tunnel. I walk by the first room and flip on the light. It's Dom's, and it's every bit the same as he left it, only a little emptier. Posters of motorcycles and his favorite hip-hop artists hang the walls, and some of Uncle Adam's old mechanics books line the small bookshelf in one corner. Motorcycle magazines lie piled on the desk and on the seat of the pushed-in chair. The bed is made, and there's not a single article of clothing to be seen, my only indication that Mama was in here at some point.

I turn off the light and move past the bathroom to the next room—Michael Jr.'s. I clench my jaw as I flip the light switch. I don't know why I decided to come in here. Everything about that coward pisses me off. It's fitting that he bears our father's name. Serves him right. Michael's room is tidy as well, thanks to Mama. His walls are bare, other than a "Basic Striking Points" chart that shows all the vital areas on the human body and a shelf lining one of the walls, displaying dozens of martial-arts trophies and gold medals. A pair of dumbbells and a steel bench press bar with two twenty-pound weights are tucked under his bed. A picture of me and Dom as kids sits on the night table.

Fuck this. I shut off the light and leave.

I turn on the bedside lamp in my room. My old basketball posters are barely held to the walls with age-old tape. The bookshelves are bare. I used them to hold all the vinyls I collected when I was first learning how to mix. I pull open the closet. Only a few of my middle- and high-school clothes hang there, organized by color and pressed—more of Mama's doing. In the corner of the closet, I spot a bag, which holds my old two-channel mixer and turntable. Smiling, I pull out the bag and plop down on the bed with it. I uncover the equipment, which no longer works due to over-usage. This shit's junk compared to what I own now, but I guess I'll keep it around a little longer for its sentimental value. I stuff the equipment back into the bag and set it on the floor next to the bed.

Sticking the earbuds back in my ears, I switch to a new song on my player and lie back. I instinctively reach my hand under the bed, groping for the basketball I've always kept there. Palming it, I pull it out. The ball had seen its uses in the many pickup games I've played in at the parks. It's the same ball that got me my full-ride scholarship at the University of Washington. I toss the ball up with a perfect free-throw technique and catch it. I *do* miss the game. Sometimes I feel bummed that I've lost my scholarship.

But I'll never regret quitting school to save my brother.

About the Author

Marie Long is a novelist who enjoys the snowy weather, the mountains, and a cup of hot white chocolate. She's an avid supporter of literacy movements like We Need Diverse Books (WNDB) and National Novel Writing Month (NaNoWriMo). To learn more about her, visit her website: www.marielongauthor.com.

Made in the USA
Charleston, SC
18 May 2016